"A Very Special Sort Of Mystery Writer . . . Never Before Have His Strengths Seemed So Strong!"

—Kirkus Reviews

"They are all dead now. There's only me left."

"All of them?" asked the commissaris.

So his sister told him the grisly tale—six elderly residents living on the south shore of Cape Orca in Maine had either died or disappeared. The last to die was her husband.

In an alien land, with only de Gier and the local sheriff to help him, the commissaris went in pursuit of a murderer. Or would it turn out to be murderers? It meant delving into the private affairs of an eccentric island hermit, a sharp real-estate broker, a shady Boston holding company, a lovely widow and her ex-Marine gardener, an oddly philosophical youth gang and a beautiful young woman who had her seductive eyes on de Gier. . . .

"The combination of Dutch sense and Buddhist sensibility gives van de Wetering's detective novels a special appeal."

—Publishers Weekly

Books by Janwillem van de Wetering

The Blond Baboon
Corpse on the Dike
Death of a Hawker
The Empty Mirror
A Glimpse of Nothingness
The Japanese Corpse
The Maine Massacre
Outsider in Amsterdam
Tumbleweed

Published by POCKET BOOKS

Janwillem van de Wetering

THE MAINE
MASSACRE

PUBLISHED BY POCKET BOOKS NEW YORK

**POCKET BOOKS, a Simon & Schuster division of
GULF & WESTERN CORPORATION**
1230 Avenue of the Americas, New York, N.Y. 10020

Published by arrangement with Houghton Mifflin Company
Library of Congress Catalog Card Number: 78-10185

ISBN: 0-671-82865-7

First Pocket Books printing September, 1980

10 9 8 7 6 5 4 3 2 1

POCKET and colophon are trademarks of Simon & Schuster.

Printed in the U.S.A.

To J. O. Jeppson,
with love

THE MAINE
MASSACRE

1

The telephone call interrupted a pleasant conversation that hadn't been leading anywhere apart from stressing the point that the three men, gathered for the ceremony of ten o'clock coffee in the commissaris' stately room on the second floor of Amsterdam police headquarters, weren't alone that morning but could face the bleakest time of the early December year together.

The telephone's irritating jangle cut through the sergeant's lengthy explanation as to how a begonia can be made to flower in the midst of winter. The commissaris* was interested, and the adjutant, from the depth of a comfortable armchair upholstered in velvet, had been polite enough not to yawn, or cough, or suck noisily on his soggy cigar stub while the sergeant held forth. But now there was the telephone and the two detectives listened to the commissaris' side of the conversation with some interest. It could be business, but it was unlikely. There hadn't been any business for weeks, apart from traffic accidents and family fights and the usual bits and pieces that were far outside the scope of the "murder brigade" or the criminal investigation department in which they had served for longer than they cared to remember. The heavy continuous rain, occasionally changing into an icy downpour of sleet, kept

* The ranks of the Amsterdam Municipal Police are constable, constable first class, sergeant, adjutant, inspector, chief inspector, commissaris, chief constable. A commissaris is usually in charge of a division. Sergeants and adjutants are noncommissioned officers.

tempers down in the city. The citizens were spending their days at work and their nights at home. Public order couldn't be more orderly. Nothing to do but read files and drive the gray Volkswagen, unmarked, dented, and disreputable, through wet streets. Nothing to do but stare at the cold, bored faces of pedestrians. The pedestrians would stare back. The pedestrians only saw a car, and they wouldn't notice it until it happened to be in their way. And even if it were in their way, they wouldn't notice its details or occupants. The faces behind the Volkswagen's restless and squeaky windshield wipers would be gray blobs to them. But the faces belonged to live beings, to large, quiet adjutant Grijpstra, accepting the world with some mild misgivings from under his gray bristle of unbrushed metallike hair, and to lithe Sergeant de Gier, whose soft, large brown eyes observed whatever was going on, or not going on, over high cheekbones shadowed by carefully combed locks and thick curls. His hairstyle was a little too elaborate perhaps. A pedestrian who bumped into the car and cursed its driver, and bent down to have a closer look at the subject of his rage, might mistake the sergeant for a woman—provided, of course, that the sergeant would be blowing his nose. The sergeant's wide, upswept mustache clearly proclaimed him to be male. And so he was; an athletic adventurer with a reputation of antagonism, not so much to the world of crime as to the various systems of authority that interfered with his individualistic routines. But the sergeant was also a reasonable man and allowed his unfortunate inclination to go his own way to be checked by the adjutant's mellow mannerisms and the sly but gentle admonitions of the commissaris.

The sergeant's eyes rested on the commissaris' thin, blue-veined hand that had began to play with a pencil on the polished desktop.

"Yes, Suzanne," the commissaris said softly. "I am very sorry to hear the bad news. When did it happen?"

A vague murmur came from the telephone. There

were words and sobs. Then there was a moist whisper that could also be a fit of crying.

"Friday? But that's four days ago! Why didn't you let me know earlier? I might have been able to come out for the funeral?

"You kept on having bad connections? Poor dear."

The commissaris put his hand over the telephone and looked at the adjutant. "My sister, she lives in America. Her husband died." The commissaris' notebook was on the table and he flipped through the pages. "Yes, dear, I have your address. Of course I will come. Soon. Yes. Tomorrow perhaps, or the day after. I'll telephone you. Can you meet the plane, do you think?"

The murmuring voice stopped, sobbed, and spoke again.

"I see. Never mind, dear. I can find a taxi. Yes. Warm clothes? I'll see what I have in the cupboard. Thirty below? Yes, I'll keep it in mind. Rheumatism? No, no, Suzanne, I am quite healthy. I'll be there. I'll cable you the flight number so that you know when to expect me."

He put the phone down.

"Thirty below," the sergeant said. "That's very cold, sir. Where does your sister live?"

"On the American east coast, sergeant, close to Canada but still in the United States. She asked me many times to spend a holiday out there but I never went, a pity. She must have lived there some ten years now, ever since her husband retired. He used to work for one of our banks in New York and he got himself a vacation house on the coast, quite a lovely place, I believe. She sent some photographs once. But I don't imagine my sister liked the house, or that part of the country, and I don't think she was happy when her husband decided that they would live there all year round. Maybe that's why I never went; her letters weren't too enthusiastic. And then the cold, of course. And in summer we are always kept busy here."

"How did her husband die, sir?"

"An accident. He slipped on the ice. Tried to cut a

tree down and lost his footing and went all the way down. They live right on the shore and he fell on the rocks. Now she wants to live here again, but the estate will have to be liquidated. She isn't a very practical woman, rather dreamy. And gloomy. And she never had any children. She must feel very lonely now." The commissaris smiled. "I hardly know her, although we differ only a few years in age. She was always in her room." He imitated a little boy's voice. " 'Where is Suzanne, mother?' " " 'In her room, Jan.' " " 'What is she doing there, mother?' " " 'She is crying, Jan.' "

He moved his coffee cup to the edge of the tabletop and the sergeant jumped up, ran to a corner of the room, and came back with a silver pot. The adjutant brought a tray with a milk jug and a sugar bowl. "Thank you. And now she is crying again. But she has a reason this time. Must have been a sad experience. There are other houses nearby. She may not have been alone when she found the corpse and tried to bring it back into the house." He got up and briskly rubbed his hands. "Well, gentlemen, it seems I'll be traveling. I'd better see the chief constable and apply for some extra leave. Bring back the damsel in distress and set her up properly. I hope my brother-in-law had a good pension and proper life insurance. Life in Amsterdam is expensive these days and I'll have to find Suzanne a good apartment."

"Sir," the sergeant said.

"Yes?"

"Do you think you should go, sir? Your health . . ."

"Is bad," the commissaris said. "A fact I have been aware of."

The adjutant cleared his throat. "Thirty degrees below, sir, that's cold. You suffer from rheumatism. Doesn't that disease become worse . . ."

"When it is cold? Yes. But I can wear warm clothes. And the house will be heated, no doubt. She lives in America, adjutant, not on the North Pole. America is a wealthy country, filled with comforts. I am sure I'll be quite all right."

"Your brother, sir . . ." the sergeant said.

The commissaris sat down again and rubbed his small wizened face with both hands. They pushed up his spectacles and his faded green eyes looked at the sergeant. "Yes, my brother, but he lives in Austria now, a very quiet life in the mountains. I don't think he wants to be bothered." The spectacles slipped back on the straight little nose and the commissaris got up. "No, after all, she telephoned *me,* didn't she? So I am duty-bound to go. A sister is a very close relative, and it won't be all that much trouble. An airplane will cross the ocean in a matter of hours. I should be able to have breakfast here and dinner in America. And what is there to do? Comfort her, make her feel that there are still people around who care . . . sort through some papers, make a few telephone calls, write a letter or two, sell her house, help her pack, and fly her back to her home country. Should be nothing to it." He was on his way to the door.

"Sir?"

The commissaris stopped and turned. "Sergeant?"

"Can I go with you, sir? You were ill last week, sir. I am sure your wife doesn't want you to travel alone. I have some leave due and I'd like to go to America."

It wasn't the right thing to say. The commissaris frowned. "My wife? I tell you, sergeant, my wife *does* fuss, you know. If she had her way I would never leave my bed or my bath. And you know what that will do to me?" The commissaris' forefinger pointed at the sergeant's stylish denim jacket. "It will kill me. Anything will kill me. Nonactivity will and activity will too. What ever way I go I am faced by disaster."

Adjutant Grijpstra raised his bulk from the low chair and ambled over until he stood opposite the commissaris' frail figure. "But perhaps you shouldn't go alone, sir." The adjutant's deep voice was polite, soft, reassuring. "I would like to go too, but my English is bad. The sergeant speaks the language well. He could do the legwork while you sort out the job."

The commissaris stepped back until his back touched the wall. "Yes?"

"Yes, sir."

"No," the commissaris said. "No, no. Not at all. The sergeant should spend his leave in the sun somewhere. This is private business, and unpleasant too. A wailing old lady and a blizzard around the house. And what about the money? The trip'll cost a few thousand per person, a waste of good money if there are two of us. No, adjutant. It's a kind thought and I appreciate it."

The door closed. The sergeant hadn't moved from the straightbacked chair opposite the commissaris' desk. Grijpstra sighed and looked out the window. A streetcar splashed through a puddle on the other side of the street. Two cyclists, huddled in plastic yellow coats, caught its wave of muddy water and nearly capsized.

"Look at that," Grijpstra said. "I would rather see snow. Snow is nice and white, all I have seen for the last few weeks is gray water and brown mud. Maybe you should go all the same. He can't stop you, you know. It'll be a private trip. My young cousin spent his holidays in America. He said he had a good time, and it wasn't all that expensive either, but he got some sort of discount, a student's ticket. You may have to pay full fare. Do you have any money?"

"No," de Gier said and studied his new suede boots. "I could get a bank loan."

"It might not be enough. They won't lend much against your salary. I don't have any cash either. Hmm."

There was some cheerfulness in the "hmm" and de Gier looked up. "Hmm what?"

"An idea," Grijpstra said. "A good idea. I'll see the chief constable."

"That high?"

"That high," Grijpstra said as he left the room. "The top. It's hard to go higher than the top."

De Gier left too and wandered through the building. He stopped at the canteen, where a sergeant from the garage showed him how to obtain a free cup of coffee by pressing certain buttons in a certain combination on a recently installed machine, and at the typists' room, where his presence evoked some smiles and at least one wistful sigh. He reached his own office an hour later and found Grijpstra sitting on his desk. The adjutant beamed.

"Yes?" de Gier asked suspiciously.

"On your way." The adjutant's smile was triumphant.

"On my way where?"

"To the American consulate. They're waiting for you. I have a name. Ask for the name and you will be shown straight through and your passport will be stamped right away. There is no fee."

"A visa?"

"Yes. The chief constable was most impressed."

The adjutant's smile was now both triumphant and mysterious, and de Gier sat down on the visitor's chair, stretched his long legs, and put his feet on the desk. "Tell me," he said patiently. "I won't go anywhere if you don't tell me."

"What is there to tell? You are going to America. I saw the address of the commissaris' sister in his notebook. The town of Jameson in the county of Woodcock in the state of Maine, USA. We've been friendly with the American police ever since the junkies began to arrive here. Only last week I had to show a New York police lieutenant around, remember? Took me two days."

"Yes. You took him to the restaurants."

"That's where he wanted to go. I do as I am told. But it works both ways. We can go over there—there's a fund in The Hague* somewhere and there's money in the fund, American money and Dutch money. When they come over here their expenses are paid by the fund and if we go over there our expenses are paid by the fund, only we never go over there."

"That's for crime detection, Grijpstra, not for private adventures. Detection of crimes and apprehension of criminals. I saw something about it in the *Police Gazette*."

* The Hague houses the various government centers of the Netherlands. Amsterdam is the country's capital.

Grijpstra waved a magazine. "You didn't read the text properly. It also says that the fund is set up for the mutual benefit of the various police organizations. We can study each other's methods. That police lieutenant I had to take out to dinner wanted to know how we manage to catch suspects without harming them. It seems that most of the criminals brought into his precinct bleed. And he can't stand blood. He hung around one of our stations in the inner city and noted that all our suspects just walked in. Most of them weren't even handcuffed. Over there they have to carry them in."

"Did you tell him we try to be polite?"

"Yes. But he worried about the safety of the police officers. I told him about the constable who got shot and killed last year because he happened to stop an armed robber on a routine traffic checkpoint. The lieutenant said that that wouldn't have happened in America. They are very careful, even during routine checks. They walk up to the driver from the rear and hold on to their pistols. That's a good approach, I've been thinking about it. If you approach a driver from the rear he can't pull a gun on you so easily. Maybe we can learn something."

"Wait a minute," de Gier said and dropped his legs. "You mean that fund . . ."

"Yes. Go to the consulate. Once you have your passport stamped you can leave. You can leave tonight. The commissaris is also leaving tonight, but you can take a different plane. I have his flight number."

"He doesn't know?"

"No. I told the chief constable that the commissaris doesn't want you to go, but the chief agrees that the commissaris shouldn't go alone. Amazing, the whole thing was fixed in half an hour. He telephoned The Hague to clear you with the administrator of the fund. That only took a minute. You can pick up money with the cashier here, up to three thousand, and you have to bring back the change and a stack of vouchers. That fund is a faucet; if you know how to turn it it'll flood you with money. And then he phoned New York. He called the man 'general'—maybe he was a police general. The general said he would call back. He did within twenty minutes. You are invited to serve under the sheriff of Woodcock County, Maine. The general spoke to the sheriff. The sheriff will meet your plane once you tell him when it will arrive."

"Shit," de Gier said.

"Beg pardon?"

"Shit. You aren't serious, are you, adjutant? What does the chief want me to do there? Catch poachers? We don't have any poachers in Amsterdam—the rabbit that lived in the park behind my apartment building was run over last week and nobody wants to shoot the blue herons, they have a fishy taste."

Grijpstra got off the desk, pulled de Gier up by the lapels of his tailor-made jacket, and shoved him to the door.

"Off you go, dear boy. Nobody cares what you do out there as long as you bring back the commissaris alive. That fund is to be wasted, waste it pleasantly. Off you go."

"Thanks," de Gier said on the threshold.

"A pleasure. Be sure the commissaris doesn't find out until it's too late."

"What do I tell him when he does find out?"

"Blame it on me," the adjutant said. De Gier was in the corridor. The door closed slowly.

De Gier grinned.

2

The plane's wheels seemed bound to touch the tops of the tall pines bordering the tiny airstrip and the commissaris had to force himself to keep his eyes open. His ideas about America had changed once the stewardess walked him across the vast hall of Boston's airport and pointed at a two-engined plane. The plane looked old, with bulging lines dating some thirty years back. A young man in a heavily padded jacket and an oil-stained cap with earmuffs was wheelbarrowing a suitcase through the snow.

"Is that my plane?"

"Yes, sir," the stewardess said brightly. "Prestige Airlines, a small private company. They fly to most of the small airports in Maine. They've been going for years. I'm sure they're very reliable."

The young man had got the wheelbarrow stuck and was pushing it with all his might. He was shouting, but his words didn't penetrate through the plate-glass walls of the airport building. The stewardess giggled. "That's your pilot, sir. He'll come back in a minute; he also takes care of the desk here."

"Good God," the commissaris muttered. The stewardess studied the tired, drawn face of the little old man leaning on his bamboo cane. "Are you all right, sir?"

"Yes, miss, just tired. I couldn't sleep, they were showing a movie while we crossed the Atlantic."

"Where are you going again, sir?"

"Jameson, Maine."

18

"Jameson," she said. "That's a nice town, I spent a holiday there once. It's on the seashore, rather popular in summer but nobody would want to go there this time of the year. It'll be all snow and ice, I imagine."

The pilot had come back and took the commissaris' ticket and suitcase. "Jameson?" he asked. "That'll be three, three and a half hours maybe, hard to say in this weather, and they may not have plowed the strip. They hadn't last time and I had to circle while they pushed the old plow around. I suppose they thought I wouldn't come in and their radio had broken down again."

The commissaris' cane dug into the hall's wall-to-wall carpeting, its tip sinking away in the thick yellow strands.

Another young man, in overalls, gum boots and a peaked cap, had arrived. "Is the old crate ready, Bob?"

"Sure," the first pilot said. "As ready as she'll ever be. She was hard to start and we should really get some new cables. Another storm like this and she'll blow right away—that left cable is badly chafed, did you notice?"

"Really?" the commissaris asked.

The man addressed as Bob laughed. "Only the anchoring cable, sir. The plane itself is sound enough, old army stock and we've been looking after her. We'll be ready in a minute. Would you like to go to the bathroom before we take off? There's no toilet on the plane."

But the trip hadn't been too bad. The other two passengers, stocky middle-aged men with brilliant red hats and shotguns in leather cases, had passed a bottle of strong, raw-tasting whiskey around and nobody had objected to the commissaris' small but smelly cigars. The plane flew low and the commissaris was impressed with the landscape, or seascape, for they followed a rugged coastline with many islands dotted in a cold and wild-looking sea. The pilots had pointed and shouted names, and he looked at a map he had been given as the hunters traced a course that ended in a small spot and the cursive letters JAMESON.

"There!" the pilots shouted. The plane dived. It had

taken the commissaris a few seconds to see the airstrip, a brown cross in the all-pervading whiteness.

"Anyone meeting you?" the hunters asked as they kicked their duffelbags out the small door. "We have a truck here, can give you a ride."

But the commissaris thanked them and refused. He waved at the huddled shape standing near the wooden shed—an old woman, bent, loaded down under a fur coat and a wooly hat and wrapped in mufflers. It could only be Suzanne, he decided when the shape began to shuffle toward him and a high voice mumbled words of welcome.

"Oh, Jan, did you have a bad trip?"

He had to look the other way, for the icy wind was cutting into his face. "Yes," he heard himself say, "or no, it was a good trip. I saw the coast, very beautiful. How are you, dear?"

She cried. The pilot handed his suitcase down and his fingers hurt through the thin leather glove as he tried to grab its handle.

"Let me take that." He looked up gratefully. He was rid of his suitcase, which was carried away by a wide-shouldered man in a long coat topped by a hood. He took his sister's arm and was led toward a long, gleaming car.

"So you could come after all?" he asked cheerfully. "That's good. Is that Opdijk's car?"

"No, that's one of Janet's cars. She's my neighbor. I can't drive, Jan."

"And the man, is he your neighbor too?"

"That's Reggie, he works for Janet. He's very nice, they're all very nice. Oh, Jan, are you really going to take me out of here? To Holland? Are we going to Holland, Jan?"

The path was iced over and he had trouble staying on his feet.

"Certainly."

"I can't believe it, Jan. Opdijk always said we would stay here forever. It's so cold, Jan, and the summers . . . all the insects. We live behind double windows in winter and behind wire netting in summer. It's so *cruel* out here, Jan."

"Cruel?" the word seemed wrong to him. He had been treated very well so far. By the plane's staff, by the personnel of the airport, by the pilots and the hunters. He almost slipped again and stopped. The white silence comforted his tired mind. Huge pines towered above him and two black birds fluttered down a branch and spread their wings and soared off. Crows —no, they couldn't be. Too large. Ravens! *"Ravens!"* He had shouted the word. A species long extinct in Holland but still alive in tales and legends. And here they flew around. Amazing. One of the birds seemed to answer his shout and croaked. He thought of the crows in his neglected back garden in Amsterdam. They would cackle. This croak was very different, a powerful and majestic utterance, a promise. "Those are ravens, Suzanne." His sister turned and blinked.

"What was that, Jan?"

"Ravens, the birds!"

"Are they?"

"Don't you know? How long have you been here?"

She was pushing against his arm, leading him to the safety of the car. The man called Reggie was coming back.

"I never went out much, Jan. Opdijk liked to go out."

Reggie had stripped off a mitten and was offering his hand. The commissaris shook it, a hard hand with dirt ingrained in the lines and with strong square nails. The man's hood had fallen back. The face didn't go with the hands. A sensitive face, the commissaris thought, but reserved. A man who has been hurt many times but who perseveres. A lonely man who has found a way to live with his loneliness. The commissaris was reminded of de Gier. De Gier was a hard man too, and sensitive. But this man's eyes lacked the gleam that made de Gier's face lively. The commissaris was aware of his own thoughts as he shook Reggie's hand and heard his full name. "Reggie Tammart, at your service."

An old-fashioned way of greeting, a noble salute. Yes, nobility. He remembered American nobility, for he had met some of the officers of the liberation troops riding into Holland at the end of the war. The officers had told him that they were from the South—perhaps Reggie Tammart was a Southerner.

"Are you from the South, sir?"

"New Orleans, Louisiana, sir. Pleased to meet you."

The commissaris tried to place the name on a map. A coastal place, a port. And in the South, he had been right. He marched on, pleased with himself. A new environment, but he had some knowledge to relate to —the new facts might drop into a pattern.

"Beautiful country you have here, Mr. Tammart."

"Yes, sir. You can call me Reggie if you like. Beautiful country indeed, sir, but when the snow covers the ground there isn't much to do except hunting and logging."

"Is that what you do?"

"I am Janet Wash's gardener, sir, amongst other things. I only hunt woodchucks because they ruin the gardens, but they're asleep in their holes now."

"So you are 'logging'?" The commissaris didn't know what the word meant, but he thought the man would tell him. He had been trained not to show his ignorance but to let others fill him in, through their answers to his carefully planned questions.

"Yes. Janet has woodstoves, she doesn't believe in oil. The stoves in the house go through a quarter of a cord a day and then there are the barrel stoves in the garage and the cabins. I have twenty cords cut, but we'll need a lot more if the winter goes on like this."

"You do all that on your own?"

"No, sir, I have some help."

Reggie spoke in a slow drawl, pondering his words. His friendliness was close to politeness, not the open cordial approach of the pilots and the hunters. Not an easy opponent, the commissaris thought as he slid into the back seat of the car. But the man wasn't an opponent, of course. He thought of his object in coming to America. All he had to do was sell his brother-in-law's estate. The face of Suzanne's dead husband formed itself in his memory. He hadn't known the man well, but they had met a few times, when Opdijk was in Amsterdam on leave, or on business. A blunt man with a red face, not at all the polished banker he was supposed to be. A man who drank a lot and who told coarse but not unfunny jokes. The commissaris didn't think he had ever bothered to find out what Opdijk's position in the bank was. Ah, he remembered now, Opdijk had been an accountant, with a university degree. An expert on financial strategy. An inner-circle job most likely, checking computer charts in a room on the top floor of some New York skyscraper. An unlikely match for sad Suzanne. He also remembered what Suzanne had done during her short vacations in Amsterdam. She had bought antique chinaware in little stores, one piece at a time, after endless deliberation. Opdijk probably held her on a short leash. Well, anyway, the man was dead now. He wondered if Suzanne minded very much. She only seemed eager to get back to Holland. Perhaps Opdijk's death was a release for her.

He mistook the blurred shape in the corner of the back seat for a bundle of blankets so that the sudden words startled him.

"I am glad to see you are all in one piece. That little plane is a real bone rattler, don't you think?" A careful, pleasantly slow voice, as cool and firm as the hand that reached out for him and which he held for a moment as he lowered himself onto the seat and found a place for his cane.

"Not at all, madam. I liked the plane, and the pilots know their job."

"Good. And you had a clear sky."

"Yes, and a wonderful view. It was very good of you to drive my sister to the airport and to meet me here, but you shouldn't have put yourself out. There were some gentlemen on the plane who offered me a ride into town."

The long slender hand touched Reggie's shoulder. "Friends of ours, dear?"

Reggie had the car in gear and the commissaris saw the pines slip away while the car turned into what seemed to be a bumpy country lane. Suzanne was in the front passenger seat, turned around and peering at him. He smiled encouragingly.

"Not friends, Janet, acquaintances. The two Boston businessmen who bought that camp on Bartlett's Bay. They've come for the deer again."

The refined voice acquired an icy edge. "The deer, of course, the hunting season. Every year I forget and every year there they are again, with their horrible red hats and orange jackets and coarse faces and dirty hands and their cartons of beer and their big cannon, banging away at the poor things. How many did they get last year, Reggie?"

"Thousands, I believe, Janet."

Janet sighed. "Thousands of the lovely creatures, it's unbelievable and yet they don't die out. In the old days the predators would catch them, I suppose, the bears and the bobcats and the mountain lions. But now there aren't too many of those, so we horrible humans have to do the job. Oh well. Dear me, I haven't even introduced myself. I am Janet Wash, your sister's nearest neighbor. We were all very saddened when we heard the awful news about Pete Opdijk's accident. Any neighbor would have driven Suzanne to the airstrip to meet you, but as I am closest I grabbed the honor. We are so glad you could find the time to come out here."

The commissaris wondered whether he could light a cigar. The ashtray in the armrest was empty and clean, so perhaps not. He noted the details of the car. Old, but in excellent condition. He had recognized the car's make as he got into it. A Cadillac, of the type the mayors of Amsterdam had used many years ago before they switched over to compacts and pretended to be economizing. A smooth car, built well, with great headlights sitting on the sleekly curved mudguards. He patted the leather of the armrest.

"I should have come earlier." Suzanne's hand crept over the back of the front seat and he held it affectionately. "Suzanne asked me often enough, but America seemed so far then."

"It *is* far," Janet said, "and out here we are very far indeed. The Canadian border is close. We're almost falling out of the country. Will you stay awhile?"

"As long as it takes. There is some work waiting in Amsterdam. I would like to stay awhile but . . ."

"It shouldn't take long, Opdijk was always very meticulous about his affairs and we'll all be glad to help. My house is close and you can use Opdijk's car, I am sure, if you don't mind driving on slippery roads, and there's always the telephone."

He squeezed his sister's hand. "You'll be back in the old country soon. I wonder if your house will be easy to sell. Do you know if it is mortgaged, dear?"

Suzanne's watery eyes blinked above the little nose, which was an exact copy of the commissaris'. "I, I really don't know, Jan, he never discussed such things with me, but I know where he kept his papers. There are some boxes and files—perhaps you can find out."

"Yes," the commissaris said. The car had reached the top of a <u>hill</u> and had stopped to let an oncoming car pass. Below the hill the forest stretched as far as the sea, and the commissaris identified some of the trees. Naked white trunks of birches clustered around high maples that seemed frozen in gigantic movements of joy, and everywhere there were the strange pines that he had also seen around the airstrip, reaching up with delicate long needles, like the sleeves of an Oriental dancer in the middle of an exuberant movement. The other car had stopped alongside and Reggie pushed a button so that the window on Suzane's side eased down. The window of the driver's seat in the other car also slid open.

"How are you doing?"

"Good," Reggie shouted. "How are you, sheriff?"

The commissaris stared at the long cruiser, spotlessly polished and with an array of blue lights attached to a

bar on its roof. A very neat and a very dangerous-look-
ing car that reminded him of a pike in a Dutch moat,
a ponderous fish but quick to attack and gobble its prey.
The young man at the wheel, in a uniform that looked
like a Boy Scout's, was slender and fairly small, but he
bore his authority naturally. The commissaris noted the
clipped moustache, the clean angular lines of the face,
and the calm, clear eyes.

"On my way to the airstrip," the sheriff said.

"The plane has come and gone."

"I don't want the regular plane. The high brass in
New York are sending me a Dutch police officer; the
state police are flying him in. There they are now." He
pointed, and the commissaris opened his window and
looked up. A blue aircraft was circling about a thousand
feet up.

"A minijet," Reggie said. "Amazing, the police must
have money to burn these days."

Janet's quiet voice spoke into the commissaris' ear.
"Did the sheriff say a *Dutch* police officer?"

"Yes."

"Aren't *you* a Dutch police officer? I believe Suzanne told me so yesterday."

"I am," the commissaris said.

"But you have already arrived."

"So I have."

It was too much of a coincidence. The commissaris
wondered how many men were employed by the various
Dutch police services. Fifty thousand? More? But what
would any of them be doing in Woodcock County,
Maine, USA? He smiled. He remembered having seen
Grijpstra going into the corridor where the chief constable had his office. What would Grijpstra have wanted
the chief constable to do for him? If Grijpstra wanted to
deal with the top he would, normally, go via the chief
of his own division. That chief was he, the commissaris. So why would Grijpstra have bypassed him?

He looked back. The blue plane was coming down,
gracefully. An elegant machine.

"If you like we can go back," Janet Wash was saying. "Whoever that man may be, you are sure to know him, don't you think so? Wouldn't it be nice for two Dutch police officers to meet in the middle of nowhere?"

"Yes," the commissaris said, "but I won't delay you. I will meet my colleague later on, no doubt."

So they were flying Sergeant de Gier in. He thought a little further. The chief constable knew a number of high American police officers. Amsterdam had become a city of interest, ever since it had been classified a throughport for drug traffic. The chief constable also knew the American CIA chief in the Netherlands. A single telephone call from the chief constable's desk would arrange a temporary transfer for the sergeant. He frowned. Something was wrong. He wouldn't accept official recognition of his own invalidism, even if he was an invalid, even if his rheumatism was crippling him. He didn't need a bodyguard, or a nursemaid. He was traveling at his own expense, in his own time. He felt that he was falling asleep and struggled to stay awake.

"We'll have you in bed soon," Janet's low voice said, "with a cup of good strong tea. You must be exhausted, poor man."

"I am a little tired," he said and fell asleep. His last thought was that he would find a way to deal with the sergeant. It wouldn't do to disappoint de Gier, but he certainly wasn't going to encourage him either.

3

The blue jet's engines roared while its wheels screamed to a stop on the carelessly plowed and badly leveled strip. The hands of the impeccably uniformed pilot moved over his controls and the engines whined into silence.

"Jameson," the pilot said gruffly and pointed at a weathered sign dangling on a long rusty nail. "One of the world's forgotten assholes. You sure you want to come here, sergeant?"

"Jameson, Maine," de Gier said. "Yes, that's what they said."

"And that's where you are."

The sheriff's cruiser showed its nose between a shed that housed the strip's machinery and office and a corrugated iron hangar, and an old man in a shapeless coat and an old-fashioned airman's leather cap with form flaps seemed hesitant as to whether he should go to the plane or acknowledge the sheriff's high station by opening the cruiser's door. He finally decided to stay where he was and let things sort themselves out. The cruiser inched forward, then suddenly leaped away, coming to an abrupt halt near the small aluminum staircase that the pilot was sliding from the plane. The pilot jumped down and shook the sheriff's hand.

"Here he is, all in one piece."

The sheriff's regular white teeth showed. "You guys spending the night here?"

"Can you put us up?"

"I only have the jailhouse."

The pilot laughed. "No thanks, we have our own jails and there'll be a storm tomorrow. We'll get back while we can."

De Gier waved at the second pilot and tried to pull his stylish short coat closed with his free hand. His suitcase was leaning against his leg.

"You sure you want to stay here now?" the pilot asked, turning back to his plane.

"Sure."

"Okay, it's your party, let us know when you have enough and we'll come and save you—if the weather lets us."

"Get into the cruiser," the sheriff said and whisked de Gier's suitcase off the ground. "It's too cold here—there's more ice than air in the wind. Is that the coat you're planning to wear here?"

De Gier lifted a foot, slipped, and was yanked back upright by the sheriff's wiry arm.

"What have you got under your shoes?"

"Leather."

The sheriff grinned and pushed his guest around the cruiser, holding on to him while he opened the door. As the car moved off de Gier noticed that the sheriff's mustache had become white and that ice had formed on the end of each hair. He felt his own. The icicles tinkled together. He tried to pull them off. The sheriff shook his head. "Don't do that. They'll come off by themselves. Ice melts. What do I call you? Sergeant? The general said that was your rank, how come a general is sending me a sergeant?"

"Sure, sergeant. Sergeant Rinus de Gier."

He had to say it again, since the sheriff had trouble with the sharp G of the surname. "Like getting a fly stuck in your throat and trying to bring it up. You have more sounds like that in your language?"

"A few."

The sheriff's tone was cold, but de Gier hardly noticed. His thoughts were still in the sky. The small jet had moved like a dragonfly, and the pilot had obliged when de Gier pointed at one of the hundreds of islands and circled the conglomeration of overgrown rocks dotted with a few white wooden houses, going so low that they could see the foam break on the waves, rolling in to froth over the jagged shore. The transition from the even routine of Amsterdam's ugly police headquarters and the gray steady rain of Holland's swampy winter that had made his brain sodden and slow to the sudden explosion of clear colors on the American coast had been too quick, and he felt elated but also stunned. One day with nothing but the prospect of thumbing through a file of lengthy reports on events hardly worth noting and the very next day this. He mumbled and the joined inarticulate words sat on the steady purr of the cruiser's engine.

"What's that?" But the sheriff forgot his question as he asked it. They had left the road leading to the airstrip and were on a narrow highway, reasonably clean of snow and mud. A car came roaring toward them, cutting through the double yellow lines in the middle of the road.

"Watch it." But de Gier had seen the car and stretched his legs and held on to the dashboard. A head-on collision seemed possible, but the other car swerved. "Close," the sheriff said and braked and made a U-turn.

"You mind?"

"No," de Gier said.

"Good."

The sheriff had grabbed the microphone stuck close to the shaft of the cruiser's wheel. "Route One, going south, pursuing subject in black Oldsmobile, speeding, possibly under influence, just passed Billy's farm."

The radio responded immediately. "Want any assistance, Jim?"

"Not yet, ten four."

"A little chase. I'll call it off if you're tired. You had any sleep lately?"

"Enough," de Gier said. The cruiser's siren was barking just above his head, short urgent blasts, threatening like the howl of a pack of wolves.

"Motherfucker," the sheriff said.

"Pardon?"

"Motherfucker, must have been going over eighty. There's a fifty-mile limit here."

De Gier thought about the word as he watched the cruiser's speedometer touching a hundred. The low trees on the sides of the speedway had become a continuous fringe of gray green streaked with white where snow clung to the evergreens' needles. The cruiser's purr changed into a controlled roar. The dark eyes in the sheriff's narrow face betrayed no excitement. There was no traffic on the speedway and the only other moving object was the Oldsmobile. The battered rear of the black car was growing. De Gier could see the registration plate, but the numbers were unclear, partly covered by dirt and rust.

The cruiser's speed grew somewhat and the fleeing car's back fender came closer. The microphone popped back into the sheriff's hand.

"You there?"

"Yes, Jim."

"You got that complaint about the missing Olds yesterday?"

"Right here on the desk, Jim."

"Number?"

"Four-five-two, seven-four-six."

"Could be, this plate starts with four-five. Sixty-nine black Olds, right?"

"Right, Jim. Sure you don't want assistance? Bob's cruiser is on Route One too. I can raise him."

"Sure, raise him. Ten four."

The cruiser's engine made its doors vibrate as the two cars raced side by side. The sheriff put his foot all the way down and began to steer to the side. There was a squeal of brakes. De Gier looked round. The Oldsmobile skidded and seemed to be ready to overturn, but it touched a snow bank and dug itself in, its rear wheels spinning frantically.

"Right," the sheriff said and opened his door. De

Gier got out too. "Careful, sergeant. You're not too steady on your legs."

When de Gier reached the Oldsmobile the driver was facing the sheriff, dwarfing the tight upright figure that stood nailed on the glistening asphalt. Very nice, de Gier thought, a three-hundred-and-fifty-pound suspect. Like many big men the driver seemed pleasant, jolly almost.

"You're not taking me in, sheriff." The voice boomed and came from a pink slit in a thick beard that grew up to the man's deep-set eyes. De Gier stopped, his feet slightly apart, his arms dangling. The giant turned to look at him.

"Who are you?"

"A rider," the sheriff said.

"So why is he here?"

"A curious rider. I'm taking you in, Leroux. Speeding."

"Curiosity killed the cat." A strong waft of whiskey hit de Gier's nostrils. It hit the sheriff too.

"You've been drinking, Leroux. That's another charge. And I have a third. You stole the car."

The pink slit in the beard curled. "No, sheriff. The car belongs to my buddy. You know him—Charlie, young Charlie Bouchier. Charlie had the loan of my chain saw, but he didn't give it back. He gave me some parts back, not the chain saw. He owes me a couple of hundred to have it fixed again, but Charlie has no money."

The sheriff walked to the Oldsmobile and looked in. He came back. "There's no key in the car. How did you start her, Leroux?"

"I can start a car without a key."

"So you stole it. Charlie didn't give you the key, right?"

"You're not taking me in, sheriff." Leroux hadn't raised his voice, but his eyelids dropped halfway and the fist on his right arm swung, just a few inches forward, then dropped back again.

"Yes I am, Leroux. Get into the cruiser."

"Not unless you pull your gun on me."

De Gier looked at the gun. It stuck obscenely from a narrow holster on the sheriff's belt, secured only by a thin leather strap that would spring open if the sheriff flicked a finger. A wicked gun, an oversized revolver, the wooden butt shining in the low sunlight.

"I won't pull a gun on you, Leroux."

Leroux's throaty laugh rumbled around the sheriff. "You want to fight me, sheriff?"

"Get into the cruiser."

Leroux's hand came up slowly and a forefinger poked out of the fist. The finger touched the sheriff's nose and pressed down. The nose flattened. The sheriff hadn't moved.

De Gier's reaction wasn't conscious. His mind had appraised the situation and determined it to be dangerous. The suspect was big and undoubtedly strong. He was also armored, for the thick jacket, padded with down or plastic fluff, would absorb any blow. The only exposed part of the suspect's body was the face, but Leroux had his chin down and his left arm was free to block the sheriff's punch. The sheriff didn't have enough weight to resist the pressure of the suspect's hand. Leroux's action constituted a charge: harassing an officer. There was little the sheriff could do except try to stand his ground, but de Gier could attack. Leroux's neck was free. De Gier's knees buckled slightly and his left hand chopped upward, forming a blade, and hit Leroux's arm a half inch below the elbow joint. Leroux's forearm snapped up and the bearded head turned slightly, but the movement was arrested by a second chop when de Gier's right hand hit the side of the big man's neck. There was less force in the second chop, but it had enough strength to block the flow in Leroux's artery. Leroux's eyes closed and he fell slowly. He rolled over once, as if he were trying to find a more comfortable position on the cold road. Then he sighed.

"Out," the sheriff said. "Thanks. Good move. I hope you haven't killed him."

"No."

"You've hit subjects like that before?"

"Not too often."

"I usually hit them with my flashlight." The sheriff showed the flashlight. The stem was a foot long. "Give them a swipe on the temple. Knocks them out and it doesn't hurt my hand. Let's move him."

They dragged the body to the cruiser and maneuvered it onto the back seat. Leroux groaned and smacked his lips. His eyes were still closed as his hand rubbed his bruised neck.

"Did the rider knock me out?"

"He did. How do you feel?"

"Bad."

"You going to behave now?"

Leroux's groan became a bark. "No! I'll kill you both."

"Handcuffs," the sheriff said and ripped the metal rings from his belt. "Hold him, sergeant."

Leroux's hands were fists again, but they had no power and de Gier's long, muscular fingers pried them open and applied a twisting pressure so that the body on the backseat turned halfway and the arms met in the back. The handcuffs touched his hairy wrists and snapped shut. Leroux slumped back.

"Watch him, sergeant. I'll get the Oldsmobile started and drive it to the jailhouse. Can you handle the cruiser?"

De Gier looked at the controls. "Perhaps."

"Have you driven automatic cars before? They have them in Europe, don't they?"

"Yes, I have. Not often. The P is Park, isn't it? What's the N?"

"Neutral. Shift in D for Drive and be gentle with the accelerator. If you have to brake, pump it—just touch it with your toe. Can you do that?"

"Yes."

The sheriff walked over to the Oldsmobile, opened the hood, and adjusted the cable Leroux had used to start the car. When the engine caught, he reversed the big car out of the bank, allowing the engine to idle so

that the wheels just moved and didn't spin. De Gier
eased the cruiser behind the Oldsmobile. The radio
crackled and he fumbled with the microphone, having
trouble finding its button.

"Caught him, sheriff?"

"The sheriff is in the suspect's car. We are on our
way back."

"Who are you?"

"Sergeant Rinus de Gier, Amsterdam Municipal
Police."

The radio crackled emptily.

"Come again?"

De Gier came again.

"You the guy the sheriff went to meet on the airstrip?"

"Right."

"You got the subject?"

"Yes, man named Leroux."

"Leroux. He's big. Did he fight?"

"A little."

"Okay, ten four."

De Gier put the microphone back. "Ten four," he
mumbled.

"Means 'acknowledged,'" Leroux said. "Ten three
means 'go ahead.' Sheriff's talk. I have a CB radio.
Everybody has. It's fun to listen in sometimes, not always. They talk a lot of shit too. You really from the
Amsterdam police?"

De Gier adjusted his rearview mirror so that he could
see Leroux's face. The small beady eyes twinkled back
at him.

"Yes."

"That's close to France. How come you're here?"

"An exchange. I am learning."

Leroux laughed. "On me, hey? I would have murdered that little bastard."

"Maybe not. How do you feel?"

"Bad. Take the cuffs off and I'll feel better."

"No."

Never trust a suspect when he's just been arrested.

A golden police rule. An arrested suspect feels threatened, his nerves are ready to break, his reasoning is impaired. Better to humor him.

"You French?" de Gier asked.

"Not French French, local French."

"American."

"Yes, everybody is American. But I'm French. They don't like us here; they say that we are niggers but we've been sandblasted so the color doesn't show."

"What's wrong with black?"

"Black isn't white," Leroux said. "Take my cuffs off. Bastard put them on too tight."

"In a minute."

Leroux leaned forward. The sheriff had left the glass partitioning open. Leroux's chin rested on the barrel of the shotgun that was clipped to the two front seats.

"I can bite your neck off."

"Don't bite my neck off," de Gier said. "It'll be another charge. You have enough already. Did you steal the car?"

"Borrowed it."

"Will the owner say you borrowed it?"

"Sure. Charlie only wants his car back, and I won't give it back unless he gets my chain saw fixed."

"You'll give it back now. Are you drunk?"

Leroux grinned slyly. The Oldsmobile was still ahead. There were houses on both sides of the road now, and the dainty steeple of a clapboard church pointed at the clear, pale blue sky. Great elms flanked the street. A store sign glided by: ROBERT'S MARKET. Two pickup trucks were feeding off the pumps under the awning of the store. An old woman pushed a rusty supermarket cart through the caked snow on the sidewalk. A fat black dog limped behind the woman.

"Jameson," Leroux said. "Good old Jameson, nothing but trouble. I haven't made money, not even in the summer. Broke my leg and the bill from the hospital is still on the shelf. They'll be pulling the house from under me soon. It's a good thing they're feeding the kids at the school or I'd have them whining around me.

There's a deer in the freezer for the holidays, but they eat a deer in a week and there'll be another week after that one. If the judge fines me heavy it'll be all over."

The cruiser turned sharply, following the Oldsmobile. A small sign, overshadowed by a twisted pine, and JAIL. The sheriff stood next to the cruiser.

"How is our friend? Quiet now?"

"I'm quiet, sheriff."

The sheriff opened the rear door. Leroux didn't move.

"I'll be real quiet, sheriff. Take them off."

The handcuffs snapped free.

"Walk."

"Yes, sheriff."

"Bernie McDougal," a fat man said and shook de Gier's hand. "Good to meet you, you did some work, that's good, loafers get very cold here. Shall I take him, Jim? I couldn't raise Bob's cruiser, but you had enough help."

"All yours."

Leroux was led to the rear of the building. The big man was rubbing his wrists. There was the clang of a metal door and Bernie came back. He wore the same uniform as the sheriff but there was a plastic disc above the left tunic pocket: "Chief deputy."

"Are you going to hit him, Jim?"

"Speeding," the sheriff said. "Fifty-mile limit, he was doing eighty but maybe we'll drop it to sixty-five. That'll be a twenty-dollar fine. He won't have much more."

"Drunk?"

"He wasn't too drunk."

"Stolen car?"

"Phone Charlie. Tell him we found his car and to bring the key. Leroux used some silly wire. It may short-circuit the system. Charlie won't want to press charges, but we should talk to him about Leroux's chain saw. Leroux is a logger in winter. He needs the saw. L Charlie has broken it he should do something."

"Coffee?"

"Yes," de Gier said. "Coffee. Is there a place to eat nearby?"

"Be my guest," the sheriff said. "We have a cook in the jailhouse. What's he got, Bernie?"

"Pea soup and there's bread in the oven. No eggs but there's bacon. Four frostbitten green peppers from the greenhouse but enough lettuce. Tomatoes. Clam chowder."

The sheriff nodded. Bernie went back into the jail and returned with a barefoot young man with long shiny brown hair.

"You had your bath?"

"Yes, sheriff."

"Won't have a dirty cook. Did the bread rise?"

"Yes, sheriff. But you got the wrong yeast. I don't want little chunks, I want the little bags."

"Chunks are cheaper. Meet the sergeant."

De Gier and the young man nodded at each other.

"The sergeant is our guest. A police officer from abroad. Call him 'sergeant.' His name will give you a sore throat. Sergeant, this is Albert, second man of the BMF gang. He'll be out tomorrow, but we have another cook. How is he shaping up, Albert?"

"His soups are better than his stews."

"He'll have to learn."

The meal was served on the room's only table. It was a big room, pine paneled on all sides and with a high roof carried by dark brown rough beams. Half a dozen rifles and shotguns were chained to a rack on the wall. A modern radio transmitter and receiver stood on a shelf next to two old black telephones. Uniform jackets and stiff high felt hats hung from hooks near the door leading to the jail. The sheriff unbuckled his gunbelt and lowered it carefully into a drawer under the table.

"You want a gun, sergeant? I can let you have one, but you'll have to wear it so that it shows. There's a law against hidden guns here and I can't make you a deputy. Only Americans can serve in a sheriff's department. I can call the general—maybe there's an exception to the rule I don't know about."

"No, I don't want a gun."

"Good, you shouldn't need one. I hardly ever touch mine. It antagonizes the locals. They've all got guns too. If I pull mine it may give them ideas. What were those chops you used on Leroux? Karate?"

"Yes."

"You good at karate?"

"No, I am trained in judo. It's a gentler method, but the suspect was big and I thought I might lose my footing if I moved around him."

"Yes," the sheriff said, cutting the bread, then pushing a steaming bowl of soup across the table. "I really thought you had killed the motherfucker."

"Motherfucker," de Gier said and held up his plate so that Albert could serve the salad. "Does the suspect have a perversion?"

"Not that I know of. It's just a term. We deal with two types: subjects and motherfuckers. Everybody is a subject until we have a charge against them that will stick. Charges make them motherfuckers. And the judge may change their status again. If he confirms the charge they become prisoners."

"I'm a prisoner," Albert said. "Take this pepper, sergeant. It looks a little back on the edge, but it's okay."

"What did you do?"

The sheriff stopped eating. "I'll tell you what he did because he won't tell you. He did very well. Old Bernie likes a good chase and he likes to make the cruiser jump, and Albert, here, he knows that. So Albert does a number of things. First he comes to see us, all meek and pleasantlike, and he says his motorcycle is stolen. Just disappeared. One minute it's in front of Robert's Market, sitting quietly in the sun, and the next minute it's gone. Very strange, for Albert's motorcycle is some outlandish contraption and nobody knows how to start it but Albert. But anyway, it's gone and Albert comes to see us. It's a red bike, easy to spot. Then Albert goes and gets himself a big beard made out of twine or something, and he hangs it over his face and gets some funny clothes and puts them on, and he finds his bike where

he has hidden it, and he races up Main Street. Just as
Bernie is coming out of Beth's restaurant. Bernie
jumps for his cruiser and tries to yank its door open.
The door is stuck. Bernie puts his foot against the
cruiser and gives a mighty heave and the whole door
comes out, on top of Bernie, who's sitting on the sidewalk. Okay. Bernie gets up and into the cruiser. He
starts the engine. Fine. But the shift is locked in park.
Bernie gets mad and tries to force the shift, and meanwhile he has his foot on the gas. The shift works after
a while and the cruiser jumps away, into a parked vehicle. Okay. Bernie backs up and takes off. But then the
cruiser has four slow leaks and Bernie doesn't get very
far. I didn't see it but I listened to people who did.
They were still laughing and it was hours later. Like a
Laurel and Hardy movie, only better. Full color and
three dimensions. And Albert was gone. Eh, Albert?"

"That's what you say," Albert said.

"That's what I say and what everybody says. The
cruiser needs a lot of county money and a couple of
weeks to get fixed up again. The sheriff's department
pays for the car Bernie hit. You laugh and all your
buddies laugh."

"No proof?" de Gier asked.

"No proof."

"But the next day Albert telephones to say that his
motorcycle has shown up again. We say that that is
very nice. Albert says yes and hangs up. Then he goes
for a ride. He doesn't wear the funny clothes or the
beard. And he passes a state trooper in a curve, on the
gravel shoulder, at a hundred and ten miles an hour.
When he sees that he's playing with a police car it's too
late, eh, Albert? You got away but we picked you up a
little later and the judge liked the charge. Dangerous
driving. Ten days. Thirty suspended. You are a good
cook, Albert, we'll miss you, but we'll have you back."

Albert smiled. "You won't, sheriff."

"You can't drive at fifty-five miles an hour, you can't
do it, Albert. Only the good citizens can do it, and you

aren't a good citizen. You'll be speeding and we'll catch you. That's not a probability, that's a fact."

"I'm selling the motorcycle."

The sheriff held up his bowl. "If you do we're getting somewhere, Albert, but it's winter now and your bike is useless. When spring comes around you'll have forgotten. But we still have thirty days for you."

"More soup?" Albert asked.

"He is a motherfucker," the sheriff said, "but he admits it. He is a *bad* motherfucker. The name of his gang. The BMF gang. How is the fox these days, Albert?"

"The fox is fine, sheriff. He has been visiting."

"We'll have him here too," the sheriff said. "Tell him to brush up on his cooking. I've got a freezer full of mushrooms and I like them sautéed. With a pickle on the side and plenty of gravy. I haven't asked you to try so far because you're still a little coarse, but the fox should do better. Make sure you tell him."

"Yes, sheriff." The young face smiled again. De Gier studied it. An intelligent face with more depth than could be expected of a village rowdy. The clear blue eyes sparkled above a strong jaw.

"That'll be all, Albert. We'll do the coffee ourselves."

Albert's bare feet shuffled over the boards and the metal door clanged.

"You keep the door unlocked, sheriff?"

"Yes. Call me Jim. That door is open, but the cells inside are locked. Albert is a trusty, he can move around. Leroux is in a cell now, but he'll be out in an hour, if we can get the chain saw business with Charlie fixed. He'll have bail."

Bernie had finished his call. "Charlie is on his way, Jim. He's borrowing a car."

"Good."

"This BMF gang," de Gier asked. "Just fun or are they dangerous?"

"They're dangerous, but we keep them in check. The fox is clever and he gets bored sometimes. The fox is the boss—he looks like a fox too, hairy ears and all.

If he went to New York he could beat the Mafia, but he likes it here so he gets his gang to try and beat us. We're the only other power around."

"They got my cruiser," Bernie said. "That was bad. It took a lot of brown-nosing to talk it right with the authorities."

"I'll show you your room," the sheriff said. "Upstairs, next to mine. The motel has closed for the winter. The general said to make you comfortable, but comfort is hard to get around here, although we try at times. And you'll need some clothes. I wouldn't know how. You aren't my size, and Bernie is fat and Bob and Bert are sort of square. You'll need a car too. How about the Dodge, Bernie?"

"Sure, the Dodge was meant to be a detective's car, but the detective never showed up."

"A Dodge Dart, sky blue, about new, got a receiver and a transmitter and no markings. We can clip a shotgun into it. Will that do, sergeant?"

"Yes, thank you very much. But without the shotgun, please."

"Then we won't clip it in. You're welcome, sergeant."

The upstairs room had a dormer overlooking the jailhouse grounds and the town sloping away beneath them toward a bay. The bed was covered with thick patchwork quilts and the whitewashed ceiling contrasted pleasantly with the rough boarded walls. The sheriff sat on the bed and de Gier sat in the room's only chair. He got up and felt about in his suitcase. He brought out a cheese and gave it to the sheriff. "With the compliments of the Amsterdam Municipal Criminal Investigation Department."

"That's a big cheese. What's it called? Edam?"

"Yes."

"Good. That's good cheese. We'll have to keep it away from the prisoners. They steal, you know. Stole my salami the other day. Sat around munching in their cells and didn't know what happened to the salami. Big salami too. Let's have a piece of that cheese now. I'll get the trimmings."

De Gier cut two good-sized slices with the knife the sheriff had left on the table.

"Here we are. Keep it in a strongbox in my room. Bourbon. You drink bourbon over there?"

"Not too often, but we would like to."

The sheriff poured. "Try it, you'll like it, as the dealers say to the junkies. But they give them shit. This is the real stuff, hundred proof, a present from a grateful subject because we caught another subject with twenty thousand dollars' worth of antiques taken from the first subject's house. I've been hoarding the bottle, but it'll have to go."

They drank.

"Yes?"

"Yes." De Gier's eyes shone.

The sheriff smiled. "That's better. I thought that maybe you wouldn't fancy the good stuff and then it would be hard to get to know you. Right. Now tell me, sergeant, what brings you here?"

De Gier told him about the fund financing exchange of American and Dutch police officers.

The sheriff sipped, lowered his glass, raised it, and sipped again.

"Yes," he said slowly, "but I don't buy that. You'll have to credit me with some intelligence, sergeant, even if you find me in Jameson, Maine. Why would an Amsterdam murder brigade police detective be sent here? There are such cities as New York, or Chicago, and there is a place called Los Angeles. There is crime over there and the quality of the crime could be compared to what you have in Amsterdam. But in Jameson . . . No, sergeant. This town is barely on the map. So tell me, if you want to tell me. What have we got here that makes you interested, so interested that a general troubles himself to phone the Woodcock sheriff all the way from his shiny office on the eighty-fourth floor of his Manhattan plastic palace?"

The bourbon oozed down to de Gier's stomach and warmed his blood on the way. He felt tempted to tell the truth. The truth is the best lie. He took a deep breath and told the truth.

"I see," the sheriff said a few minutes later and got up and refilled the glasses. "And this *commissaris,* this goldbraided gentleman with the pain in his legs, he is due soon, is he?"

"He should be here now."

"A little old man with thin gray hair and grandpa spectacles?"

"That's right."

"I saw him. He came in on the regular plane before the state troopers dropped you off from their space-craft. Is he staying with a lady called Janet Wash?"

"Don't know that name. He'll be staying with his sister, Mrs. Opdijk. Her husband died a few days ago. They have a house on Cape Orca."

"Ah," the sheriff said. "So you are finally telling me. In your own way, of course. My predecessor left a file on Cape Orca; the file is mine now. Cape Accident it should be called, for he wrote them all off as accidents. The old sheriff wasn't too fond of work I believe, although I wouldn't spread that belief around, even if he lives in Boston now."

"The old sheriff?" de Gier asked. "Are you the new sheriff?"

"Oh, yes, sergeant. Very new. Three months now and I still don't know the county at all. I was born and raised in the capital, a long way from here. But I know Cape Orca because I read the file. And Pete Opdijk died under my supervision so to speak. An accident. The fifth. Schwartz just ran away, but he might have been another if he had stopped to wait."

"Schwartz?"

"Captain Schwartz. The name is not familiar?"

"No."

"Maybe not, suit yourself. Maybe you came in on the Opdijk angle. Opdijk was a Dutchman and Captain Schwartz an American, even though he professed to be a Nazi. The others were Americans too, but their deaths link them to Opdijk, your client."

"Client," de Gier said.

"I'll tell you what I know. You can read the file later. A third and last glass?"

They had the third glass and the sheriff told his story while they drank it.

It wasn't a bad story, de Gier thought, with some good open leads. But his interest was academic, a foreign tale told in a foreign country. He would be no part of it. He would take the commissaris back to Amsterdam and he would see what he would see in the meantime.

Yes, de Gier thought, as the baseboard radiators popped and rattled in the warm room, the snow on the spruce outside glowed a deep red in the gentle touch of the setting sun, and the bourbon seeped through his tall body. It was a good story. Cape Orca.

"What's an orca?" he asked when the sheriff finished and got up to show him the bathroom.

"Orcas are killer whales," the sheriff said. "They are intelligent and skilled animals, as intelligent and skilled as the contract killers in New York. And their only aim is to kill. The orcas hunt in groups, and they corner their prey and rip it apart. They used to come into the bay here, but the Coast Guard fought them and now they're scarce. The bay and the cape are still called after them. They are silent and quick and always deadly. Yes, sergeant, that's what orcas are, deadly. And mighty hard to catch. Especially when the sheriff doesn't know his way about and the chief deputy is fat and the other two deputies are about as eager as hound dogs raised on bone glue and sawdust. Another drink?"

"Yes," de Gier said. "Please."

4

The commissaris was awake, but not quite. He struggled to remain in the in-between state of awareness where thoughts are sharp and definite and abstractly pure and can be experienced and enjoyed without the necessity of bothering to translate them into the always-false world of activity. He wriggled his toes and tensed and released the muscles of his hips and back. The padded blanket dropped back and a warm draft drifted over his body. There was no pain, not even the slightest twinge in the nerve ends of his legs, the heart and ever-productive source of his rheumatism. But happiness, by definition, cannot last and he knew that his hand would raise the blanket and his brain would order his body to step into the room, and he dreaded the moment.

The door opened.

"Jan?"

"Yes, Suzanne, I am awake."

"I brought you some coffee and orange juice."

"Good."

"I'll put it down here. When you're ready to come down we can eat. I have some frozen *hutspot* that can be warmed up quickly."

He shivered. *Hutspot,* a stew of carrots and potatoes and shredded meat, always reminded him of vomit drying on the cobblestones of an Amsterdam alley.

The little shape padded over the carpet. He heard the tray click as it hit the night table.

"You slept for eight hours, Jan, but you had such a long journey. Why don't you go back to sleep again?"

He sat up. "No. I think I'll start on your husband's papers. You said you had them all together. Would you mind bringing them up?"

She came back with a briefcase filled with different-colored cardboard files, and he opened them and glanced through their contents. He grunted miserably. All so simple and straightforward and Suzanne hadn't even looked at the policies. He totaled the monthly payments the pension funds and insurance policies would render and raised his eyebrows. Suzanne would be able to live in style. He checked the last bank statement and the stubs of a checkbook. A few hundred dollars' balance, but his eyebrows shot up again when he saw the total of Opdijk's savings account. Very nice indeed. No trouble there.

"Suzanne?"

She answered his shout and came into the room again.

"Do you know if the doctor sent you a death certificate? I will need several copies to make the insurance policies pay out?"

Suzanne began to cry quietly.

The commissaris cleared his throat. He had forgotten that he should commiserate. "I am sorry, dear, but I do need the certificates."

"Yes, Jan, I understand. I'll get them. They were addressed to me and they're in my cabinet. Just a moment, Jan. Do you need paper and envelopes and stamps too? To write to the insurance companies?"

"Yes, please."

He got up and put on his dressing gown and slippers and winked at himself in the mirror. Suzanne still had her wits about her. She would cry, but she would also get her money. Oh well. He sipped the coffee and rushed out of the room. He spat the coffee into the toilet. Boiled, weak, too much milk. He came back and tried the orange juice. That was fine. Perhaps he could live on orange juice for a few days. If only the house could be sold quickly. He hoped that the furniture could be auctioned. There would also be the car he had seen when they arrived, a sturdy four-wheel-drive vehicle, a station wagon, in good condition but hard to sell he supposed. Everybody around would already have a car. He would have to persuade her to make some sacrifices, but he could always work on her fear of staying. Fear and greed, two powerful urges he might be able to manipulate to everybody's benefit.

She brought the writing materials and he sat down and wrote the letters and licked the stamps. He might be able to post them after dinner if she would let him use her car. He lit a cigar and ambled about the room. A nice room, but the wallpaper was a little elaborate. Suzanne would have bought it in Holland. A farmer and his wife, in folksy clothes and wooden shoes, doing a jig against the background of a windmill. Good God. He looked away, but the design repeated itself. The jig continued on all the room's walls. The commissaris stared in horror. The farmer and his wife were smiling inanely, a thousand times, many thousands of times. He would have to try to stay away from the walls. But what else was there to look at? The windows. He pulled the shades and sighed with relief as the opaque linen snapped up and rolled itself on a bar.

The view destroyed the jig of the imbecilic couple. He sighed with wonder as he admired the bay below, its ice mirroring the starlight. An icy, immense wasteland of pure beauty, stretching away to a shore covered by a growth of what appeared to be evergreens surrounding an island. The island sloped up to a hill. There were no lights, but a high jetty stuck out into the bay. He looked up just as a moving cloud revealed the half moon, and when his eyes dropped down again the ice of the bay had become a light shade of, of what? Mauve? A very soft blue? The color seemed hard to define. He forgot the question. Why name the color? He stayed in front of the window until his sister called him, and he had time to see the narrow channel in the ice between the island and his side of the shore. The channel would run out to the ocean. He also saw the ridges and domes where ledge and rocks had been frozen over and become raised when the tide went down. He shook his head when he remembered the simple beaches of Holland, a hundred miles of yellow sand protected on one side by monotonous dunes and attacked on the other by steady breakers. He had always liked the Dutch beaches, but this was a different beauty, a distorted beauty almost, dating back to the beginning of the planet, when the first shapes were created out of turmoil.

"Jan?"

There was a sob even in that one-syllable word. He promised himself not to be irritated by his sister's gift to find suffering in anything. He remembered Suzanne as a child, a girl, a young woman. He had been able to find a way to put up with her misery then. All he had to do now was remember the recipe and repeat the performance.

"Yes, I'll be coming down, dear. Just let me shave and dress. It won't take long."

"The food is on the table, Jan."

"Very well." She would get her way. He wondered how Opdijk had put up with her sniffling approach. Would he have hit her from time to time? But Suzanne didn't look battered. Perhaps Opdijk had found ways of keeping himself busy.

"What did Opdijk do here, Suzanne?"

"He did everything, Jan. He chopped wood and he worked in the garden and he often went to town. He was the president of the club—that took a lot of his time. They have boats and things, and there were dinners and parties. I didn't always go."

"Club? What club?"

"The Blue Crustaceans. Opdijk was always very social. The doctor said he should be more careful, his heart . . . But he just slipped on the rocks."

"Had he been drinking?"

"No, he only drank after five. It happened in the morning. He had gone down to cut a dead tree, and when he didn't come back for coffee I went to look for him. The chain saw was still going. I couldn't understand it. The saw was halfway in a log, but he wasn't there and when I looked down I saw him, a long way down, on the rocks. He was looking at me, but his eyes were dead. Oh, Jan . . ."

"Yes. We'll have a look at the spot tomorrow. Slippery down there, I suppose."

"Yes, Jan."

After dinner he looked through the rest of the files and checked Opdijk's bookkeeping, which had been kept up to the day preceding the man's death. He found the deed of the house stating that the total property was just under three acres. There were no mortgage payments in the tidily kept records. Opdijk owned his property outright. It would make the sale easier.

"Is there a real estate agency in town, Suzanne?"

She looked up from the sock she was knitting. "Yes, Jan, Mr. Astrinsky's office."

"I'll see him tomorrow."

"He is a nice man, Jan, also a member of the club. Opdijk knew him well. They sometimes drank together, too much I am afraid. I was always so worried when he would come home late, but he would drive slowly and he always made it."

"Any other realtors?"

"No, there's only Mr. Astrinsky."

"I see. So I can't make them bid against each other. Well, there's no hurry, dear. You are well off. We can have the house listed, and it can be sold later."

"But I do want an apartment in Amsterdam, Jan, not a room. Will there be enough to buy an apartment?"

"There's a lot of money in the savings account."

"Will it buy me a nice apartment?"

He thought, clicking the pencil against his teeth. "Yes, there is enough for a down payment. You can easily get a mortgage for the difference."

"I don't want any debts, Jan. I always hated debts, and I would like a three-room apartment."

"There isn't enough cash for that."

"Can't you sell this house right away?"

"Yes," he said. "Yes. Don't worry, dear. I'll see what can be done and then I'll do it."

"I am so glad you came, Jan."

He had his doubts. A forced sale would drop the value, but it would be useless to try to advise her. Under the sadness there was an iron will, misdirected of course, but that wasn't his affair. He had committed himself to be of help and it had to be the help she wanted. The apartment she had in mind might cost over fifty. Still, he wouldn't throw her money away unless she forced him to. And there was the matter of time—he couldn't stay too long. He sighed, got up to look out the living room window, and sighed again. The moon was higher now and the bay had subtly changed. He mentioned the island, and she came and joined him at the window.

"That's Jeremy's Island. I've never been there. Opdijk went a few times, but he didn't like Jeremy; called him a filthy old man."

"Is he?"

"Yes, in a way. He lives there by himself, and I suppose he doesn't have a bathroom or electricity or anything. But he is very polite. He always waves when he comes by in his boat."

"You know him at all?"

"Not really, Jan. I don't know anybody except Janet. She comes to tea and I've been to her house, not often."

He left the window reluctantly. "Can I use the station wagon, Suzanne? I'll mail the letters. I've asked the pension and insurance people to send the money to you care of my address in Amsterdam. Once you have your apartment you can contact them again or I'll do it for you."

"Yes," she said. "How nice. In Amsterdam. I've been so homesick, Jan."

He looked at the stacks of Dutch magazines, at the reproductions of paintings of canals, bridges, dikes, views of Amsterdam streets looking cheap in plastic frames. He had seen the kitchen and looked at shelves filled with Dutch cans, jars, pots. She hadn't even changed her food, after that many years in another en-

vironment, in America, the land of plenty. An expensive
household to run if everything has to be imported. He
was surprised that Opdijk had allowed her to waste
money like that. Perhaps the man hadn't been as tough
as he had imagined him to be.

She went with him to the garage and waited until the
station wagon's engine caught, then opened the doors.
He drove too fast at first and the wheels spun, but he
shifted down and only one wheel sunk into the ditch
at the side of the path and the car growled back again
on firm ground. The mailbox was at the end of the
road. He promised himself to drive around again in the
morning to determine the layout of the land. It would
be silly to face the realtor without any ideas at all. The
man might be honest, but even an honest man gets
tempted when faced by an idiot.

When he got back Suzanne was sitting in front of the
fireplace wringing her hands. Her original misery
seemed to have acquired an additional twist. She seemed
close to hysteria. He sat down next to her and held her
hand.

"What is it, dear?"

"They all died, Jan, all of them, I *must* get away.
They are all dead now. There's only me left, me."

"All of them?"

She told her story in bursts, trailing off every now
and then until he patiently guided her back. He asked
as little as possible, waiting for the information to fit.
Gradually the pattern emerged, a definite report with a
beginning and an end. The end was Opdijk's death. But
the event seemed to relate to other events. When, two
hours later, she had calmed down and they had drunk
coffee he had made himself and he had seen her safely
to her room, he went to his own and made some notes.
The notes had six headings and each heading was a
name. He read the notes to himself and lit a fresh cigar
and puffed and underlined a word here and there. Then
he wrote them again, slowly and meticulously.

Six houses on one line, south shore of Cape Orca.
That was the main clue of course, the connection, the

thread. *Only one house occupied now; the Opdijk house. The others empty and two of them burned down.* Strange, wasn't it? Valuable property, left to rot, left for storms to blow through, for vandals to desecrate and ultimately destroy, to burn. Burn, that was the limit; they wouldn't burn by themselves. Right. Now the former occupants.

Case number one. A *Mr. Jones.* He couldn't put a face to the man. Suzanne had hardly known Jones, but Suzanne never knew anybody except herself, her poor suffering self. The commissaris wondered if Suzanne had known her husband. The bedrooms were separate; they might have been separate from the start. Why would Opdijk have put up with Suzanne? Did he want a housekeeper and no more? But Suzanne wasn't much of a housekeeper either. The house was clean of course, and fairly luxurious but otherwise—a hellhole of bad taste. Well, never mind. Mr. Jones was dead. An old man living by himself in a small, good bungalow set at the end of the Cape, overlooking the water like the other houses. A man who kept to himself. Found dead in his own woods, shot through the head. Two years ago. During the hunting season. Bullet came from a deer rifle. Accident, pity. According to Suzanne the house wasn't sold. Nobody else moved in, and eventually it burned down.

Case number two. The death of *Mary Brewer,* a woman about sixty years old, also retired. Miss Brewer liked to sail and to take her eleven-foot boat out on the bay. The Coast Guard had warned her several times and she had been fined for not wearing a life jacket or taking proper precautions, but she kept on sailing for the horizon and one day she didn't come back. Her corpse turned up bashed by the waves and the rocks and partly eaten by sharks or raccoons. Raccoons, the commissaris said, and he remembered how Suzanne had pronounced the word. Clearly the animals disgusted her. The commissaris had seen raccoons in the Amsterdam zoo. Very likable, he had thought, small dainty bears with agile hands. But they ate Mary's corpse. Well, why shouldn't they? The lady was dead. Another accident. And again the house found no new occupants. It still stood there. The furniture and trimmings had been removed by the heirs, but the empty shell was left.

Case number three. The disappearance of *Captain Schwartz.* But there was a difference to the pattern here and more was known. Schwartz, a genuine captain of some U.S. army outfit, retired, became a Nazi, and liked to march around his grounds with a swastika band around his arm. He also wore a German-style cap. There were no other Nazis in Woodcock County, but the captain occasionally went to New York to meet friends. He also wrote articles for the party monthly in which he propagated Nazism as the solution for American crime and corruption and urged his countrymen to conquer the world and kill the Jews. An evil man, but, as far as he had been able to deduce from Suzanne's incoherent rambling, probably insane and unable to realize his preaching in any way besides writing to be read by other madmen. His neighbors would have no contact with him and the local store wouldn't serve him, but he didn't mind and did his shopping in the next county. If he wanted any conversation he talked to a portrait of Adolf Hitler, hung in the hall of his house. But his activity attracted hostility from Jameson's rowdies. Suzanne talked about a gang. She even had a name for the rebels of Jameson: the BMF gang. The commissaris didn't know what the letters stood for. A motorcycle gang if he interpreted Suzanne's information correctly. And the leader of this gang, a young man called the fox, a particularly nasty character according to Suzanne, was reputed to have visited Schwartz and possibly threatened him, for the Nazi suddenly left and was never seen again. The captain was supposed to be living in New York now. A relative had come out and perhaps sold the house, but it was still empty. Suzanne wasn't clear about the timing of Captain Schwartz's troubles and subsequent flight. Some years ago, she'd said.

Case number four. A gentleman by the name of *Carl*

Davidson who lived by himself after his wife died of a heart attack in the hospital. Davidson liked to walk in the woods and might stay out camping for a few days. Because he lived alone and had few social contacts he wasn't missed until his frozen corpse was found by wandering locals. It had been snowing heavily and there were no tracks.

Case number five. Another old man, by the name of *Paul Rance.* Unlike the others, who all originated in New York or Washington, D.C., Rance was a local, a retired carpenter who had built his own small cabin between the bungalows of his neighbors. He had been an alcoholic but managed to stop drinking when told to do so by his doctor. Rance was sickly and liked to stay on his own grounds. Toward the end of his life he was running short of money. After not drinking liquor for several years, he suddenly died of alcoholic poisoning. His cabin burned down some months after his death.

Case number six. Pete Opdijk, sawing down a dead tree, slipped, fell off the cliffs, and broke his spine and head.

The commissaris reread his notes and added a few full stops and commas. Then he whistled, blew a smoke ring, put his finger through it, and made some joyful but inarticulate sounds. But then his expression changed and became a mixture of sadness and indifference. He remembered that he wasn't in Amsterdam and that the detectives of the murder brigade weren't around to be summoned to join him in a conference. This string of deaths had nothing to do with him. It might be of interest to the local authorities and the local authorities wouldn't be altogether witless. He recalled the face of the small sheriff, impassive in the sleek cruiser. A fine pair of eyes, calm and penetrating. Surely the man wouldn't just float around in his power symbol while willful death repeated itself in house after house on the shore of a peninsula well within his jurisdiction. Or would accidents really happen in such an alarming, repetitious pattern? The victims were all elderly.

He studied his cigar carefully. Elderly. Statistics

proved that the elderly often want to die, so they become accident prone or actually commit suicide. Suicide requires an act of will. It is easier to become careless. And to be careless in Woodcock County might be very dangerous. Why on earth would Pete Opdijk pick a cold day to cut down a dead tree, walk on slippery ice to get to the tree, and work on the tree while he was balancing on the edge of a precipice? And why would an old man like Carl Davidson wander about in the woods? Did he want the blizzard to sneak up on him and kiss him to death?

He put his cigar between his thin lips. No, no. Opdijk wouldn't have spent a fortune on a comfortable bungalow if he meant to have an accident. And what about the other houses? Why wouldn't anyone move into them? Why were they left until they burned down? And who was burning them down? Vandals?

He rubbed out his cigar. "Bah."

"Yes, Jan? Anything wrong?" He shivered, he hadn't noticed her coming in.

"No, dear, just going through my notes."

"There aren't any complications, are there, Jan? Oh, I wish we could go tomorrow. And I wish we could go by boat. Airplanes frighten me."

"Do you want to take your furniture, Suzanne?"

He watched the struggle on her face but didn't interfere.

"It will be expensive, won't it, Jan?"

"Yes, it will have to be crated and we will have to get trunks to take it to a port and you will have to pay to bring it through Dutch customs. Freight, duty—it will add up."

"I can't just leave it."

"No. You could, but whoever buys the house will have furniture of his own."

She swallowed. "Do you think I should have it auctioned, Jan?"

"The bigger pieces, yes. Certainly you could take the small stuff."

"The chinaware?"

"Yes." He picked up a fisherman's head from the mantelpiece. A pipe-smoking old man, rough but honest. Hard-working and mysterious. Why not? The clarity of the sea mirrored in the clear blue eyes. A strong chin, a straight nose, all in porcelain. But kitsch all the same. He put the fisherman down and picked up a pink dog, a Pekingese with bulging eyes. He put it down quickly. There were other pieces on the mantelpiece. A monkey hanging by its tail from a palm tree. A Spanish dancing girl with white breasts pushed out of a frilly blouse. She had very white thighs too. "Yes, you can take your collection, but you'll have to get a lot of tissue paper."

"I have tissue paper, Jan."

"Good. I'll go to bed. Maybe you were right. It was a long trip. Can I make a telephone call to Amsterdam, Suzanne?"

She hesitated.

"I'll pay, dear. I'll ask the operator what the charges are."

"No, no, that's all right, Jan. There is a telephone in your room."

He grinned as he climbed the stairs. This was one investigation he could get himself involved in.

It took a while before the sleepy voice of Adjutant Grijpstra yawned, said hello, and yawned again.

"Sorry, Grijpstra, it's me. I knew you were asleep but I won't take long."

"Aren't you in America, sir?"

"Yes, adjutant, but there are telephones in America. It's quite an advanced country, I believe. Tell me, what happened to de Gier?"

"Isn't he with you, sir?"

"A-*ha*."

"You haven't seen him, yet, sir?"

"A-*ha*."

Grijpstra was fully awake now. "I am sorry, sir. But he really did want to go and we were all worried about your health and you being alone out there, and the cold and so on, sir, and the chief constable . . ."

"What about the chief constable, Grijpstra? Did he order the sergeant to fly out here?"

"No, sir."

"And who is paying for this personal extravagance?"

"Oh, that's all right, sir. There is a fund, in The Hague. It is set up to finance the exchange of police officers."

"Police officers, adjutant, not nursemaids."

"Yes, sir."

"I am amazed, adjutant, absolutely amazed."

"I am sorry, sir. We'll pay it back somehow."

"You better, unless we can find the sergeant something to do here, something that will help keep him so busy that he'll have no time to push me around in a pram."

"Yes, sir," Grijpstra said. "I am sure you can find him something to do."

"Sleep well, adjutant. Sorry to have waked you up."

"Yes, sir, thank you, sir, goodbye, sir."

Grijpstra put the phone down carefully and stuck out his tongue.

"You haven't seen him yet, sir?"

"What was that?" his wife asked. "Do you have to go out? Was that the commissaris? What did he want?"

"He wanted to joke with me."

"At five o'clock in the morning? Was he drunk?"

"No, dear, just sarcastic."

"They are always putting you down and you are such a hardworking man and you've been with the department for such a long time."

"Don't overdo it," Grijpstra said. "Go to sleep. Since when have *you* been on my side?"

5

The sergeant had a headache and a dry mouth when he woke up, but he could have felt worse. It was 10:00 A.M. He wasn't too sure where he was, but it came back to him. America, Jameson, sheriff, jailhouse. More details came to mind, and he remembered where the bathroom was. He had a long shower and shaved. He put on his denim suit and found the right scarf to go with the new pale blue shirt. He zipped on his ankle-length suede boots. He smiled and bowed at the mirror, but the bow brought back his headache.

America, he thought. The commissaris. The commissaris on Cape Orca. Cape Accident. A murder case. He sat down on the bed and held his head. It couldn't be. It was quite impossible that he had strayed into a murder case. But then he remembered that Grijpstra had once strayed into a murder case. The adjutant had been on holiday, somewhere far back in the provinces, on the German border. The adjutant was drinking coffee in the corner of the bar in a third-rate hotel and two local men had come in and begun to whisper together. Grijpstra had listened in from behind his newspaper. The adjutant had enjoyed his holiday. He had worked with the local police and they had solved a case that hadn't been a case to start with. The victim had been buried months before Grijpstra went on his holiday. The lady had died of asthma. Only she hadn't. She had been slowly poisoned by relatives. Clever Grijpstra.

Clever Sergeant de Gier. But did he want to be

clever? The question split through his throbbing skull. The answer split back. He did *not* want to be clever. He wanted to make sure that the commissaris survived his mission and he wanted to see America. He got up and looked out the window. He saw snow on the branches of several trees, on the ground, on roofs, and on the ice of the bay below. Well, fine. American snow. And it doesn't snow in Holland; the climate has changed. It used to snow, but it doesn't anymore. He was seeing a novelty. Exotic faraway snow, and he was right in the middle of it.

He found the sheriff in the room below. The sheriff's boots rested on the shelf between the radio and the telephones.

"How are you feeling? Headache?"

"A little."

"You went through half a bottle of bourbon. If you had drunk half a bottle of anything else you wouldn't have a head at all now, you'd have a big sore. Coffee?"

Albert came in to pour the coffee.

"Breakfast, sergeant?"

"Yes," de Gier said. "Breakfast, that would be nice."

"What would you like?"

De Gier tried to think.

"We have no eggs," the sheriff said to Albert. "But there's fresh bread and a bit of bacon and some parsley on top and a raw tomato. More coffee. That'll clear your head, sergeant."

Breakfast came as ordered, and de Gier ate and felt better.

"You remember our conversation of last night?"

"I do."

"Cape Orca?"

"Yes."

"Are you still interested?"

De Gier cleaned his plate with the last piece of toast. "Was I interested last night?"

"Yes, we both were. I still am, but I'm a little more used to bourbon than you are, so you can back out."

De Gier thought. "Yes," he said. "Let me go and see

the commissaris first. You said I could use a car, a
Dodge, I believe. I think I should discuss the case with
him. He may have ideas. He'll have talked to his sister.
If we were right, if our conversation last night was getting us anywhere, then he may confirm our, eh . . ."

The sheriff grinned. "Our, eh . . . dreams, hey? Or
our, eh . . . facts?"

"You have facts, Jim. I am not from here. What do
I know?"

"You know what you know. I can use what you
know. But go and see—what did you call him again?"

"Commissaris."

"Go and see him. The key is in the Dodge. Be careful. We had a thaw during the night, but it froze up
again. The roads are supposed to be sanded, but the
town is short of sand, although there should be some
on the way."

"Yes," de Gier said, but he hadn't listened. He
found the Dodge, started it, and waited for the engine
to warm up. He wondered what the commissaris would
do if he saw his trusted sergeant appear out of the snow.
What sounded like a good idea in Amsterdam might
turn out to be a very bad idea in America. Perhaps the
commissaris was perfectly capable of looking after himself, even if he had been very ill a week ago and even if
he was under doctor's orders not to exert himself in
any way.

The Dodge slid out of the parking place and into the
road. De Gier turned the wheel, but the car didn't respond. It responded a little later, but it overresponded
and slid to the other side of the road. Then it spun and
de Gier was facing the jailhouse for a second. He saw a
stop sign and braked, but the car continued, just missing a truck. It spun around once more, heeled over on
two wheels, hit a snowbank, and fell back. De Gier reversed and touched the accelerator, but the rear wheels
wouldn't grip. He tried another time. The engine
whined, the wheels whirred. He switched the engine off,
got out, slipped, and fell on the ice. He was trying to
get on his feet again when a red station wagon stopped

behind the Dodge. A small old man in an oversized fur-lined overcoat and a raccoon hat complete with tail came out of the station wagon and shuffled toward the Dodge on enormous rubber boots held together by bright yellow laces. The hat was in the old man's eyes, and he tried to push it up with a hand covered in a mitten that reached to his elbow.

De Gier pushed himself up. He stared at the little old man in the coat and the hat and the boots and the mittens. His eyes grew until they were perfectly round. He put his hands over his face and breathed in deeply. He dropped his hands.

"Need some help?" the old man asked. "Maybe I can pull you out with Opdijk's station wagon. It has four-wheel drive. I've just figured out how to operate the extra gears." The old man spoke Dutch.

"Morning, sir," de Gier said. "Yes, that would be nice. I've got this car stuck. It's slippery."

"There is a chain in Opdijk's car. I'll get it."

The sergeant tried to help the commissaris, but his leather soles had no grip on the ice and he skated around, getting in the way until the commissaris told him to sit in the Dodge. The station wagon pulled and the Dodge made feeble attempts to extricate itself from the snow bank. When the commissaris stepped on the gas the chain snapped. He reversed the wagon and got out and knotted the chain. The second attempt made the chain break again and the station wagon got stuck in the bank too.

The commissaris and the sergeant got out of their vehicles and stood on the ice, arms linked, studying the situation.

"It's very good of you to come here and help me out, sergeant."

"Do you think so, sir?"

"No," the commissaris said. "I don't think so, but I am polite sometimes and try to say the right thing. You have a chief constable and God knows what American superstars behind you. Grijpstra told me a

little last night. He moved heaven and earth to bring
you here. Do you think he spoke to the queen too?"

"No, sir."

"So you are helping me out. That's nice. But I got the
Opdijk car stuck too now. I am on my way to a real
estate agent called Michael Astrinsky to sell the Opdijk
house. Do you know where Astrinsky's office is?"

"Yes, sir."

"You do?"

"There's only one important street in Jameson, sir,
Main Street. Mr. Astrinsky will have his office on Main
Street. Main Street is over there, sir."

De Gier let go of the commissaris and pointed. He
slipped and fell and dragged the commissaris down with
him.

A jeep stopped and a thin-faced young man jumped
out, a lanky young man in a short leather jacket, an
open-necked thin cotton shirt, and no hat. His light
brown curly hair had been cut in a strange fashion and
stiff tufts pointed above his ears.

"You from California?"

"No," the commissaris said. "We are from Holland,
the Netherlands. Over there." He pointed at the bay.

"Really? No ice over there?"

"Not much."

"Is that so? Want me to pull you out?"

"Please. If it's not too much trouble."

"It's trouble all right," the young man said and
walked back to the jeep and backed it to the station
wagon. It took a little over a minute to free the wagon
and a little over five minutes to extricate the Dodge.
The young man put his spade, ash bucket, and chain
back into the jeep, waved the commissaris' thanks
away, and drove off. De Gier noted the registration on
the jeep: BMF ONE. Only letters, no figures. The commissaris had read the registration too.

"BMF," the commissaris said. "Sunzanne said something about BMF, a gang of sorts. Troublemakers. How
did that helpful young man get his registration? Are
they made-to-order here?"

A small red compact passed. The license plate said
CUTE. There was a middle-aged woman at the wheel,
heavily made up.

"Made-to-order," the commissaris said. "Incredible.
But true. BMF."

"BMF ONE, sir. That young man was number one.
The boss. Boss of the gang. The sheriff told me about
the gang."

"What else did he tell you?"

"A lot, sir. He made me tell him what I was doing
here, and I thought that the truth might answer all his
questions at once. He didn't believe me. He has a file
on Cape Orca. Your brother-in-law is the fifth corpse,
sir, and a sixth victim ran away."

"Is the sheriff doing anything about that file?"

"He is new, sir. Three months in office. The old
sheriff didn't care perhaps. He retired. He lives in Boston now."

"No," the commissaris said.

De Gier nodded energetically. "Yes, sir."

"No, sergeant. I've done the paperwork for my sister.
The letters are posted. I am going to sell her house and
get out of here. We were hired to take care of a city
with one million peaceful citizens in it, in our own
cozy little country, six thousand miles away. I've never
heard of a town called Jameson. I happen to be here
and I happen to be selling a house, but it's all most
unreal, unsubstantial. Let's go to this man Astrinsky.
We can leave the cars. But I'd like some coffee first.
Would there be coffee in this town?"

They struggled across the street and inquired at
Robert's Market. A bland-faced young man directed
them to the town's only restaurant: "Beth's Diner.
Country style food, all we have." "And a store where
we can buy some clothes?"

"Next door, only other store in town."

"Good," the commissaris said when they were back
on the sidewalk. "I hate shopping around. No choice
simplifies life. You can wear these clothes, sergeant.
They won't fit you either, but they'll look better on you

than on me, especially the hat. Opdijk had a big head and you have a lot of hair. It may sit on the hair."

They got to the store holding hands and were served by a young girl. "A coat," the commissaris said. "Warm, and boots, please, miss."

"Would you look around, sir? Coats are on the racks. And there are boots under the racks. I'm minding the store. I don't know much about the stock, but everything is priced."

"Here, put my coat on, sergeant. There, the hat too." The hat turned and the raccoon's tail hung over de Gier's face. "Other way around, sergeant. It fits in a way. Take the boots."

The commissaris stepped out of his boots and began to rummage about. It didn't take long. He came back. "These boots fit. What do you think about the coat, sergeant? Not that it matters, I'll take it anyway."

"Yes," the sergeant said. "Very nice." It was a hooded navy coat, heavily lined. The commissaris' thin, small face peeped out of the hood. The sergeant looked away.

"All right. How do I look? I wasn't so nice to you just now. You can tell me the truth, Rinus. How do I look? You can laugh too if you like. I am sure I look perfectly ridiculous."

"You look like a movie star, sir."

"A comic character. A Marx Brother? Chaplin? My favorite? Buster Keaton?"

"No, sir."

"Who? Be honest, Rinus. You may not have another chance for a while."

"Walt Disney character, sir. Out of *Snow White*."

"A dwarf? Smily? Grumpy? The fellow who sneezes?"

"Dopey, sir."

The commissaris clapped his hands. There were just the two of them between the racks. The girl was waiting behind the counter for them to come out.

"*Exactly*. Well seen, sergeant. That's exactly how I feel and no doubt how I look. We are always the projection of what we think. Dopey. Here I am, with the puzzle of a lifetime staring me in the face. How many corpses? I made notes last night. If I read them I'll remember again. Five, I believe. This is America. Do you know that we get one real corpse every two months in Amsterdam? The others are accidents, suicides. These corpses are part of some web, a spider's web, with threads going everywhere, probably right into this store. But they are transparent and thin, although not quite invisible, I am sure. We'll find them if we apply the usual tested methods and persevere. And then there is this incredibly beautiful setting. I am not just referring to the landscape, sergeant. There's far more to it. You should have seen the car that picked me up yesterday, an elegant car. Who says there is no elegance in America? We've been misinformed. I have been anyway. Perhaps you know more, you read a great deal. What am I telling you anyway? *You* were flown in on a special jet. Did you see the two men who passed us in the street just now? They had guns on their belts, big revolvers. It's lawful here to carry arms. Even the police don't show their arms anymore in Amsterdam. Our pistols are hidden under tunics and coats. If you touch your gun, seargeant, you are expected to write a report and I have to countersign it."

"Yes, sir."

"All very well, of course. Our society functions in a way. But I have been thinking about other societies, and their possibilities, and here we seem to have the superb example of everything we haven't got. A bay. Hills. Mountains even. Gun-toters. Corpses. Lawmen in out-dated uniforms. And you, of all people to pop up here, in that *hat*."

"Yes, sir."

"And I have to sell a house. There's nothing I can do here, sergeant, and there's nothing I will do either. I'll sell the house and go back and see what Grijpstra has been doing. A corpse in the canal, no doubt, some young man who uses drugs and had an argument with a friend and they poked at each other with knives. No identification, so we'll search about for a week and get a dozen well-trained detectives on the job and turn up all sorts of other misdemeanors that will interest other specialists. And meanwhile this has been going on here. Five corpses. Or six? I forget."

"One of them is your brother-in-law, sir."

The commissaris stopped waving his arms. "Yes, sergeant, thank you. I hardly knew the man, of course, and I suspect that my sister is quite pleased about the whole thing, since she can go back to Holland now. If I can sell the house. I'll pay that young lady and we can go and have coffee and see the real estate agent. You'll have to carry your coat. Didn't you bring any warm clothes at all?"

"No, sir. I don't have any. Just a short coat. I never had a hat."

"Neither did I. I always hated winter sports, but this is different."

The commissaris paid and the girl took de Gier's coat. "I'll drop it off at the jailhouse on my way home."

"You know I stay there, miss?"

She smiled. "Aren't you staying with the sheriff?"

"Yes."

"Are you Canadian? I thought I heard you speak Canadian just now, when you were between the racks."

"No, miss, we spoke Dutch. We are from the Netherlands, in Europe."

"I don't know languages. We only hear Canadian here."

"Don't Canadians speak English?"

"Some do I believe, but not here they don't."

"French Canadian," the commissaris said when they had arrived at Beth's Diner and were eating cream pie near a large square cookstove in the middle of the small restaurant.

"That's right, sir. I helped arrest a French Canadian yesterday, on the way from the airstrip. Speeding, drunken driving, and theft of the car. The suspect harassed the sheriff, but he was only charged with speeding. The other charges somehow disappeared. The sheriff said that the suspect wouldn't be able to pay the fines and released him on bail."

"Don't they jail suspects for car theft?"

"May have been joy-riding, sir. The car belonged to a friend."

The commissaris didn't seem eager to leave the warm room and he ordered more pie and coffee.

"That sheriff, sergeant. Tell me about him. Did you get close to him at all? He showed you that file. That would be an act of trust. Did you make any contact?"

"He made the contact, sir. He wanted to know what I was doing here and he used liquor to make me open up. I didn't mind—the liquor was whiskey, a very good brand, and I have nothing to hide. I don't think I convinced him; I am sure that he still thinks that I came in on the Orca angle. He must be supposing that your sister told you that she thought her husband was murdered and that you rushed out here to see for yourself and that you got the proper authorities to back you up. I came as a bodyguard and to be of help perhaps, a liaison between you and him. He asked me questions and I answered them truthfully. He knows that I work for the Amsterdam murder brigade and that you are a division chief, specialize in homicide, and are my direct boss. So . . ."

"So he talked too. Well, tell me what he told you, any detail, anything. My interest is theoretical of course. Did the two of you get drunk?"

"Yes, sir."

"Well," the commissaris said an hour later. "Maybe there is something *you* can do, but I don't see where I fit in. I don't have a general who makes telephone calls on my behalf. Was the name Astrinsky mentioned at all?"

"Not last night, sir, but I saw a plane land, a very small plane, earlier on today, on an island just off Cape Orca. The jailhouse is on a hill and has a good view of the bay. I asked about the plane and the sheriff said that it belongs to Michael Astrinsky, the real estate agent here, and is often flown by his daughter, Madelin.

She is friendly with a man who lives on that island. The man is old, used to be a New York businessman, and has been living here twenty years. Madelin sometimes flies in supplies. The man on the island is called Jeremy, and the island is called Jeremy's Island. He lives like a hermit, but he has some contact with the town."

"I saw that island, sergeant, from my bedroom window. Very beautiful, especially at night. I saw no lights, but there is a jetty. A hermit, you say. I've always wanted to meet a hermit. I could go and see him. Try to see him. Maybe he doesn't want visitors."

The commissaris asked for the bill and Beth brought more coffee. The two hunters who had flown in with the commissaris came in, sat down at the same table, and talked. Beth sat down and talked too. The commissaris said something pleasant about the large woodstove and Beth, a big-breasted woman in a tight sweater, took him by the hand and showed him the stove, explaining its various functions. The stove didn't just give warmth and cook food, it also baked bread, dried socks, and had what Beth called a waiting area for simmering soups and boiling water. The hunters joined the audience and everybody learned about what to use for firewood and what not, unless there was nothing else. Pine crackles, Beth said, and spruce pops, and alder burns too fast and gives so much heat that the stove may come apart. Birch, that's what should be used, and maple. Oak? the hunters asked. Yes, oak, but oak is expensive. Beech is even more expensive. There was more coffee again, and finally the commissaris was allowed to pay.

"Why don't we stay here?" the commissaris asked when they were back on Main Street. "That came to half of what any Amsterdam restaurant would have charged and some sloppy waiter would have popped the bill under my nose before I had finished the pie. Good pie too. She must have baked it herself in that museum piece."

"But they seem a little slow here. We spent hours in there."

"What's time, sergeant? There must be a lot of time here; back home there isn't anymore. The telephone rings it away and people like you grab it. With questions and bits of paper. Grijpstra takes my time too. With his scheming and conniving."

"He meant well, sir."

"Yes. Here we are, sergeant. I haven't got my glasses on. What do those cards say? Here, they are stuck in the door."

De Gier read the signs. The first said, "Out, back in ten minutes," and the second said, "Closed for the winter."

The commissaris tried the door and found it unlocked. A girl opened the second door for them. "Come in, gentlemen. It's very cold out there. I've finally managed to get this office warm. Please sit down. What can I do for you?"

De Gier gaped at the girl while the commissaris stated his business. He knew the girl, he knew her very well, he knew she wouldn't be in his day-to-day memory, but he had gone deeper down already. His dreams, but further back. Madelin's face seemed to be all eyes, large dark eyes. He had seen the eyes before. And the small slender body too, in tight corduroy jeans and a soft sweater, so supple that he was sure it would wilt if he breathed out with force. He guessed her age, twenty-five perhaps. He admired the smooth skin, stretched over small cheekbones and a dainty but firm jaw, and her pointed chin, a perfect base for the triangular face. He looked back at her eyes and recognized the girl: the princess caught and kept by the dragon. He had lost the book but the page came back in full detail. The girl was in a cave, chained to a rock, and the dragon was breathing foul fumes at her. She was staring bravely into the dragon's face. When he had the book he couldn't read—he must have been four or five years old. His mother and his older sister had read the story to him so many times that he knew the words by heart, but he still carried the book around and made them read the tale. The dragon was slain by a knight with long black hair. He had hated the knight almost as much as he had hated the dragon, and he finally destroyed both by rubbing the page with a wet finger, patiently, until the images faded away. But he hadn't rubbed out Madelin.

She was dressed differently then, in a semitransparent dress. She had excited him then. She still excited him now.

She wasn't in a cave now. He looked about. The office could have been anywhere. The best and most expensive metal and imitation wood desks. A thick wall-to-wall carpet. Brand-new office machinery. Walls paneled in veneer. One wall carried a map of Woodcock County, an antique map, cracked in places, with a wealth of detail and handwritten place names. He got up and found Cape Orca and the bay and studied the fish that had been drawn into the bay's waves. A large fish, black on top, white below. Smooth, sleek, with a wicked mouth full of grinning teeth, on its leisurely way to take another tasty morsel off the rapidly approaching shore.

"The Opdijk house," Madelin said thoughtfully. "And you are Pete Opdijk's brother-in-law. What a terrible accident that was. We were all very upset. Dad went to the funeral. I didn't know Pete so well and I didn't want to see his wife cry. I am sure my father is interested in the Opdijk house. I'll telephone. We live in a house just behind this office. Just a minute, please."

She replaced the telephone. "He's on his way. So Suzanne wants to go back to Amsterdam, does she? I've heard about Amsterdam, a magical city, I believe. Are you and your friend from Amsterdam, sir?"

"We are, miss."

"You're in business out there?"

"No, Miss Astrinsky. I am a police officer and so is Sergeant de Gier."

Madelin's voice stayed on the same polite level. "Police officers? How exciting! What branch of the police, sir?"

"Homicide, Miss Astrinsky."

Madelin smiled at the seargent, and de Gier was

preparing to return the smile when the back door of the room opened.

A blusterer, de Gier thought when it was his turn to shake the heavy man's hand. The realtor had a loud, deep voice that hooted sonorously, as if he had swallowed a Swiss Alpine trumpet. Michael Astrinsky said the right things. Very sorry that the accident happened. Opdijk had been a good friend. Good old Pete. A fellow Blue Crustacean. Friendship based on many years of mutual understanding. Would sure miss him. Poor Suzanne. Glad to meet her brother. Suzanne often talked about her brother. Here he was, all the way from across the ocean. House to be sold. A pity that Suzanne would leave too, but understandable under the circumstances. Yes.

"Did you know that Suzanne's brother is a police officer, dad?"

Astrinsky lit a cigarette. He dropped it. "No, are you really?"

"Yes, Mr. Astrinsky. From Amsterdam."

Madelin looked at de Gier. "Homicide, dad. Mr. de . . ."

"Gier," de Gier said.

"The sergeant is also a police officer, dad."

Astrinsky had lit the cigarette at the wrong end. Madelin took it out of his mouth and killed it in the ashtray on the desk.

"The sergeant is studying with the local police, Mr. Astrinsky, and I came out to help Suzanne. The house is to be sold as soon as possible. Suzanne asked me to come and see you," the commissaris said.

Astrinsky lit another cigarette and looked sad. "A quick sale, yes, that could be arranged. I might be interested myself, but unfortunately, values aren't what they used to be some years ago. This is a cold corner of the country, with a very short summer season. We used to have a lot of people summering up here, but the fashion has changed. They seem to prefer the warmer states in the South; Florida, California. The sun states offer holidays all year round and here, well, you can see for yourself. The climate is so fierce that it seems to be out to kill us all some times. Just too damn cold."

"I see."

"I could list the house, of course, and try to sell it in the summer."

"No, Suzanne wants to buy an apartment in Amsterdam, and she needs a lot of cash now."

Astrinsky walked around his desk, his hands in the pockets of an immaculate tweed jacket. A well-dressed man, but flabby.

"I could take the house off her hands for cash, but I couldn't pay more than, say, thirty thousand."

"Thirty thousand," the commissaris said.

"In summer I might get a little more perhaps, but it wouldn't be cash. The trouble with the Cape Orca properties is that they don't seem to move at all. There are a number of empty houses on the cape. There's some problem with the right of way. The rest of the cape belongs to Janet Wash, and, technically she owns the roads. They're maintained by the town, but Janet gets the bill. She has never been difficult about allowing other residents to use the roads, but newcomers don't like to feel restricted."

"I see."

Astrinsky brightened up. "But I would like to do something for Suzanne. The station wagon will be for sale too, and I can buy it at a good price. My own car is ready to be junked. I would pay whatever it's worth. The car is a year old. I would spend, say, sixty percent of the new price."

"Thank you. Very good. I can't decide without consulting my sister, of course, but I will contact you soon."

Madelin showed them to the door. When de Gier turned, he saw Astrinsky studying the map on the wall. The muscles in the realtor's big face were working.

"Your statement as to what we do for a living shook him somewhat, sir, but he recovered quickly."

The commissaris marched on, enveloped in his coat.

"So what, sergeant," the commissaris said when they had reached their cars. "So Astrinsky feels guilty. But

we all feel guilty. Don't you remember that you would
feel a tremor down your back when you were a little
boy and a constable passed you on his bicycle? You
hadn't seen him, but suddenly he is there. It is drizzling
and the road is wet and the bicycle's tires make that
soft nasty hiss. And there's the uniform and the man's
eyes, watching you. Didn't you feel guilty?"

"Yes, sir."

"About something you had done a long time ago.
Maybe you broke a window and didn't tell anyone. Or
you stole something. The constable doesn't know,
doesn't care. He is just riding his bike. I am just selling
a house."

De Gier opened the door of the Dodge.

"What are your plans, sergeant?"

"Nothing in particular, sir. The sheriff told me to
familiarize myself with the scene."

"Fine. Leave your car and come with me. My sister
and I are invited by a lady called Janet Wash, any
time this afternoon or evening, for a drink. Since she
owns most of Cape Orca, we should meet her. I already
have, but I was half asleep then. I am sure she won't
mind if I bring an extra guest. She is curious about you
anyway, since she saw your plane and the sheriff said
something about you."

"Ah, so *that's* how you knew, sir."

"Yes, sergeant, and Grijpstra confirmed my suspicion.
I phoned the poor man."

"The scheming and conniving poor man, sir."

The commissaris put a hand on de Gier's arm. "All
right, sergeant. I know I am a cripple, but I can still
get around. And I was pleased to see you. It's just that
I get a little depressed sometimes, as you well know."

"Yes, sir. I know, sir. I understand."

"That's very good of you. Now, we'll go and have
this polite drink with Mrs. Wash. We should also find
our way to that island, Jeremy's Island. What did you
think of the price Astrinsky mentioned?"

"Thirty thousand, sir?"

"Yes, it sounds like a lot, but I am sure it isn't.

I don't share Opdijk's taste, and I certainly won't have anything to do with Suzanne's complete lack of taste. But the house is comfortable, well built, spacious, with several bathrooms and central heating and more rooms in the basement and a garage and a woodshed and a swimming pool even. What would they want with a swimming pool? The bay starts at the end of their grounds. No, thirty thousand can't be right."

"You might get somebody else to look at the property, sir. Jim would know, the sheriff I mean."

"You have a radio in your car. Didn't you say so just now?"

"Yes, sir."

"See if he can send out another realtor. Even if the man doesn't want to buy it, we can get an idea of the right price."

"Certainly, sergeant," the sheriff said. "I have a friend in the next county. I'll ask him to come over tomorrow morning."

"Thank you, we'll ask the commissaris' sister to be sure to be home then."

"Okay. I am glad you've started. You're doing well so far. I am glad you met Madelin. She's the local beauty, but she would be a beauty anywhere. Did you like her?"

"Yes, Jim. We're going to have a drink with Mrs. Wash now, and the commissaris is thinking of visiting Jeremy's Island some time, maybe tomorrow. We lost some time at Beth's Diner."

The sheriff chuckled. "That place is a trap. You're a true deputy already. If I can't find any of my men I phone Beth, they're sure to be there. Did you say Jeremy's Island?"

"Yes. We'll visit the hermit."

"If the old gopher lets you. Be careful, he keeps dogs. You know how to make contact with him?"

"No."

"Go down to the shore. There's a path leading down close to the entrance of the cape. A path marked by red reflectors on rods. You'll find a shed at the end of the path. You'll find a Very pistol in the shed. Fire a green shell over the island and he should come out. He has a rowboat to cross the channel with."

"Thank you, Jim."

"You're welcome. Good hunting."

6

A sudden bump knocked the raccoon hat into de Gier's eyes and he took it off and put it on the empty seat next to him. The station wagon was performing well. They had been driving for some minutes through the interior of Cape Orca on a narrow lane that followed the contours of the land, winding wildly. The commissaris was handling the car as if it were a vehicle on a planet in another galaxy. He kept on changing gears and only braked if there seemed to be no choice. De Gier amused himself by watching the old man's antics. Suzanne sat next to her brother, and her small head bobbed with the movements of the car. From the back the two heads looked identical. De Gier felt a deep admiration for the commissaris, an admiration that had grown through the many years that he had worked under him, and he had difficulty in accepting that the commissaris' sister was stupid. But he could find no other word. The woman seemed to have no interests at all, with the exception of her craving for porcelain objects. He had entered her house briefly. The commissaris had introduced him. Suzanne had smiled. How nice, another Dutchman. She had touched his hand but hadn't bothered to memorize his name. She had prattled on about her coming departure and had asked about her brother's visit to the real estate office. De Gier had seen her living room and its fearful quest for coziness, for protection, for being away from bad things and clinging to good things. Everything in the room was nice, nice and warm, nice and colorful, nice and tasty, nice and comfortable. He had studied the woman's screwed-up, wrinkled face and darting glinting eyes and pronounced her crazy, like a hundred thousand other Dutch old ladies back home who mumble their way through supermarkets, tram rides, happy-end movies, and each other's everlasting company. But he couldn't shrug the woman's craziness away, for it concerned him because it concerned the commissaris, and he was supposed to be assisting his chief.

The car stopped.

"Look, sergeant!"

He gasped. Two deer stood in the path, a doe and her almost full-grown fawn, two delicate shapes, high on their thin legs. The animals stared at the car, immobile for a moment, and then jumped. Their movements were synchronized into a single leap, and he saw their white tails melt away into the undergrowth.

"Dear," Suzanne said. "It's the hunting season again, isn't it? I've heard bangs quite close to the house. But there are always bangs; the hunters come out of season too. That's why I don't like to go out so much. Mr. Jones was near his own house when he got shot. Reggie says that rifle bullets travel for miles. It's just like the war when we couldn't go out because the antiaircraft guns splattered shell fragments all over town. Do you remember, Jan?"

"Yes, dear. Are we close now?"

"I think so, Jan. Drive carefully. There are so many accidents here. I don't know whether this car is insured. Opdijk sometimes forgot things."

"It is insured, Suzanne. I saw the policy last night with your papers in Opdijk's briefcase."

De Gier made a face and patted the raccoon hat, running his fingers through the thick fur of the tail. There would be raccoons in the woods. The sheriff had told him about the animals and about the locals who hunted them. He wondered how he would go about hunting a raccoon, a wild animal at home in the woods. He imagined himself crashing and tumbling about be-

tween the trees, shooting at shadows. His hand strayed
to his armpit, but the familiar bulge of the small automatic pistol wasn't there. He could hunt a man in
Amsterdam. He supposed the same principle of hunting
would apply here. Study the prey, find out what its
habits are, track its paths, and then get in its way and
shoot it down, aiming for the legs.

But here the hunters were out to kill. They skinned
and boned the corpse, and ate the meat and used the
fur. A different routine, a different environment. A city
slicker in the wild woods. He didn't think he would be
able to help the sheriff much. He thought of the sheriff's
heartiness and hospitality. A friendly man, but also a
calculating man. The sheriff meant to get to the murky
bottom of the Cape Orca file, left to him to sort out.
No, not to sort out. To put in a drawer and forget.
But meanwhile Pete Opdijk had died and two foreign
policemen had popped over the horizon. The sheriff
meant to use his visitors. The sergeant had already
been converted into a useful tool, a spy sniffing about
and reporting back to the jailhouse. If anything went
wrong the sheriff wasn't to blame. If anything went right
the sheriff would reap the credit. De Gier remembered
one of Adjutant Grijpstra's early lessons: "Always look
for the lowest possible motivation, sergeant, and then
you are usually right. If you are proved wrong you have
looked too high." A tough truth, but a truth all the
same.

The station wagon moved on slowly. De Gier lit a
cigarette. Suzanne coughed and waved at the smoke.
He stubbed the cigarette out.

"There!" the commissaris said.

De Gier was impressed. The mansion was big, two
stories high and L-shaped, but not by any means
clumsy. The long white clapboards covering its structure
gave it an austere touch, but several cupolas broke the
long lines and the wing had its roof softened by graceful dormer windows. The main cupola grew into a
spire topped by a weathervane, a golden bird sitting on
a cross. The heavy snow smoothed the general impres-

sion of imposing sternness, and rows of long icicles attached to gutters and the small roof of the porch reflected the light of several lanterns illuminating a cleared driveway and parking lot. A battered pickup and a new station wagon of the same make as the Opdijk car were parked near the fieldstone steps of the porch leading to the front double doors, sculptured in oak and adorned with simple garlands. There was no sign of the Cadillac that had caught the commissaris' fancy.

Reggie Tammart opened the doors and Janet Wash awaited her guests in the hall. The commissaris explained the sergeant's presence and introduced him. De Gier held the old lady's long cool hand. A graceful woman, tall and straight but without any stiffness, splendid in a long woolen dress of a rose color that contrasted with her long white hair. De Gier liked her even more when she walked ahead, sweeping through the hall, guiding her guests to a room warmed by an open fire in which four-foot logs hissed and crackled. He thought of pictures in old English country magazines. Faded sepia pictures of a world that seemed unbelievable and very likely no longer existed, now that castles had become state property and lords and ladies were public servants, paid to prance about at set times while the crowd was herded along under the watchful eyes of uniformed custodians. But here the scene was alive. He found a corner near the fireplace and warmed his back while Reggie poured drinks from crystal decanters with silver labels on chains and stirred sausages in a copper saucepan heated by a burner.

The commissaris stood in the middle of the room, with his cane stuck in a bearskin rug and Suzanne had become lost between tasseled cushions on a divan upholstered in the same material that had been used for the ten-foot-square curtains hiding windows on two sides of the room.

"Beautiful," the commissaris said. "Superb, madam, as superb as your country. I had forgotten what space is like, as I come from a place where fourteen million people are crowded into an area half the size of this state."

Janet Wash inclined her head. "Thank you. Fourteen million you say. How frightening. There are a million of us in Maine, I believe, but when I flew over the land in Michael's plane some weeks ago it seemed there were houses everywhere. We are very fortunate, I suppose, but we have come to the end of things here too. This house can no longer be kept up. I keep most of it closed. Perhaps with half a dozen servants something could be done, but the only servants are Reggie and myself and there's a limit to energy, especially to mine. And Reggie has his own cabin to worry about. I can't expect him to help me push a vacuum cleaner. Do we all have our drinks? A toast of welcome to you, gentlemen!"

De Gier sipped and bowed. Janet smiled at him. "How do I address you? As Mr. de Gier?"

"The sergeant is a detective on our force, madam," the commissaris said. "Out here on an exchange trip. I knew he was due to travel to the States, but I had no idea we would meet here, an amazing coincidence."

Janet found her purse, opened it, and put on her spectacles. "Come closer, sergeant. You look so well in that denim suit. Is that the latest European fashion? I haven't been to Europe in years, and the last time the general and I went the fashion was double-breasted suits. This is so much better. I always thought men should wear scarfs instead of ties. And your boots! How *chic!* Reggie, really, I must take you to Boston. Suede boots would look magnificent on you. Just step over and look at the sergeant's boots. Don't you think they're marvelous?"

Reggie came, looked, and attempted to smile. De Gier felt embarrassed and took refuge in his whiskey, raising his glass and grinning at Reggie. Reggie looked away. De Gier thought the man looked very well in his faded brown sports jacket, corduroy slacks, and white shirt. The knot of Reggie's tie had dropped an inch, revealing the absence of a collar button and a thick growth of curly chest hair.

"Never mind, Reggie. I am only teasing. You even remembered to put on a tie. But a trip to Boston wouldn't be wasted. You haven't been out of here for so long. Reggie is a military man," she explained to the commissaris. "He came here after his return from Vietnam and he says that he prefers nature, any nature, to the cities. I should be grateful. Reggie is an accomplished gardener and an excellent woodsman."

"Vietnam?" the commissaris asked. "What outfit were you with, sir?"

But Reggie had gone back to the sizzling sausages and Janet answered. "Reggie was with the Green Berets. He fought in trouble spots where the regular army wouldn't go. It's such a pity that the Vietnam war turned out to be a flop. Reggie should have come back as a hero, but now we are all supposed to be ashamed about what went on there. My husband was luckier. He fought in the Second World War and returned sporting his medals, but he came back as an invalid, the poor dear. It happened in the last week, somewhere in Germany. A bullet in a very wrong place. He was paralyzed, and I had to push him around in a wheelchair. Such a shame. But he was very good about it, and he loved the life here. Another drink, sir."

Reggie collected the empty glasses and refilled them. He served the sausages on little saucers and de Gier helped. When the sergeant had found his corner near the fireplace again he took a minute to study the man. A commando, a professional superman. De Gier felt jealous. He had often thought that he had been born in the wrong place. He saw himself gliding through a tropical forest, carrying some ultra-automatic weapon, a ripple among leaves and trailers and creepers. He tried to stop his fantasy, but it continued by itself. De Gier had traveled somewhat, but he had never been to the tropics and knew the jungle of Indochina only on film. And this man had actually lived in such an enchanting location. In a tent. Tigers growling outside, and small yellow men in black cotton pajamas crawling everywhere. Hmm.

"You do gardening here?"

"Not now. The snow will be on the ground until April. I've been working on the tractor all day. I need it for pulling logs, but the machine is getting old. I keep on taking it apart, but it is just as old when I put it together again!"

"How long were you in Vietnam?"

"Three years. Until it was all over."

Janet came over and made de Gier sit next to her on a settee. "Will you be going on patrol with the sheriff, sergeant?"

"Yes, madam. He gave me the first day off, but tomorrow I am supposed to be working."

"That must be an interesting experience. I wonder if we have crime here. Reggie, do we have crime here?"

Reggie bent down and adjusted a woven rug on the shiny hardwood floor. "Of course, Janet. Jameson houses the biggest bunch of cutthroats this side of Manhattan. I'm glad you keep me on the estate most of the time. I wouldn't be sure of my life in town. The last time I walked down Main Street every second man carried a six gun and Beth was saying that she would rename her diner. The OK Corral I believe it's going to be called."

Everybody laughed except Suzanne.

"Ah yes," Janet said. "I mustn't forget to ask. You mentioned the sale of Opdijk's house yesterday. Did you see my old friend Michael Astrinsky? He is such a nice man, and he was such a good friend of Pete's. I had wanted to give you Michael's name, but I forgot. I am sure he could be of help."

The commissaris put his glass down and shook his head when Reggie wanted to carry it to the table. "No more, thank you. I have to watch my habits these days. Yes, madam, we saw Mr. Astrinsky and he made an offer, but I would like to have another evaluation and the sheriff was kind enough to ask an expert friend of his to come and have a look at the place. Somebody from the next county, I believe."

"Can I ask what Michael offered?"

"Certainly. Thirty thousand."

She shook her head sadly. "I don't know about values anymore, not since inflation has changed everything. Some years ago such an amount would have been a good price. That would be for an immediate sale, I imagine, with Michael buying for his own account?"

"Yes, madam."

"It might be better to have the house listed. Although I don't know. The other houses on the Cape are empty and Michael hasn't been able to sell them, and he is an excellent businessman, the only rich man around we always say. He has done very well here. Our trouble is that we are too far from the shopping centers. Even in summer we don't have enough of a crowd to have our own supermarket. We have to drive over sixty miles to get groceries. Robert's Market only stocks the staples, some canned food and local produce and flour and so on. Of course many of us have our own vegetable gardens and we keep goats and even cows and have them slaughtered in the autumn to stock up the freezer. And we get fresh lobsters and fish all year 'round, but, still, it isn't the easy life the city people are used to. Only the tough dare to settle here. Don't you agree, Reggie?"

"Sure, Janet." Reggie looked polite.

Poor fellow, de Gier thought. Dancing attendance on a refined old lady in a palace in the woods must have its drawbacks.

"So you may sell to the other realtor? I wonder if he would be interested. If he is in the next county he may be too far away."

"I may," the commissaris said. "And we may end up accepting Mr. Astrinsky's offer. He also said he would buy the car at sixty percent of the new price."

"But that's an excellent offer. The hardest thing to get rid of in America is a used car. The banks lend everybody money to buy a new one. Even high school kids can get a limousine these days. Sixty percent, my word! That would be the insurance value. Reggie just wrecked a one-year-old station wagon, bounced it off the road and turned it over so many times that the poor thing was beyond repair. It was a wonder he survived the accident himself. That's what we got, sixty percent of the new price. But Michael always liked Opdijk's car. He even borrowed it a few times. I would advise you to accept his offer."

The commissaris smiled. "I am afraid the two offers go together, Mrs. Wash. I don't think he'll take the car if he doesn't get the house."

"Yes," Janet said. "We Americans are tough dealers, and Michael is a true American, although his fore-fathers were gentle scholars in Poland, I believe. The scholarly part has missed him, but it got through to Madelin. She has an M.A. in philosophy and is work-ing on her Ph.D. now. That's why she came home for the winter. Did you meet her?"

"Yes." De Gier's affirmation was a little too enthusi-astic, and Janet looked up and smiled at him.

"Astrinsky left," Reggie said. "I saw him drive to the airstrip just now, as I came back from Robert's Market. We stopped to talk. He's off for the Bahamas again."

"Yes, he said he might spend another week or so there. The slow progress of winter is getting him down and he is engaged in some big deal over there, I think. Or maybe he is using business as an excuse to loll about in the sun. Good old Michael. I envy him."

The commissaris coughed. "So we won't see him again. Will anyone take care of his business while he is away?"

"Madelin. She is a partner in his real estate business. Michael was divorced many years ago. He lives alone with his daughter."

"I see."

They stayed for a last drink, then Reggie walked them back to the car while Janet waved from the big double doors. The commissaris asked about the Cadillac.

"Inside," Reggie said and pointed at a low building in the field bordering the house. "Locked and chained. The BMF gang managed to steal it last year, or I think it was them. The Cadillac came back undamaged. We found it sitting on the lawn in the morning. But Janet has made sure they won't get it again. We even have an alarm system now with bells that will ring both in the house and in my cabin. The cabin is in the woods, about half a mile from here."

"The BMF gang," the commissaris said when they were halfway home. "Amazing, don't you think, sergeant? A gang in a small, pleasant town like Jameson. I thought that only cities bred gangs."

"They may get bored around here, sir."

"Yes, bored. But I did meet that young foxlike fellow with the BMF ONE number plate on his car. Such an efficient and intelligent young man. Perhaps his gang is different from the ones we deal with. Do you know what BMF stands for, sergeant?"

"B is *bad,* sir. M is *mother.*"

"And F?"

"A four-letter word."

Suzanne stirred. The commissaris drove on.

"Ah," the commissaris said. "I see." He tittered. "How interesting. Twice interesting. To add the prefix 'bad.' Most interesting indeed. To have intercourse with the mother would be the ultimate bad thing to do, I suppose, although the mental attitude behind such a belief seems retarded. Perhaps Americans are retarded in certain ways, in spite of the wealth and the push buttons. They may have developed too quickly and the Victorian fears clung on. Yes, that could be. But to name the worst and then to add *bad.*" He tittered again.

"Yes," he said after a while. "This foxman could be a genius of sorts, like some of the American cartoonists. Did you ever study American cartoons, sergeant? Some of them are really funny, outrageously funny."

"*Bad boys,*" Suzanne said.

"What's that, dear?"

"Bad boys, Jan. Not funny at all. You would know if you had been here longer. Pests—Opdijk was afraid of them. In summer they roar about on their motorcycles, and in winter they come in on snowmobiles, still roaring about as if the cape belongs to them. Even Reggie can't deal with them, and the sheriff would never come out. I telephoned several times. They would come into our garden. They have no regard for private property. Once they even cut down a tree and rolled the logs down to our beach and another boy was waiting with his powerboat and took them away."

"The sheriff? This sheriff?"

"No, the old sheriff. Every time I called he said he didn't have a cruiser available and when the deputies showed up they were always too late. One of the gang is a girl."

"A girl? On a motorcycle?"

"Madelin has sold her motorcycle. She flies her father's plane now. She buzzed Opdijk when he was fishing last summer. I telephoned her father, but I couldn't get through to him. Madelin should know better, but she is as bad as the others, master's degree or not."

"Madelin," de Gier said, and his voice vibrated on each syllable of the name.

Suzanne's small head turned around. It seemed she saw the sergeant for the first time.

"Pah!" she said. The exclamation cut through the overheated car.

The sergeant looked guilty; the commissaris had smiled, briefly, for the station wagon skidded again and claimed his attention.

7

"No," the commissaris said and looked critically at de Gier. The sergeant hung on to the lowest branch of a pine tree growing at the side of the path leading down to the landing. "This is ridiculous, sergeant. You keep on falling over. Here, let go and then grab me."

He poked his cane into the snow and reached out. The sergeant slithered down to him. "There, that's better. We are at a disadvantage here, sergeant, but we can make use of the situation. It's good if things can't be taken for granted. Put on your hat."

The raccoon hat had fallen onto the snow and the commissaris picked it up with his cane. They walked on slowly.

"Tell me more about the BMF gang, sergeant. If there's anything to tell. That's another disadvantage. It's hard to obtain information. No computer that spits facts at you, no informers in little pubs or on benches in the park, no prisoners who get bored in their cells and welcome company, even our company. Just us, sergeant. The two of us. Well? What do you know?"

"Not much, sir. There is a young man in jail by the name of Albert. Convicted on a charge of reckless driving, but the sheriff claims that the prisoner, on another occasion, deliberately damaged the chief deputy's cruiser."

The commissaris sat down on a stump. "Go on, sergeant, details, you must have details."

He listened. "That's all?"

"Yes, sir."

"Good. Very clever. And this Albert is the jailhouse cook now? What is his cooking like?"

"Excellent, sir. He even bakes bread. The dinner he served was first class, and his breakfast was even better. And he doesn't slop the food on the plates, he arranges it."

The commissaris was nodding and smiling. "And the girl, another member known to us, has a master's degree in philosophy and is working for a Ph.D. And she flies an airplane. And she had the audacity to buzz a retired banker fishing off his own shore. Ha!"

"She may have killed him too, sir."

"Oh yes, sergeant. Why? To enable her father to make a profit on the Opdijk house? To help Suzanne be rid of a husband who kept her here against her will? Or just for the hell of it?"

The sergeant grinned.

The commissaris' cane shot out and hit him in the stomach. The sergeant fell, rolled over like a cat, and got back on his feet.

"Well done, sergeant. You haven't wasted your thousand hours on the judo mat. Have you considered Suzanne as a suspect yet?"

De Gier was looking for a position where he would be out of reach of the commissaris' cane and where he wouldn't be standing on ice.

"Sergeant?"

"Yes, sir. She may have pushed her husband, but I don't think she would have touched the others."

"Do you think she is clever, sergeant?"

"No, sir."

"I agree with you. But she isn't that stupid either. She is stupid in certain areas only. I am sure she realized that her husband was keeping her here and that his death would release her. But to make me come out here . . . no. She could have asked my brother. Or perhaps she is a genius too, in her own single-minded, superbly egocentric way. Perhaps she is thinking that I will sell her house at the right price. You see, this death may have nothing to do with the others. She saw the neighbors die and thought about Opdijk joining the party."

De Gier pondered the proposition.

"Would you arrest your own sister, sir?"

"On United States territory? Certainly not, sergeant. The very idea! Perhaps the sheriff can, but he might need proof. There is no proof, sergeant. And her confession will mean nothing if it isn't supported by circumstantial evidence. If she went up to Opdijk and pushed him and went back into the house, and if nobody saw her . . . eh?"

The commissaris smiled. "Let's go on, sergeant. There's the island and there's a hermit on the island. Hermits like to be alone. They don't like noisy people around. Let's see what he looks like."

They walked down the path, holding their arms free in case of a sudden slip. The commissaris' cane hit frozen clumps of snow, making them roll down to the bay below.

"There's the shed the sheriff mentioned."

The morning was clear and the snow glittered on the trees and on the pack ice that reached a few hundred feet into the bay. A flat motorboat chugged toward the open ocean, through the narrow channel between the jetty near the shed and the island. The island rose up gently from layers of ledge and great rocks. They could see a rowboat left out on the island's shore. The commissaris waited while de Gier went into the shed and came back with a pistol that had a short gaping tube instead of a barrel. The silence of the bay was so vast that the boat's putter seemed like a line of small dark specks on an immense sheet of white paper. A large black bird came gliding from the island and its croak startled the two men, leaning on the jetty's railing. The raven was clearly interested in the men's presence and circled above their heads, flapping its huge wings, before it suddenly turned and wheeled back toward the island's hill.

"A spy," de Gier said. "Here you are, sir. I put a

shell in it. That shed is a sort of emergency hut. It has a dinghy with paddles and a first-aid kit and other equipment. Do you want to fire the gun, sir?"

"No, you can handle the gun, sergeant. But wait for the raven to get back. We don't want to startle the bird with a display of fireworks. Let me have a look at that shed first."

The sergeant waited, weighing the gun in his hand. The commissaris came back. "Well-organized hut, sergeant. Usually vandals interfere with that type of emergency arrangement, especially if it is provided by the municipality, the enemy. One might expect our gang to monkey with the boat and the pistol and the lines and grapples and so on. But it hasn't. Everything is spick-and-span in there." He shook his head. "We must be misinformed, or we have jumped to the wrong conclusions."

The sergeant pointed at the channel. The powerboat was turning out of sight behind the curve of the cape. "There's part of the gang now, sir. I think I recognized them. Our friend the fox and Albert. Albert was released from jail today."

"Really? On their mischievous way, eh? Go on, sergeant, fire away."

De Gier aimed for a point a hundred feet above the top of the island's hill and pulled the gun's heavy trigger. There was a sharp retort and the flaming projectile whizzed off, slow enough to be followed by the eye. It disintegrated above the hill into a burst of bright green sparks.

The commissaris whistled softly. "Most impressive, sergeant. So now we wait. If the hermit doesn't want to see us he doesn't have to show himself, but I hope he does. Fascinating, a man living by himself in the midst of nowhere. How big would that island be?"

"Ten acres the sheriff said, sir."

"Acres? Let's see. We used to measure in acres when I was a child. There was a vegetable garden next door to my father's house and that was supposed to be a half acre. Twenty times that garden; that's quite a sizable area and Jeremy has it all to himself. That must be him now, that black dot coming down the path on the hill, but there's something following him. Can you see what it is? My eyes aren't what they used to be."

"A dog, sir. A big black dog. And the raven is with him too, flying a little to the side."

The commissaris peered at the island, screening his eyes with his hand.

"Must be a Doberman pinscher, sir. Nasty dogs."

"Because we train them to be nasty. Can't blame the dogs, sergeant. Cigar?"

They smoked peacefully while the man on the island pushed his boat off the ice and came rowing toward them. The dog was left behind, the raven hovered above the boat.

"Now what are those spots next to the boat, sergeant?"

The sergeant peered. Two round objects, bobbing on the waves.

"Seals," the commissaris said when the boat was much closer. "Must be seals. Silver seals too. They are particularly beautiful. I saw them off the British coast once. And they swim with the boat. Our hermit must be very good with animals. Look at those whiskers on them."

The seals turned abruptly when the boat stopped some ten feet off the jetty. The man spun the little boat around and leaned on his oars. An ageless man with a smiling face, dressed in a checkered jacket and heavy blue trousers. The face was weathered, a red rough face with a web of wrinkles that tightened around the eyes. A woolen cap had been pushed back on his shiny bald head.

"I'm called Jeremy, gentlemen, and I saw your signal, a green signal so there's no emergency, which is good. There's enough trouble in the world. What can I do for you?"

"I am Pete Opdijk's brother-in-law, a police officer from the Netherlands, and this is my assistant, Sergeant de Gier. We would like to visit with you."

"Police officers," Jeremy said. "A breed I've tried to steer clear of. Are you here in your official capacity?"

"I am here to take care of my sister, sir. She wishes to return to Holland. The sergeant is temporarily attached to the sheriff's department."

"You wouldn't have brought a warrant, would you?"

"No, sir."

Jeremy laughed. There was a glint of strong white teeth between the man's cracked lips. "Very well, so I can refuse. I won't refuse and I am sorry about your relative's death, although I never knew Opdijk well. I don't know too many people. Please get into my boat, gentlemen, but be careful not to tip her over for it's a cold sea. The seals would try to push us back into the boat, but they'll only manage to push us under again. It's happened to me before, but it didn't matter then, it was summer. If they try their tricks now they'll kill us."

The seals had ventured closer and their large luminous eyes stared curiously between the long glistening hairs sprouting sideways on the smooth, earless heads.

"They are tame, are they?" the commissaris asked once he had settled himself in the bow of the boat.

"No, they're quite wild, but they've known me a long time. I've been here twenty years now and I tried not to scare the animals off when I arrived. The animals are good friends. That's more than I can say for most of our own species."

Jeremy rowed back in silence broken only once when de Gier mentioned the small airplane that he had seen from the jailhouse at daybreak the previous morning and that had landed on the island.

"Yes, Madelin. She comes once in a while. She brought the mail and a cake. We can have the cake with tea."

He ran the boat onto the ice. The silence had returned again, but the faraway crack of a rifle spoiled it.

"Hunters," Jeremy said and spat. "It's their season. Drinking themselves silly and potting away at the deer with their automatic arms."

The seals swam along the edge of the ice and turned away, diving out of sight, but the light caught their glistening sides and their short, hairy flippers waved. The raven hopped down to Jeremy's feet. The dog danced around in the snow by the rocks. Jeremy bent down and touched the raven lightly on the head.

"Clever. You saw the green light and came to tell me about it, didn't you? You always worry when there are strangers about."

"He is yours, sir?"

"No, I share the island with him. I don't own anything, just the ground here, and I really only have the use of it. The Indians had the right idea about ground. That's why they couldn't understand when we tried to buy the land from them and just gave it away. How can land be sold? But I live with the times and I have a paper somewhere with words on it that says that the island is mine, all mine. Bunk, but I can use the paper to keep the idiots away."

The commissaris was waiting patiently.

"Don't you agree?"

"Yes."

"But my ideas may be silly and hypocritical. I made the money to buy this island out of real estate. For twenty years I wheeled and dealed in the State of New York. Every penny I spend is made out of land deals and here I preach idealism and forgotten insight. All I can say for myself is that I got away and try to ignore the stink, a possibility when a man lives by himself. I had a drunken friend once who was a biologist and who claimed that we are a mistake. Nature should never have allowed apes to become people and people to become a plague. He was a logical man and he blew his head off one nice spring afternoon in his garden. Used a shotgun. I thought of following his example, but then I took the sly way out. I had an idea that there was beauty about and I set out to find it. In a way I succeeded. It is beautiful out here, although it takes a while before it can be fully appreciated and I'm still learning.

"Well, gentlemen, would you care to follow me? My

cabin is on the other side. It used to be here, but when the shore got built up I decided to move my living quarters."

The path circled the hill and Jeremy and the sergeant regulated their speed to the slow progress of the commissaris, who was limping badly. The sergeant didn't mind the slow pace. He looked at the smooth, wide curves of the snow, covering glades between the trees, and at the bay below, shimmering between the island and the cape. The dog ran ahead and waited for them on the path. De Gier extended a hand, but Jeremy held him back.

"Don't trust the dogs. You'll see another two on the other side. The young ones like to stay near the house. They have to get to know you real well before you can play with them. Now they'll attack without warning, and they bite to hurt. I had to save a hunter last year. The man had been stupid enough to ignore my KEEP OUT signs. The bay was completely frozen over then, so he could walk across. The dogs attacked him all at once and pushed him over and held him down until I came. They bit him too, but fortunately he had thick clothes on and had rolled over so they couldn't get at his face."

"Didn't he have a gun?"

"He might have shot them if they'd barked or showed their teeth, but Dobermans don't waste time, not if they have been properly trained."

"Did you train them, sir?"

"Yes. I got the mother as a puppy and her puppies were born here."

They had to cross a steep ravine in order to get to the house. The drawbridge over the ravine was narrow. The cabin stood on posts, in a large clearing, and a small peninsula had been leveled so that it could be used as an aistrip. Smoke crinkled from the cabin's chimney and from a small shed at the edge of the clearing.

"The doghouse. I have a potbellied stove in it that will burn for a whole day if I put the damper on. But the door is ajar so that the dogs can get out. They don't like to be cooped up."

Two big dogs, larger than the one that had met them on the path, were running around the clearing, keeping their distance. Jeremy whistled and they darted up to him, touched his legs with their noses, and shot off. The first dog joined them and they barked briefly and pushed each other and split up again, each seeming to take responsibility for his share of the grounds.

"My home, gentlemen. I'll go ahead, and you can try your luck with the ladder."

The ladder was well made, and de Gier noted how it could be pulled up to slide underneath the cabin floor. He turned in the open door to take in the view. The horizon, broken only by a few small islands, was packed with puffed clouds. The open sea seemed like a gigantic, quiet pond and moved only with the swell, rising and falling away without a ripple on its smooth surface, stretching away forever.

Jeremy looked at the clouds. "More snow tonight or tomorrow. I'll have some shoveling to do. Some of the paths must be kept open. I've been snowed in before. It's not a bad feeling, but I have to buy stores from time to time and I don't want to repeat the ordeal of being without salt and tobacco for a week on end."

"You go to town often, sir?"

"As few times as I can possibly manage, but this old body of mine houses a lot of desires. I grow my own vegetables and potatoes and I keep summer goats for meat and I fish, but some of the staples and luxuries I have to buy and in winter my stocks run low."

He had taken off his jacket and hung it on a peg. An open holster was strapped to his belt and a long-barreled revolver pointed at the floor. The commissaris looked at the sidearm and at a rifle, hung from a hook above the door.

"You are well armed, sir."

Jeremy smiled.

"And well protected. It would take an amphibious attack by a number of men to dislodge you."

"Yes, it would. The water is on the boil and the cake is on the table. If the sergeant cuts the cake I'll busy myself with the tea."

The commissaris made no further efforts and let the quietness of the cabin seep into his mind. The tea was hot and strong, and he sat back, grunting with pleasure. The cabin was sturdy and beautifully finished with paneling on all sides and a high whitewashed roof, carried by rafters of handhewn pitch pine. The paneling consisted of assorted boards, but their shades and colors blended well. There were several bookcases and more books piled on the floor. Several shelves were filled with jars containing grains and dried herbs. Smoked meats and fish hung on strings attached to the rafters.

"You see why I won't let the dogs in here. They're good jumpers, and they like a change of diet every now and then. I feed them on what's called trashfish here, suckers and alewives, but they thrive on it."

"You built the house yourself?"

"Yes. I had a bit of help, but not too much of it. It took a long time though. I wasn't a handyman when I arrived. I was the opposite, in fact, the proverbial idiot, the man from the city who knows it all but can't do anything. I had to live in a tent for a year or two, an army arctic tent with a kind of funnel for an entrance. Hard to get in and out of, but it was the only thing I could find that would allow for local conditions. I was very grateful when I could move into the cabin, even if it was drafty. I hadn't learned about insulation. I thought I just had to nail a lot of boards together. I had to wreck and rebuild the house twice and get help from shore, and all in all it's cost me five times as much as I calculated. And the best joke was that I had to pull it down again, just when I'd decided that it was perfect. That was when the neighbors began to arrive and to litter up the cape with their noise and monstrosities. I pulled it down, moved it bit by bit, and built it again, for the third and last time, I hope. A monotonous occupation. It took all spring and all summer."

"Excuse my curiosity, sir," the commissaris said, "but I am a police officer and addicted to asking questions. Did you buy the island from Mr. Astrinsky when you arrived?"

"Through another agency that used to have a branch office here. The previous owner was a gambler who had no idea of what he was throwing away. The poor fellow liked the pink, crumpled hills around Las Vegas. I paid what was considered to be a high price in those days, but I imagine I could get a good deal more now. Islands are in short supply, and the summer people all seem to be millionaires. They'll give a thousand dollars for a rock with a tree on it. I have ten acres of rocks and trees."

"But you wouldn't sell, I take it."

"No, I'm here for the rest of my life."

De Gier had got up and was looking at the airstrip.

"You had an airplane once, sir?"

"I intended to have one. I thought it would be fun to fly around, but it turned out to be too much trouble. Or perhaps I was too old to learn. The instructors gave up on me after I broke the wheels of one plane and the wing of another. It doesn't matter. I have the rowboat, and when it gets really cold, in January and February, I can walk across. I have a backpack and any car will give me a ride into town. But the airstrip was made and I left it. Michael Astrinsky used to come out and visit me until I told him that his blustering bored me. Now Madelin comes sometimes."

"You don't mind her visits?"

"On the contrary, she's an exception to my rule. She doesn't talk much and we share a meal and we go for a walk. She's good with the animals and she never stays long. I keep the strip clean for her."

"I see. And you have no other contacts?"

"Very few. If the Indians were still around I might be tempted to be sociable again, but what can the people here teach me? Your brother-in-law was high up

in the Blue Crustaceans, a club. Bah. To sit around and
try not to get drunk and then make the effort to try
and get home in one piece. I can get drunk here by
myself, just by watching the bay. I get a lot drunker
here than I used to in New York and I don't need a
bottle to do it now. It took time. The first few years
were hard."

"Indians," the commissaris said. "They've all gone?"

"Yes, to the reserves. We have the land. An Indian
needs land, lots of it. An Indian could go into the woods
naked and come back a week later with a suit of clothes,
good shoes, a bow and arrows, a canoe even. And all
they used were twigs and bark and the furs of the animals. They didn't need shotguns that take five shells
and fire them all in three seconds."

"About those people on the shore," the commissaris
said, "the people that made you move your house. They
aren't there anymore. My brother-in-law fell and slipped
and died. His neighbors got shot, drowned, were chased
away, froze in the woods, drank themselves to death."
The commissaris' voice was low and sleepy.

"Yes, so I heard."

Jeremy shifted in his chair. His gnarled hands played
with the mug.

"Do you have any idea how all these accidents came
about, sir?"

"Oh yes," Jeremy said, and the words came calmly
and matched the slow turning of the mug. "Ideas I
have, the ideas of a moron marooned in Orca Bay. The
old sheriff may have had better ideas, and the new
sheriff may be having them now."

"Murder," the sergeant said quietly. "Wouldn't you
think so?"

"But I won't tell you what I think," Jeremy said, his
eyes gleaming, "although I might give you some advice
if advice is wanted."

"We are new here," the commissaris said and stuck
his fork into his cake. "As new as you were once. But
we are interested, of course, and your advice will be
appreciated. We looked just now at the chain saw my

brother-in-law was working with moments before he died. An unfamiliar tool to us. The Netherlands have few woods left and we try to leave them alone. The chain saw was stuck in a tree."

"Nipped it. He probably didn't make a proper cut and the weight of the tree was leaning on the saw so that it couldn't be moved."

"Exactly. So he pulled and pulled and slipped and fell. The snow was frozen hard, turned into ice. There wouldn't have been any tracks had somebody been with him."

"He would have worn gloves. With gloves the hands don't slip on the saw's handle." Jeremy was staring at the commissaris. He seemed fascinated and amused.

"He might have slipped all the same. Perhaps he wasn't a good man with the chain saw," the commissaris was saying.

"No, he wouldn't have been. But even so, hard to prove something, isn't it?" Jeremy got up and stretched, rummaged about on the table, and found his pipe. "You might, mmpf mmpf, try to work on another victim, mmpf mmpf, seems you have choice enough."

"Another victim? Which victim would you recommend?"

The pipe was lit and sweet smoke crinkled through the cabin. "Let's see now," Jeremy said. "Who would I recommend? Mary Brewer, I think."

There was a tap on the window. Jeremy opened it and let in the raven, which flew up and sat on one of the rafters, peering down at de Gier.

"The lady who was drowned."

"Yes. I saw her go out that day. The wind was getting stronger and she wasn't wearing a life jacket, as usual."

Jeremy paused and dug about in his pipe with a penknife. "I can tell you a little, but I'm curious too. You're police officers, you say, from the Netherlands. Would you be cooperating with the sheriff here?"

"The sergeant is here on an exchange program, sir. I am a relative of one of the victims on Cape Orca."

"But you're a police officer too?"

"Yes."

"I see. As I say, I was just curious. Well, this is my tale. Mary used to like to sail clear out of the bay, which is fine when the wind isn't too strong. But that day the wind couldn't make up its mind and came this way and that and sometimes it came in sudden gusts. Cat's paws we call them here, like a cat reaching down, quick as a flash, and the mouse is caught. But Mary was the mouse—I am assuming. I didn't see Mary go down, but I saw the cat's paws on the bay. I was a bit worried about her, I suppose, but not too worried. She'd always managed to come back."

"Go on, sir."

"Yes, if the tale is of interest, certainly. There's something else I should tell you. Mary capsized once and her boat sank. She had a silly boat, not designed for these waters. I saw her go over and I rowed out. She was close to the island. I got her aboard and we lifted the boat out later. It had sunk in a shallow spot. But Mary got a fright then, and she had the stern and the bow of her boat filled with plastic foam. The carpenter made some nice wooden bulkheads to hide the foam."

"So the boat became unsinkable?"

"Oh yes, quite unsinkable."

"And did the boat come back, sir?"

"Exactly," Jeremy said. "There we have my point. That boat should have come back. Everything comes back here. The current is inland. You should see the garbage I pick up on the shores of this island. And Mary's boat was bright orange, a horrifyingly bright color."

De Gier was trying to outstare the raven, but the bird's eyes didn't blink.

"I see," the commissaris said. "You are saying the boat shouldn't have sunk, but apparently it did. There wasn't a search?"

"Not really. Maybe the Coast Guard looked for the boat, but they can't have been too thorough. The corpse turned up, you see, and everybody knew that Mary never wore a life jacket. And she wasn't missed until days after the accident. I saw her go out, but I didn't check to see whether she came back. She lived by herself. I suppose the mailman alarmed the sheriff when he saw that she wasn't emptying her mailbox."

"You are sure the boat wasn't found."

"Yes."

"So if it was found now and the disappearance of the plastic foam was ascertained . . ."

"Yes."

De Gier gave up on the raven and turned to look at Jeremy. "So there could have been murder, sir. You didn't tell the sheriff about your theory?"

"Me? Never. Perhaps if he'd come to see me, but I wouldn't barge into his office. We live our own lives here. I certainly do."

The raven had hopped down and was worrying de Gier's hat. Jeremy got up, took the hat away from the bird, and gave it back to the sergeant.

"Thank you. My beautiful washbear hat. It belonged to Mr. Opdijk."

"Washbear? Oh, I see. Is that what you call raccoons in your country? Not a bad name. They do wash their food before they eat it. Washbear, hmmm."

The commissaris had got up too and stood looking out a window. The powerboat came chugging back, trailing several long logs. Jeremy joined him at the window.

"Ah, back again are they? Got a good crop."

"Local woodcutters?"

"In a way. Fox and young Albert. They often cut dead pines on the cape."

The commissaris scratched his nose. "Isn't the cape private property, sir?"

Jeremy grinned. "Sure, but the fox doesn't mind that. He's been out of bounds all his life. But there's no harm. Dead pines are of no value and the gales blow them over and they rot away."

"So what does he want them for?"

"He set up a small sawmill some years ago, after he came back from college. It's a used mill, outdated, belonged to an old sawyer who retired. The fox got it for the scrap price and the old man taught him how to use it. But the fox is original. He didn't want to compete with the big automated lumbermills and work himself to the bone for a marginal profit. He discovered that pine killed by carpenter ants has an interesting texture, and he learned to cut the dead wood very carefully so that it wouldn't fall apart. I've watched him do it. The boy is an artist."

"And he sells his product?"

"At a good price. He trucks it himself to Boston and sells to the interior decorators. I would say he's doing well, although he could do better if he used his education and went to the city. He could easily make a career."

"Perhaps he does, in his own way."

"What's that?" Jeremy asked and blew smoke at the raven, which croaked in protest and hopped to the next rafter. "Ah, I see. Yes, here are some of the boards he cut. Gave them to me last year. He's another exception to my rule. He comes and visits from time to time."

The commissaris admired a part of the rear wall of the cabin. The boards were very light, almost crumbly, and showed dark lines. Jeremy scratched the paneling with his nail. "See, it holds together. The dark lines were traced by the ants. Used to be their corridors."

"Now what was he telling us?" the commissaris asked and stopped. De Gier stood behind him, his hand out, ready to grab the old man in case he slipped on the steep path. They had almost reached the Opdijk house, and Suzanne was peering at them from the living room window. The commissaris turned and pointed at the island. "There he lives, in his island fortress, with a raven patroling the sky and three fierce dogs to guard the land. He carries a handgun and there's a rifle above his door, but apparently he hates hunting. His house is placed high and the woods around the house are cut down, about the last thing one would expect him to do. Maybe he would cut a few trees if they interfered with his view, but he cut them all. That whole part of the island is bare."

"A ravine," de Gier said, "and a drawbridge and a ladder that he pulls up when he is in his cabin."

"So he feels threatened, doesn't he? By what?"

"He didn't seem nervous or fearful at all, sir. His eyes laughed even when he was trying to be serious."

The commissaris' cane scratched the snow viciously. "Yes, he seemed rather flippant. But what he told us about that unfortunate woman may have been true. If it was he was helping us. But he wasn't helping us all the way. I am sure he knows what goes on here. Quite a few people know, but they aren't going to tell us. And you know why not, sergeant?"

The commissaris looked at the small part of de Gier's face that wasn't obscured by the sergeant's hat and upturned coat collar.

"Because they don't care at all. These people got killed and the rest watched them being killed, one by one, in various ways, and they went on with whatever they were doing."

"Like the muggings in New York, sir? I read an article about street killing out there. The passers-by will pass by."

"No, sergeant. Perhaps, but I don't think so. We've run into something else. As I said before, this is a different society. A small town in a forgotten corner. It may come to life in summer, but the summer people have no idea what goes on. They do their vacationing and go home. The local people stay, and they aren't all yokels. No, no, not at all."

"So what's their game, sir?"

"Jan," Suzanne's voice wailed through the window.

"Yes, dear," the commissaris shouted. "We're coming."

"Of course he may have been lying through his teeth, sergeant," the commissaris said a minute later when he was stepping out of his boots in the spotless hall, "and cackling with that raven now, about the fun they had with us. Jeremy of Jeremy's Island. He may be a very sinister man. And intelligent, unusually intelligent. But whatever he is, he knows what he is doing, and saying."

"Jan!"

"Yes, Suzanne. I just want to wash my hands."

They sat down and Suzanne came in carrying a big bowl of steaming soup.

"Pea soup, Jan. Just like Mother used to make it, with bacon and pigs' trotters. We'll have gelatin pudding afterward."

The commissaris looked at the soup.

"That gentleman came about the house, Jan."

"He did? Did he say what he thought it was worth?"

"Yes, Jan. Ninety thousand dollars."

The commissaris tried to move his spoon through the soup. There were some thin slices of white bread next to his plate.

"Do you ever bake your own bread, Suzanne?"

"No. Opdijk always wanted me to, but it's such a lot of work and quite expensive, really. I bought forty loaves last time we went to the city and froze them. They taste very good, I think."

"Ninety thousand the man said?"

"Yes. I was very pleased. Surely that much money will buy me a good apartment in Amsterdam. I would like to live in the south of the city, in one of those big blocks of flats. I am sure I can afford it now."

"The house isn't sold yet, dear."

"I'm sure you'll sell it soon, Jan. Oh, I'm so pleased you're here. I've been so worried. But that's all over now. Tomorrow I'm going to pack some of the porcelain, but I'll need some crates. Do you think you can get me some crates, Jan?"

The commissaris yawned and checked his watch, after having pulled it from his waistcoat pocket. The watch told him it was eight o'clock, he frowned at it and shook it irritably. "What *is* the time, Rinus?"

De Gier was yawning too. "Two o'clock sir, do you still have Amsterdam time? I've been getting mixed up too. Last night, after we came back from the Wash's house I went home to the jailhouse and lay down to take a nap. I slept until this morning. The sheriff said he tried to wake me but had to give up."

"You look like you could use another nap now. I'm certainly going to have one myself."

"Listen," the commissaris said when he saw the sergeant off on the driveway, "do me a favor, Rinus. Buy me some cheese and crackers at that store in town, and some peanuts or something. After you've had your nap. You can give it to me tomorrow morning. Chocolate, anything. Anything, sergeant. Where's your car?"

The sergeant looked about sleepily. "Don't know sir, ah yes, I left it near the highway and walked down. I was hoping to see some wild animals, but they must have hidden themselves. I only saw tracks."

"Will you walk back or shall I give you a lift in the station wagon?"

"It's all right, sir." The sergeant strode off and disappeared behind a large spruce, its branches heavy with snow.

Suzanne's thin hand rapped against the window set in the front door.

"Yes," the commissaris shouted. "Coming, dear."

"You must be careful, Jan," Suzanne said when he had returned to the hall. "You'll catch cold. You might even get the flu. I had the flu last winter and I was in bed for weeks and weeks."

"I never get flu," the commissaris said, and sneezed.

8

De Gier walked for more than an hour, cold to his bones and struggling with his hat and branches that whipped into his face. Most of the way was uphill, and an icy breeze blew snowflakes into his eyes and froze the hairs of his mustache and eyebrows. It had also frozen the doors of the Dodge, and he had to warm the lock with his lighter. He smoked while he waited for the engine to warm up.

The road leading to Jameson seemed even worse than before, and he drove as slowly as he could, steering in the direction the car chose for itself and pumping the brakes when he didn't agree with the car's choice. The road's surface reminded him of some of the landscapes he had seen from the window of the intercontinental plane when it pierced the skies of Greenland and Newfoundland: a shiny eternity of frozen quietness, totally devoid of human life, a beautiful but frightening wasteland dominated by white or cream mountains and cut by gorges, violet in their own deep shadows. The road, properly photographed, could have been the cover of a science-fiction paperback, suggesting the weird miracle of another reality. The shock of change had touched off his perceptions, and the recent boredom of the gray days in Amsterdam was no more than the memory of an uninteresting and mostly forgotten dream. He grinned, forgetting his caution, and the car accelerated and made a sudden hundred-and-eighty-degree turn. "No," de Gier said gently, "not that way, *this* way!" He eased the car around again and kept trying until he reached the jailhouse. The compound was silent and, in the office, Bernie, the chief deputy, nodded sleepily and seemed disturbed when one of the telephones jangled. De Gier listened while he took off his coat and hat. Something about eggs. Another deputy, by the name of Bert, didn't have eggs, and Bernie thought that Bert should have eggs. De Gier went upstairs, found his bed, lay down and lit a cigarette. He put it out a few minutes later and closed his eyes, telling himself he should think about Cape Orca. When he woke up the room was dark. He found the sheriff in the office and was offered coffee. The two men had no chance to communicate, for a sudden commotion in the jail required the sheriff's prompt attention. De Gier left, telling Bernie, who was still taking care of the desk, that he meant to do some shopping at Robert's Market and would be back presently.

"You missed dinner," Bernie said.

"Never mind. I'll buy some food at the store."

Bernie grinned. "We'll get you something when you come back. The prisoners are on twenty-four-hour duty." De Gier grinned back. He could hear the sheriff's steely voice admonishing somebody behind the heavy jail door. The sheriff's vocabulary seemed most impressive, although somewhat repetitious.

The Dodge was easier to handle this time, for the town's roads had received a good sand sprinkling. The few street lights reflected on snow banks, a wan, green shine interspersed with deep, sinister shadows. He turned and stopped under the extended roof of Robert's Market.

There was a blaze of light under the porch, calling attention to some ten different signs, partly overlapping so that it was hard to understand what they were suggesting the customers should buy. Three signs mentioned beer, another ice. Why would people want to buy ice? The sign had an arrow that pointed at a metal box. He got out of the car and opened the box. Plastic bags filled with ice cubes. He still didn't understand. Iced drinks. But surely all Americans had refrigerators and each refrigerator would have at least two trays of cubes. So why did people want more? A man came out of the store, opened the box, and took out two bags of ice. "Excuse me," the sergeant said. "What do you want ice for?" The man stared. De Gier repeated his question. "Party," the man said. "Party tonight. What else?" The man shook his head and walked away. De Gier nodded. Of course. An advanced drinking country.

The lights of the store seemed to be reserved for its exterior, for the large room inside was dark and gloomy. A young man with a round red face under a compact mass of tiny, whitish curls was serving beer to three customers who sat on high stools. They didn't turn around, but de Gier recognized them and smiled. His third day and he already knew everybody. The fox fellow, Madelin, and Albert. He said good evening, but the guests didn't turn around.

"What can I do for you?" the man with the whitish curls asked. There was no warmth in the question.

"Some cheese," de Gier said. "Some crackers, candy bars, peanuts, cigarettes, a flashlight, batteries for the flashlight."

"Help yourself."

De Gier shuffled through the store, studying the unfamiliar labels on cans and plastic bags. The display of goods was haphazard. Apparently new stock was placed wherever there was room. When he couldn't find what he wanted he thought of asking the storekeeper, but the four heads in the other corner were close together. They had obviously forgotten his presence. He stumbled on, eventually located the required articles, and took them to the counter where the storekeeper grabbed a stub of pencil, wrote down figures, and came to a total.

De Gier paid and asked for a bag.

"Sorry, no bag."

But there were bags. The sergeant saw a stack of flattened brown paper bags on a shelf on the wall behind the counter.

"Give me one of those. I'll pay if you like. I can't carry all this in my hands."

There was no response, but the fox fellow slipped off his stool, went to the door, and locked it. He took the key out of the lock, dropped it into the pocket of his short heavy jacket, and went back to his stool.

"Three beers, Tom."

"Three beers coming up."

"Make it four. Have one yourself."

"Four beers coming up."

The refrigerator behind the counter opened. Four cans of beer slid onto the counter. The beer was sipped slowly, straight from the can. Nobody looked at de Gier.

The sergeant's purchases were still on the counter. He studied his collection. If he picked the articles up he could carry them to the door, but he wouldn't be able to open it even if it were unlocked. He would have to ask somebody to open it for him. He might try to grab the bag, but he would have to get over the counter to reach the shelf that held the bags. Tom might object to his climbing the counter. He could handle Tom, but the fox fellow and Albert would be on Tom's side, and Madelin had given no sign that she disagreed with her friends' behavior. Any trouble arising from his grabbing a bag could be explained as the lawful start of a fight, with the enemy on the right side of the law.

Fine.

The locked door presented another interesting problem in any further proceedings. Obviously the act of locking a customer in is illegal. Restriction of the liberty of a human being. But he would have to prove the locking of the door.

He went over the options again as he got on the last stool at the counter. Yes, there was nothing he could do. Kicking the door out of its hinges would be explained as willful damage committed by an irresponsible foreign visitor, for they would unlock the door afterward and claim it had never been locked. He might, of course, remove the key from the fox fellow's pocket.

The fox fellow would not like that. Back to base one.
A fight, four against one. No.

De Gier produced a cigarette and lit it. He thought
of asking for a beer, but Tom might not hear him. Tom
was picking his teeth with a match he had sharpened
with a long knife. He had left the knife on the counter,
within easy reach. De Gier studied the skin on Tom's
hand, soft skin covered with tiny, very blond hairs. A
good knife with a thin, wicked blade. He had fought
men with knives before. But to fight a man who holds
a knife takes concentration, and he wouldn't be able to
watch what the others were doing. Tom threw the match
into a carton filled with garbage and picked up his beer
can. He drank, looking straight ahead. The fox fellow
was tracing a crack in the counter with his forefinger.
Albert had closed his eyes and was whistling. Madelin
was reading the label on her beer can. De Gier smoked
and rearranged his purchases, the processed cheese in
front of the carton of crackers. He stacked the candy
bars and put the carton of cigarettes on top and the
peanuts on top of the cigarettes. He unscrewed the plastic flashlight and inserted the two batteries. He flicked
it on. It worked. He flicked it off again. The cigarette
had come to its end and he dropped the stub on the
floor, rubbing it out with the heel of his boot. Nothing
happened for the next ten minutes. Albert's whistled
song repeated itself endlessly. A monotonous theme,
but quite exact. De Gier listened to every repetition.
He wasn't particularly worried. He had found the answer to the puzzle. There was nothing he could do but
wait. There was nothing the enemy could do but wait.
They would have to outwait each other. But the enemy
was several steps ahead of him. The enemy could drink
beer and be together, he could do nothing and he was
alone. And the enemy could call the end of the game.

What next? Another cigarette? But he had just put
one out. He felt in the side pocket of his jacket and his
hand came up with an Amsterdam bus ticket. He held
the ticket at arm's length and read its text: *"This ticket
is valid on the day of issue for any distance on an*

Amsterdam streetcar or bus including transfers provided that . . ." He crumpled the ticket and threw it into the garbage carton. Not too interesting, no plot, no characters. He glanced at the enemy. The enemy wasn't doing anything in particular, but Albert still whistled. Even so, there had been some subtle change. Albert's pouted lips blew a variation on the theme and his foot tapped twice. The taps seemed to set off the fox fellow, who got up, walked to a position halfway between the counter and the door, and began to click his fingers. Madelin's right hand became a fist, and her knuckles hit the warped and stained counter. Tom did something too. He picked up his knife, turned it around, and made the handle repeatedly touch his beer can. The sounds didn't blend at first, but Albert's whistling became a little louder and he held a note, broke it, and held it again. The rhythm fell into place.

De Gier got off his stool and unbuttoned his jacket. The enemy turned toward its prey, but the whistling, clicking, knocking, and rapping continued. De Gier's hand reached into his inside pocket and produced a flat black leather case. The whistling stopped, then started again. He opened the case and took out a small metal flute and screwed its two gleaming parts together. He blew his first note. It fitted into a missed beat of the knocks and clicks, and the sergeant breathed in, held his breath for four bars, and blew a higher, much longer note. When it broke, Albert's whistling caught up and spread and de Gier made the flute go down and become the whistle's shadow. He wouldn't dominate the enemy, he would be content to follow. He knew the tune. "Straight, No Chaser." A very good tune, created and played by the best musicians on the Coast and in New York City. He had the tune on at least twelve records. He had played it often with Adjutant Grijpstra accompanying on his old set of drums. But perhaps the present rhythm section was more of a challenge than the methodical approach the adjutant, the faraway adjutant, had offered on previous occasions. He knew the adjutant's style well and liked to adjust to Grijpstra's ways, but the enemy was new and bound to produce surprises, sudden changes, a whole new way of making use of the tune's possibilities.

He started the high note again but cut it into slivers and got back into the theme, repeating it to give the others a chance to fit in. Madelin was the first to start the chant. There was a word to the chant: *Cannonball*. Tom chanted with her, using the word's syllables to stress the main theme of the tune. Madelin's voice reminded the sergeant of the iced landscape he had seen in the Orca road surface, but the emptiness was no longer void. There were beings in it now, transparent and floating. The hoarse, thin voice of the fox fellow gave the beings more form and de Gier began to recognize some of the creatures on the edges of his mind, but not quite, for they were of his dreams and wouldn't enter into actual, definable existence. *Can-non-ball*. The word seemed logical, the only word that could be used in the chant. He remembered that he should follow rather than lead and Albert's whistling filled the store again, reaching into its dark corners. Tom had left his protected nook by vaulting across the counter. He no longer held his knife and the beer can. The fox fellow was no longer clicking his fingers. The chant had become powerful. Even quiet Albert was chanting, and Madelin's voice rose and broke the limitations of the room. She sang the last syllable of the chant's word. *Ball*. High and eerie but also sweet. A holy sound, de Gier thought, but truly holy, cleansed of the goodness that clings to angels and saints, approaching the purity that can no longer be named.

He was facing the door when it opened and the sheriff and chief deputy came in and stood between the shelves holding giant cola bottles that formed a corridor into the store. The store's scanty light reflected in the blue metal of their guns and the silver badges on their Boy Scout tunics. The tune halted abruptly when the flute dropped away from de Gier's lips, and Tom vaulted back to his place behind the counter. He faced his customers and smiled.

"What can I do for the law this evening?"

"Any sandwiches left, Tom?"

"Yes, sheriff. Turkey or salami? Eat here or take out?"

"Turkey. What do you want, Bernie?"

"Turkey."

"Turkey, twice, to take out."

The sandwiches appeared from the depths of the refrigerator and looked fresh and tasty. Tom wrapped them, pulling the plastic from a slit in the counter, pulling and cutting the thin film in a single movement. The sheriff paid and the two men turned and began to walk back to the cruiser waiting under the awning, partly visible through the door's glass. The cruiser's wide nose nudged the timid shape of de Gier's Dodge.

"Evening, sergeant," the sheriff said as he eased his way past de Gier. "See you later in the jailhouse. I still have an hour of patrol to get through with."

De Gier nodded. The door closed and a hand touched his wrist. He looked up into the light yellow brown eyes of the fox fellow. The door's key rested in the fox fellow's outstretched hand. De Gier took the key, walked to the door, inserted the key into the lock, and turned it. There was a click, but no latch moved out of the lock.

"A trick lock?"

"No, just old."

"You have used it before?"

The fox smiled, a pleasant slow smile. "Not too often. It tends to upset people."

"Sergeant?"

Tom had joined them. He held a brown paper bag. "Your things. The bag is on the house. I like your flute, come again."

The fox laughed. "You don't have to say that, Tom. You've got the only grocery store."

De Gier carried his bag to the door. The girl slipped past him and opened it.

"Thank you."

"Do you remember where I live, sergeant?"

He remembered. The house behind the realtor's office. He also remembered that her father had gone to the Bahamas.

"Yes."

"I'll be waiting for you."

Her feet hardly touched the snow as her slender body, wrapped in a tight fur coat, flitted to a large car parked in the yard by the store.

When he switched the Dodge's radio on the sheriff was talking to the deputy called Bert. "But we've got to get eggs, Bert. You know that the egg truck overturned. Robert's Market won't have any eggs for a week. The prisoners want eggs for breakfast."

"I can't get them, Jim. I tried. Nobody has eggs to spare, it's winter. They've slaughtered most of the chickens." The radio crackled.

"I may get some duck eggs from Smithtown. Would the prisoners eat duck eggs, Jim?"

"Get duck eggs, Bert. Get them tonight. Ten four."

"Sheriff," Bert said. "Jim, please. That's thirty miles each way and the roads are bad. Maybe he's out of eggs too. He's got no phone. You don't want me to go nowhere for nothing, Jim."

"Ten four, Bert."

"Jim!"

"Ten fucking four." The sheriff's voice was low, almost loving, but it had a frazzled edge.

De Gier pressed his microphone. "Sheriff?"

"Ten three, sergeant."

"I may be late, Jim. Madelin Astrinsky has asked me in for a drink. I am on my way there now."

The radio chuckled. "Good for you. Are you still on Main Street?"

"Yes."

"I want to talk to you for a little while. Don't go to her just yet. Go up Main Street and keep on going. There will be some elm trees on your right. You know what elm trees look like?"

"I think so."

"Tall straight trunks that only fork high up. They

died some years ago, but the town hasn't allocated money for cutting them down yet. Died of your Dutch elm disease. Stop there. Keep your engine running. I'm out of town now but coming back."

The elm trees reached up with great surging gestures. The bark was peeling off and waved slowly in the dying breeze. The naked ghost trees impressed the sergeant. Corpses, skeletons almost, but still expressive of the life power that had made them grow into huge symbols of the planet's urge to join the sky. The small blue car had slid to a stop facing some dried-out weeds that threw shadows on the snow, a moving bristle of sharp black lines. The windows were icing over and de Gier scraped them. He saw the white glow of the landscape stretching away on both sides of the deserted road. The cruiser's lights appeared in the curve ahead and approached rapidly. Its growing bulk seemed evil, a disturbing entity about to interfere with his bliss. He got out of the car and the frost bit into his face. He impatiently adjusted his raccoon hat, but the tail still dangled over his face. The hat had been bothering him in the car too, but he hadn't dared take his hands off the wheel. He couldn't take the hat off now either, as it was protecting his ears.

The sheriff waved invitingly, and de Gier stumbled to the car's rear door, which had swung open. The cruiser's back seat was a simple wooden bench, and the windows on each side of it were barred. There were no handles on the insides of the doors.

"Hope you don't mind sitting in the prisoners' quarters, sergeant, but we won't keep you long. Just wanted to fill you in."

The sheriff had opened the thick glass partitioning behind the driver's seat. The chief deputy filled the right side of the front seat. He was eating his turkey sandwich.

"They did the trick of the door on you, right?"

"Yes."

"They've done it before, a perfect trap. I asked you to meet me because there's a CB radio in the store and they have our channel. Was it on while you were there?"

"No."

"It'll be on now. I've asked for a scrambler, but the state can't afford it. Everything we say on the radio is public knowledge. The door trick didn't work, did it? You all seemed quite merry when we came in. What happened?"

De Gier told him.

"Yes, I thought I heard music at first, but that store is so dark you can't see what's going on. Good, so that's the first round won. But the gong sounds again. Now Madelin wants you, right? That's good too. You should be able to get some information."

"How long has she been with the gang, Jim?"

"I am not too sure. Bernie's an expert on local history. Tell him, Bernie."

The fat deputy swallowed and turned. "Ever since the gang formed, sergeant, ten years ago maybe. They were youngsters then, and we used to run them in for slashing tires and breaking windows. They used to be a public nuisance, but it was all easy stuff. They're different now."

"Do they have records?"

Bernie looked at what was left of his sandwich. There was nothing left. He folded the plastic, making the crumbs run into his hand, and ate them. "No, not really. That early stuff got wiped out because they were underage, and after that it was just speeding and drinking in a vehicle parked in the public road." He yawned and looked at his watch. "Another half-hour, Jim."

"I did a little work today, sergeant," the sheriff said. "I saw the town clerk. Cape Orca has three present owners. There's Mrs. Wash, of course, she owns the bulk of the land. Then there's Michael Astrinsky, who has bought all the vacated properties, and Suzanne Opdijk still owns her house and land. You might count Jeremy as a fourth owner since the island is his and the island is in Orca Bay and Cape Orca embraces that property."

"Astrinsky? Did your realtor friend tell you about the real value of Mrs. Opdijk's house?"

"Yes, ninety thousand. And Astrinsky offered thirty you said."

"So Astrinsky is playing Monopoly, trying to get a whole street. What would he want with the street?"

"A marina perhaps," the sheriff said. "He could build a jetty with a little port for pleasure craft. It wouldn't be a bad proposition."

The sergeant looked at the metal bar separating him from the driver's seat. The bar was worn smooth by sliding handcuffs. "Yes. And Astrinsky took off for the Bahamas. Any chance of getting him back for questioning?"

Bernie laughed. "Astrinsky? He's a big shot, sergeant. He knows the governor. He's a town selectman. He's the president of the Blue Crustaceans. Everybody owes him favors. Astrinsky is a big fish in a small pond."

The sheriff nodded. "I could make him come back if I asked the state cops to start an official investigation, but what do I tell the state cops? No, sergeant, it's just us, puttering around. You did some puttering today. How is Jeremy these days?"

The sergeant reported on that morning's visit. The radio came on and Bernie answered the call.

"Game warden here," the radio said. "That you, Bernie?"

"Yes."

"Got that dog?"

"I thought *you* were going to kill that dog."

"No," the radio said. "And you know it. We agreed twice now that you were going to do it and this is the third time we're agreeing. Let us know when you've got the dog. Better let us know tomorrow."

"Ten four," Bernie said. He pushed the microphone back into its clip and cursed.

"Same ten sixty-four again, Bernie?" the sheriff asked.

"Yes, Jim, same old ten sixty-four. They're passing the buck to me and I pass it back."

"Not this time, it seemed to me," the sheriff said.

"What's a ten sixty-four?" de Gier asked.

Bernie was studying the dashboard. His face was impassive but there was some movement in the rolls of fat in his neck. "Dog-deer complaint, sergeant."

"Dogs hunting deer?"

"Yes, sergeant," the sheriff said. "The dogs go after the deer but so do the tourists. We like to sell them hunting licenses and cabins and supplies and anything else they think they need. It's part of the business of the county. The game wardens are supposed to patrol the woods, but they use helicopters. They don't like to work on the ground; they reckon we can do that. If they see a dog hunting deer they'll track the dog and find out who owns it, and they'll warn the owner once. The second time they shoot the dog from the chopper. But the dogs are getting clever, and hide when the chopper is around so we have to come in and do the job."

"Right," Bernie said. "And we're busy. Everybody has a dog here and nobody ties the dog up. The dogs chase anything they see and deer are the biggest thing they see, and they don't kill the deer, they just cripple them. One dog can cripple a dozen deer in a day."

"So you shoot them?"

"Sometimes. The locals don't like us shooting their dogs; they like us to warn them. So that's what we do. We go around warning dog owners. I've warned the owner of this particular dog a dozen times. And every time old Bill says, 'Sure, Bernie, won't happen again. I'll tie him up.' But he never does. And I never see the dog. Bill hides him when he sees the cruiser. Bill has lived here all his life. He runs a saltwater farm. A very crafty man, old Bill Thompson, too crafty for me. But the game wardens don't want to know. They speak to me every other day."

"Yes," de Gier said. "What do you think about these murders of ours, Bernie?"

The deputy crumpled the plastic from his sandwich into a little ball, opened the window, and threw the ball out. He pressed the window's button and the glass zoomed up. "Littering, a one-hundred-dollar fine. Every-

body does it all the time. You tell them it's unlawful
and they laugh. You write a ticket and they slash your
tires. Murders? What murders? Seems to me you've
got to prove them. Just one would be enough. Then you
can call in the state cops. Homicide is not the sheriff's
business. He can spot it, but he can't work on it too
much."

The sheriff seemed bored. His small, narrow hand
moved over the controls of the cruiser's dashboard and
touched a button. The siren barked once, tearing at the
silence outside. "You heard what the sergeant said,
Bernie. Mary Brewer's corpse was found, not her boat.
Maybe we can find the boat."

Bernie pointed at the bay. "That boat is out there,
Jim. The bay is freezing up. We can't look under the
ice."

"The boat is orange. Orange is a good color. If it
hasn't sunk, it'll show up from the sky."

"We don't have an airplane, Jim."

"We don't have many things, but others do. I have
a friend in the Coast Guard, an officer. The Coast
Guard has dozens of choppers. Maybe they need exer-
cise. I can ask for a favor; they've asked us for favors.
I don't need an official investigation to make a few
choppers fly around."

Bernie belched.

"You don't think I should ask the Coast Guard?"

"Sure, Jim, go ahead. Maybe the boat will turn up.
Maybe we can connect the boat with the gang. The
gang is bad, Jim. Look what they did to my cruiser.
Look what they did to poor Captain Schwartz. Sure
the guy is a Nazi and sure Nazis are bad, but Schwartz
was nuts, just nuts, harmless. He would walk around in
that crazy uniform and he would foul-mouth niggers
and Jews, but it was all talk. He didn't do no harm.
He was a quiet old guy, but the fox visits him and the
next thing we see is Schwartz hotfooting it out of town.
His son or nephew or somebody comes out and sells

the house and has a yard sale and all the captain's goodies go for a nickel and a dime."

"The fox," de Gier said. "Does he have any particular reason to dislike the Nazis?"

Bernie shrugged. "Don't we all? Old Fox died in the war, got shot in France. A few hundred thousand other G.I.'s got shot too. Why hold that against Schwartz? I tell you, the fox is bad. All of them are bad. They hang around and smile and get their college degrees and cut boards out of stolen timber, but when they get a chance to be real bad they take it. Look at what happened to you tonight. Okay, so they didn't make it with you, but they scared the shit out of many another. They've kept people for hours in that store, locked behind an unlocked door."

"True," the sheriff said. "Maybe you better go, sergeant. You've a pleasant appointment waiting for you, but take care. Madelin is a bit of a vampire. She may suck your blood when you nod off. I'll open the door for you."

He winked when de Gier got out of the cruiser. "Have a good time, sergeant. Take your chance, although I suppose you get enough opportunities in Amsterdam. Do you?"

"It comes and it goes," de Gier said. He felt too tired to respond to the wink. The raccoon hat had turned around again and the fluffy tail was getting into his mouth.

9

De Gier dropped, rolled away, and kept on rolling until he was covered by a large rock. He knew he was on its safe side. The rifle's crack had come from the woods, and the woods were on the other side of the rock. Not a bad shot at all. The bullet had been close to his neck. He took off his hat and peered over the rock. He could see a dark spot under the trees, moving away. The rifleman seemed hampered in his movements. There was something strange about his feet. That's right, snowshoes. He sat back and thought. The rifleman was perfectly safe. There was no point in following the man. He wasn't armed.

He got up and looked at the driveway of the Astrinsky house. Something lay near the spot where he had stood when the bullet whistled past. He found a stick and poked at the object. The raccoon tail. He looked at his hat. The tail was missing. He tried to grin, but his teeth chattered instead. A slight case of shock. He had been shot at before and had experienced the same reaction. Chattering teeth. Most annoying, but they would stop after a while.

The light on the porch was on. He had been in the light when the rifleman pulled the trigger. Set up again, just as in Robert's Market. They created their situations. He fought the little wave of self-pity that threatened to overflow his brain; so all right, he was here, in their territory, and they were playing their game. He would have to adjust to their tactics. He looked at the Dodge parked a little further down the driveway. He could walk to the car, get in, drive back to the jailhouse, have a bath and some coffee, and go to bed. Or he could visit the girl who had invited him.

The door opened and Madelin's voice reached out to the rock.

"Sergeant?"

"Here."

"Did I hear a shot?"

"You did."

"Why don't you come in?"

He sprinted across the driveway, picking up the tail on the way. She stepped back to let him jump through the doorway and closed the door. He showed her the tail.

"Came off my hat."

Her lips pouted. "That was close, sergeant."

He took off his coat, and she made him step out of his boots and slip into sheepskin moccasins. She stood very close, and he felt the curve of her breast and the pressure of her thigh. She was making him welcome, or perhaps she just happened to be standing close by. It was still a little too early to judge.

She led him into a room with a fireplace. He sat down on a settee and reached out to the burning logs.

"Have you had dinner, sergeant?"

"No, but I am not too hungry."

"Don't they feed you at the jailhouse?"

"Certainly, but I wasn't in the right place at the right, time."

"Aren't you hungry at all?"

"A little."

"I'll fix you a drink and make you a sandwich. Would you like a sandwich? A steak sandwich?"

"Yes, please."

She poured him a drink from a large brown bottle with an orange label and raised her own half-full glass. "Your health, sergeant." They drank. "I'll be right back."

He studied the flames and tried to recollect what he

knew about Americans. He had arrested dozens of
them, all on the same charges, drugs. He recalled the
vague young men, bearded, in rags, and their female
counterparts, in long dirty dresses, often barefoot. They
hung around in the center of Amsterdam during the
summer. Sad innocents, dropouts, usually on the verge
of starvation, often close to death. They would be jailed,
go to court, be convicted and flown back to the States,
under escort of the Dutch military police. He had also
dealt with other Americans, the middle-aged tourists
who came in groups, flown in daily by hump-backed
jets. The tourists often lost their way or their posses-
sions, and sometimes they were robbed.

He had also been in contact with deserters from the
American occupation army in Germany. And he had
read books and seen movies. But the actual encounters
and the fantasies of stories and the screen hadn't prepared him for meeting Americans on their home ground.
A U.S. bullet had missed him a few minutes ago. The
next one might not miss.

He shook his head and looked around the room without taking in any details. "Straight, No Chaser." The
BMF gang. A rifleman on snowshoes, plodding quietly
away into the dark woods.

He sipped his drink, put it down, stretched, and began to amble through the room, his hands in his pockets.
The same elegance as the Wash mansion but on a
smaller scale. A bare room in a way, but each piece of
furniture seemed to be a collector's item. The settee and
the matching armchairs, the dining table pushed against
the far wall, the bookcase, all seemed to date back to
the quietness of the pre-rococo era. He admired the
stern, solid lines and the superb workmanship that had
created not only the furniture but also the room itself.
Rough heavy beams, plastered walls, a hardwood floor,
not nailed but pegged. The bricks of the fireplace
seemed so old he thought they would crumble. He
studied the room's only decoration, a fairly large painting hung above the mantelpiece. He stepped back and
grunted approvingly. No mean work of art, and most

macabre. He moved back a little more to take in the overall impact of the scene. Death. A tall skeleton riding a black horse. The skeleton was dressed in a flowing cape, a purple cape the same shade as the long skirt Madelin had been wearing just now. The horse galloped. Rider and steed were on their way to do some work, on a battlefield perhaps, or in a city succumbing to the plague. He approached the painting. The horse ran through a field of wildflowers. There were wooded hills in the back and a pale sky, shot through with flames.

He shook his head again. This would be the room where Astrinsky ate and read his newspaper, comfortable in front of the fire. He couldn't imagine the talkative, sociable man under this painting. He moved it a bit. The painting didn't fit the lighter space underneath. Some other painting should hang here. This skeleton, grinning madly, holding a scythe, its body thighs pressed into the flanks of the gleaming horse, had been hung here for his benefit. It might be part of the trap, a follow-up to the bullet in the driveway just now and to the encounter in Robert's Market.

He adjusted the picture, picked up his drink, and sat down. How very nice. What next? Poison in the steak sandwich? Was she going to drag him into a dank cell in the basement and chain his sleeping or dying body to a cannonball?

Cannon*ball*. He heard her voice touch his spine in the dark store.

She came back carrying a tray with two plates.

"I felt hungry too. Let me freshen your drink. How do you feel now?"

"Better, thank you. Who fired the shot you think? One of your friends I met in Robert's Market?"

She sat down on the carpet, close to his legs.

"Could be, but I don't think so. We had our joke tonight. Why go on? You behaved very well, sergeant. We were impressed. And I love your flute. I didn't know our jazz is still appreciated in Europe. You knew the tune, didn't you?"

"Yes."

She ate and he watched her. He wondered if she always wore see-through blouses in the evening. Her breasts were firm and tilted. He looked at her feet, very small under the thin black strips of high-heeled sandals. And the face of the princess, the dragon's girl. He was sure it was the same face, small, triangular, and dominated by the dark and fluid eyes.

"Eat your sandwich, sergeant. It'll get cold."

He ate the sandwich, a salad, and some pickles. He started on his second drink and studied the orange label on the bottle of bourbon. A good situation, but unreal, like the full-page advertisements in magazines. He wondered what they were advertising now. The bourbon? Of course. The orange label was the most conspicuous spot in the low-key room, as the painting hung in the shadow. Two models on a flat sheet of paper. The male model handsome and foreign, the female local but exotic. A cleverly thought out ad, selling a beverage distilled in the South demonstrated against a Northern setting.

Whoever flipped the pages of the magazine would stop a second and fantasize about what the couple would do after, say, the third drink. Copulate. But the image was veiled, hinted at, suggested. Maybe the photograph wouldn't be too clear. The models would appear in a hazy light, dreamlike. Drink this particular brand of bourbon and just see what will happen to you. And he was in the photograph. Performing. And that's what he would continue to do. It was his only chance to get at the dragon's princess. But the dragon might still be prowling nearby, carrying a deer rifle.

He picked up the bottle and read the label: *The unique marriage of body and flavor has been the standard by which all other bourbon whiskeys are judged.* The words didn't inspire him, and he put the bottle back.

"Another drink? Go ahead."

"No thank you."

He got up, put on his half glasses, and studied the painting. She laughed.

"Anything funny?"

"Yes, you. How old are you, sergeant?"

"Forty-one."

"You look silly with those spectacles. They destroy your image."

"I don't use them much, only when I read a lot, but my eyes are becoming weaker. I believe most people over forty need reading glasses."

She smiled. "You're straight, sergeant. I like that. The fox calls straight people cunning. Why don't you come straight with me? What are you doing here, in this one-horse town in the sticks?"

"I'll tell you the truth, but you won't believe me. The commissaris, the old man now staying with Suzanne Opdijk, came out here to help Suzanne, who is his sister. Suzanne wants to leave America and her brother is helping her to sell her property here. He is a police officer, chief of the homicide division of the Amsterdam Municipal Police. I am a sergeant working for the division. He has been very ill, and I've come out to make sure he is all right. His legs bother him. If he gets too ill he is in pain and becomes lame. He didn't want me to come, so my colleagues interfered and had me sent out officially, making use of an exchange program that has been in force for some years. Since we arrived we have become suspicious of a series of deaths on Cape Orca and we found that your sheriff shares our suspicion. As I am here in a more or less official position the sheriff has asked me to cooperate."

"The truth, so help me?"

"I said you wouldn't believe me."

"I think I do, sergeant."

"You invited me here tonight to find out?"

"Perhaps I did."

"Why did you hang the painting?"

She got up, took his plate and her own, and set them on the dining table. When she sat down on the carpet again she was a little closer and he wanted to bend down and kiss her. He didn't because he would have had to make an effort. It would be better if she flung herself into his arms or undressed in front of the settee.

"I always hang that painting when Father is out of town. The fox and I bought it together, in a New York junk shop. I like the painting. Father hates it."

"Good, so it is not just for me."

She nodded seriously. "But perhaps it is, sergeant. Death is a fascinating subject. Perhaps it's the basis of all thoughts. The deaths of the Cape Orca residents fascinate me too. I like to experiment, to see what happens if certain moves are made. To hang that painting was a deliberate move."

"You experiment on others?"

"Yes, and on myself."

"Were you involved with any of the Cape Orca killings?"

"Only with one. I bought the whiskey the fox gave to Paul Rance. Paul used to drink, but he gave it up on doctor's orders. The doctor wanted to prolong the old man's life, but Paul was miserable, dying slowly, and he had always been such a marvelous old man. He was living on handouts and he hated accepting them, and he was too sick to do anything in return. The fox thought it would be a good idea if Paul had one last fling and got out happy. I agreed. The fox went out and spent a few days with Paul. They were drunk together until Paul died."

"Were you there?"

"No, I don't like getting drunk. The fox does. I would have been bad company."

"You didn't kill or help to kill the others?"

"No. I did attack Opdijk. I buzzed him with my plane when he was fishing, but I came from the seaside. He was perfectly safe. If I had come in from the cape he would have fallen on the rocks, as he did later on. I don't think he hurt himself, but he had a bad fright."

"Why did you attack him?"

She laughed. "Because the man was such a slob. Fa-

ther likes me to go to the Blue Crustaceans' club sometimes, and I can't constantly refuse. I was always sure
to find Opdijk there, and he always grabbed me. An
uncle's friendly petting, but the bastard was feeling me
up. I don't like to be felt up by slobs. It was good to
see him jump and run and fall over. But I overdid it a
bit. I nearly flew the plane into the Opdijks' house."

"Do you have any idea who killed Opdijk and Mary
Brewer and the other two, a man called Jones and another called Davidson?"

"I have an idea."

"Would you tell me?"

"Shouldn't you find out for yourself? It must be interesting to find little clues here and there and try to piece
them together. Why should I help you?"

De Gier reached for his empty glass and she refilled
it. His teeth chattered again and he held his jaw.

"If you cooperate you may clear yourself. Now you
are a suspect. So far we are just bumbling about, but
the sheriff may call in the state police, who might use
different methods. They wouldn't be hampered by local
conditions."

She smiled and he saw the tip of her tongue and her
moist lips. "Why should I want to clear myself, sergeant? I'm sure I couldn't be arrested and I'm sure nobody can be arrested. I am playing my game, which is
watching your game, and the way you play it, you and
the sheriff and your chief. And you can watch our game
again. You've been taking part in it. It's all very involved and rather exciting, don't you think?"

Watching the bear in the circus, he thought, while the
bear watches the audience.

Her head was close to his hand and he stroked her
hair.

"Yes," he said. "The game is exciting. My chief
thinks so too. He was so excited that he almost danced
in the snow. He looked very funny. He has been trying
to understand your gang. He likes its name, especially
the prefix *bad*. You say you like experimenting. Your

membership in the gang must be an experiment. You study philosophy, don't you?"

"Yes, but the books and the lectures are just words. If I attend all the lectures and do my utmost I'll get letters after my name, and perhaps one day I'll write something clever and my genius will be acknowledged. But that part of it is just silly. The true philosophers have always experimented. I was fortunate that I grew up with others whose minds were similar to mine. It's fashionable to be rebellious when you're young. Most American kids have a destructive period, but the fox always wanted to go further and he continued refusing to accept values that he hadn't tested. We became a gang and destroyed things for a while, material things, but the activity didn't get us anywhere. It was boring. He selected the biggest, New York, and we went down there for a few weeks.

"We were in our late teens and early twenties then. We found what we thought was the best part for our purposes, the Lower East Side. There were lots of gangs, most of them uniformed in some way. They didn't touch us, not even when we provoked them. The fox tried various methods. He used me as bait, but they just thought I was a prostitute. Finally Tom got us into the required trouble. He was a little drunk and he walked by himself and some Puerto Ricans mugged him. We got into the fight and the P.R.'s got help too. It was a true fight, with one corpse on their side and one on ours. The fox knifed a boy, a beautiful boy in dungarees and a black leather jacket. Gérard, a French Canadian from Jameson, caught a knife that had been thrown in his chest. He didn't see it coming. We left Gérard's body. We carried no identification, and his corpse wasn't there when we came back later. The police probably took it away. We all had a crisis then I think. We nearly gave up, and the fox stepped back and let us make up our minds. There were six of us left. Two gave up later on—they left the city and went out of state. I've lost contact with them. They married, got suburban homes in some city or other. They do the normal thing. Only the fox and Albert and Tom and I continued."

"Gérard wasn't missed when you got back to Jameson?"

"No. His parents had got divorced and left. He hadn't been living with them. Nobody cared I think, and we didn't tell anyone what happened. We said he had stayed in New York."

"But you are telling me."

"Sure, why not?"

"Do you do everything the fox tells you to do?"

She laughed. "No, sergeant. When we were in New York we ran out of money and he suggested I work in a porno studio. Some old man with a hairpiece and polished fingernails offered me two hundred dollars a day. The fox thought that was a splendid idea, but I refused."

"And the money?"

"I telephoned my father and got a check and flew home. The others came back much later. Maybe they worked or robbed a bank. I never asked them how they got money. We are very secretive, even with each other. It's part of the game. Perhaps we aren't really a gang but just individuals linked in some strange formation. If I disagree with an experiment I don't take part in it. 'Gang' is a childish word, but we've been using it."

"What's on the number plate of your car?"

"BMF ZERO."

De Gier laughed as she got up and put more logs on the fire. She came back and stripped. De Gier still felt cold. She pulled him to his feet and helped him undress.

"Do you like me, sergeant?"

"Yes."

"Most men do."

"It must make your experiments easy."

"Kiss me."

The loveplay took a good while. He controlled himself to make it stretch, but he still felt part of the advertisement, and the orange label on the whiskey bottle stayed in his mind. The dragon hadn't released the princess. It had made the princess available, and not for the first time.

De Gier was lured into various postures and all the while Madelin was submissive, inviting, seemingly passive. But he knew that she granted him no initiatives and that he was taken through a preconceived program. A good program, with a good end.

"I'll show you where the bathroom is. We might take a shower."

She let him go first and he went down again and dressed and sat near the fire, watching its glow hollow out the birch logs. Madelin returned a little later in a housecoat. She made coffee and they drank it on the settee.

"The sheriff tells me your father owns the shore strip on Cape Orca now."

"Did he check with the town clerk?"

"Yes."

"The records may not be up to date. When land is sold the title is transferred officially, but only when the new deed is registered. Land taxes have gone up lately. A new name on a deed usually alerts the assessor. It may be better to put off registration for a while."

"But what if the previous owner sells the land again?"

"That's a risk, but not when the previous and new owners are friends, or trust each other."

"So your father may have sold the land again and the town clerk doesn't know who the new owner is."

"That might have happened."

"Has it?"

She put a finger on his nose. "It might have and he may not have told me. I'm the *junior* partner. He's the head of a rival gang, the Blue Crustaceans. His ideas differ from mine."

"Do you like him?"

"I've fought him all my life."

"Another experiment," de Gier said. "I see."

She moved away from him. "Don't sneer at experiments, sergeant. It's the only way we have to find out, to really find out. The reason that you are here tonight is because I saw something in you, the way you played your flute. The fox did too. He's considering you as an honorary member."

De Gier got up. "Are you serious?"

She smiled. "Yes. Are you leaving? Better be careful, it isn't safe outside. You can stay the night if you like."

"I'll be careful."

She caressed his arm and he waited patiently.

"Why are you a sergeant? Shouldn't you be an officer?"

"I didn't have the qualifications to go to the academy. I went to the police school. I'll probably be made an adjutant in due course."

"An adjutant is an officer?"

"No."

"Do you mind?"

"No. Officers spend most of their time behind desks. I prefer to experiment in the field; maybe you and I are alike in some ways. Goodbye, Madelin. Thank you."

She laughed. "Don't thank me. I'm a country girl. Foreign males don't come my way too often. I think I should thank you. You did very well."

She walked him to the door and melted into his arms when he reached for his coat. He kissed her in return, but he still felt that he hadn't been anywhere near her.

"Come again, sergeant."

"Yes, thank you."

When he pressed the microphone in the Dodge the sheriff's response was immediate.

"Ten three, sergeant."

"On my way home."

"I just had a call. I'm leaving the jailhouse now, coming your way. You should be hearing my siren in a minute. There's a man in the road and an overturned car. I'm alone. Bernie is watching the radio in the jailhouse. You can come with me if you like, or are you exhausted?"

The sergeant looked at the microphone.

"Ten three, sergeant."

"I'll come with you."

"Ten four, sergeant."

10

De Gier didn't hear the sirens when he pushed the microphone back into its clip, but he heard them when he got the Dodge out of the Astrinsky driveway. The long, plaintive howl of the cruiser was activated by the yap of its barker, boring into the sergeant's eardrums with impatient, self-centered, aggressive barks. De Gier smiled. He liked the yapping. He thought he might try to buy one of the machines causing the weird sounds. A good gift for Grijpstra's next birthday. They could screw the gadget into the Volkswagen patrol car and split the peace of Amsterdam with it, say in the early hours of a Sunday. He waved when the cruiser's array of blue flashing lights came into view. The cruiser slowed and its passenger door swung open. De Gier jumped in and fell against the back of the seat as the sheriff accelerated. De Gier leaned over and watched the speedometer. It moved his way until it rested on eighty. Eighty, de Gier thought, and we are on a sheet of ice.

"There are snow tires on the cruiser," the sheriff said. "Studded. They'll hold. Should have chains really, but it's hard to have a chase when you're hampered by chains."

"But there is no chase. You said there was a man in the road, didn't you? And an overturned vehicle. They'll be waiting for us."

The sheriff's eyes shone. "Sure. But a little speed doesn't hurt, and the cruiser belongs to the state. We are the law, sergeant. We can move. Nobody else can these days. Why do you think we became police officers?"

De Gier held on as the cruiser skidded through a corner, slowed, and sped off again.

"Almost there now. Got the call from a man who lives in a trailer. Out-of-the-way part of the county. Nobody lives there except him. Old guy on welfare in a secondhand trailer. Looks like a cracker box that's been hit by a bulldozer, but it'll be invisible now, snowed over. Old guy doesn't like to use his shovel too much."

"What do you think happened?"

"Drunken driver, what else? Turned his car over, crawled out of it, sat down to think, and fell asleep. Old guy must have seen him and phoned us. Easy little job. All we have to do is wake up the man in the road, get him into the cruiser, and put him in jail for the night. A tow truck can take care of the wreck. Nothing to it, but I thought you could do with a bit of a change after your love affair. How did it go?"

"Yes."

"Did she say anything?"

"Perhaps. She may have been making conversation. But it could be that her father doesn't own the Cape Orca shore property. He may have been acting as a middleman and the real owner doesn't want his name to be known and hasn't had the deeds registered. The title is in Astrinsky's name, but only for the record."

"Hey," the sheriff said. "That's fine. Good. So she did say something."

De Gier was listening.

"Jim?"

"Yes?"

"Would you turn the wailer off? I'd like to hear the barker on its own."

The sheriff pushed a button. De Gier opened his window. With the wail gone the barker was very clear. De Gier grinned.

"You like that, sergeant?" The sheriff was grinning too.

"I have another sound for you. Hold on. I'm going to turn into that side lane there. It runs parallel to this road and joins it again further on."

The cruiser veered off the road and shot into the woods. A deep vibration filled the car from the rear. The sound was like a big drum being rapped by a vertical hand.

De Gier listened. His spine turned into a glowing rod and the glow eased into his entire body. The grin slid off his mouth.

"How's that?"

De Gier nodded. "Yes. What is it?"

"The radio's antennae, brushing past overhanging branches. Hold on, we're getting back into the road. Bump coming."

The bump came. De Gier was thrown out of his seat and his head hit the roof, but its insulation and his thick hair eased the contact. He bounced back.

"There!"

The cruiser stopped. A wrecked car lay on its roof, immobile in stupid helplessness. Another car was parked behind the wreck. The sheriff switched his siren and barker off, but the blue waving lights on the cruiser's roof kept on touching the trees, the shining road, and the two still cars.

"Open your window. I'll turn the radio on so that we can be reached even if we're out of the cruiser. Two cars, eh? The old guy should have put that in his message. There could be several of them, and there are only two of us. Take the shotgun, sergeant, and hang around. Don't let yourself be rushed into anything."

The shotgun jumped free and the sheriff broke it and pushed shells into its cavity. "Here you are. If you have to use the gun put one shell into the trees and the second into somebody's legs. Be easy with it. I've taken the safety off and the trigger is light."

De Gier took the shotgun and slid out of his seat. The sheriff ran to the overturned car, bent down, and played his flashlight into its interior. There was nobody inside. De Gier waited, holding the shotgun, his forefinger stretched parallel to its barrel. The flashlight lit up the interior of the second car.

"Out! OUT, you guys! OUT I SAY!"

Four men came out, rubbing their eyes, blinded by the strong flashlight, stumbling. De Gier recognized the last man. Leroux, all three hundred and fifty pounds of him. He seemed fairly sober. The others were reeling, holding on to each other like frightened monkeys.

"Who was driving the wreck?"

Only one man responded. "Don't know, sheriff."

"So what are you doing in the other car? I had a call that there was somebody lying in the road, somebody wounded maybe. Did he crawl into the bushes? Where is he?"

"Don't know, sheriff."

The sheriff's voice pleaded. "Tell me where he is or we'll have to search the woods. Maybe he's unconscious. He can freeze to death if he is. Was he hurt?"

"No, sheriff. Nobody was hurt. There were only four of us, in two cars, out visiting, on our way back. There's nobody in the woods."

"Okay, thanks. So move! *Move,* you hear! Get that car going and get out of here. I don't want any parked vehicles on the side of a dark road. The wreck'll have to go too."

Three men hesitated, but Leroux stepped forward. He took another, smaller step, and his heavy, bearded head came down and peered into the sheriff's eyes.

"We won't go. If we do you'll be after us for drunken driving. We lose whatever we do. We'll stay here and sleep it off."

"You won't. Get into that car, Leroux!" The sheriff's voice was a cold whisper.

"None of us can handle the car. We've been drinking."

"Your problem. You managed to get here. Now you get out of here again."

"No," Leroux said. "And *you* have a problem too, sheriff. I'm going to punch you in the face and walk over you when you're down. I'll keep on walking until you forget what happened here. You've got your rider again, but I don't want to fight him this time. I'll fight *you*, sheriff."

"He'll pull a gun on you, Leroux." The young man who had spoken before was standing next to Leroux, his hand on the giant's sleeve. Leroux pushed the man and the man stumbled and fell. His broad-rimmed leather hat rolled in the road.

The sheriff grinned. "I won't pull a gun on you, Leroux, but you'll be in real trouble afterward. Assault on an officer. The judge won't like that at all."

Leroux's bull neck came down and his long arms dangled. He took another small step. The sheriff straightened up.

"SHERIFF," boomed the cruiser's radio. "YOU THERE, SHERIFF?" The words thundered into the woods and echoed back.

"Excuse me."

The sheriff walked backward to the cruiser and de Gier's shotgun came up an inch and dropped down again. The sheriff reached into the cruiser's open window and came back clutching the microphone. "I'm here, Bert, ten three."

"Got the eggs, sheriff. Five dozen in a wicker basket, but I'm on the other side of the county and the roads are snowing in up here. Can I bring them in tomorrow?"

"No. Bring them in now."

"Jim! Please. The snow's so heavy I can't see a foot even when the wipers are on double speed. Let me bring them in tomorrow."

"No, Bert, right now. We need them for breakfast. Ten four, Bert."

He threw the microphone back into the cruiser and walked forward. De Gier's shotgun moved a little again, but it was still pointed at the road.

"Last chance, Leroux. I'm staying here. Think before you come."

Leroux growled. De Gier thought of interfering. A good punch from Leroux's double-size fist might snap the sheriff's head off. He would have interfered in an

Amsterdam alley. Amsterdam suspects can be talked to, manipulated by gentle words, by a friendly touch. Even the leather-jacketed ghouls can be talked to, the ghouls who lurk in alley corners, waiting for the weak. But ghouls don't want to fight. Perhaps this was a different situation. Leroux wasn't an evil force, but an individual, a workingman, a citizen intent on fighting the state that was trying to control his freedom, his rights. The sergeant studied Leroux's bulk: the leg muscles swelling under the tight jeans, the two-foot chest exposed by an open jacket, the man's vast shoulders. Perhaps he should be allowed to have his fight.

"Okay," the sheriff said softly.

Leroux lurched forward and swung. The sheriff ducked, jumped aside, and kicked his opponent's leg just above the top of his boot. The man turned and staggered, but the sheriff was in front of him again, kicking the other leg. The giant's reflexes were slow, and he ducked too late when the long, rubber-covered flashlight hit him on the side of the neck. The contact of flashlight and neck was marked by a thud. The three other men came close. De Gier's shotgun moved, but they weren't planning to join the fight. They wanted to pull their friend away. There was no need. Leroux's knees bent and he fell slowly. The sheriff let him fall.

"Right," the sheriff said and yanked an arm free and bent it back. The other arm followed. The polished metal of handcuffs shone blue in the cruiser's revolving lights and there was the small, ominous click of the handcuffs' lock.

Leroux tried to roll over but was stopped by de Gier's boot. De Gier stepped over the man.

"I don't believe it."

"What?"

"Help me up."

De Gier put out a hand. There was too much weight and the sheriff got behind his victim and pushed.

"I should have broken you into pieces, you little bastard," Leroux said, still in the same surprised voice.

"But you didn't. You guys, you all drunk?"

"Yes, sheriff."

"Got any money?"

"Some."

"Enough for a taxi? Which one of you lives nearest?"

The young man in the leather hat answered. "Me, sheriff. I'm from Jameson."

"Can you put your buddies up for the night?"

"Yes."

"Okay, all of you get into the back of the cruiser. Sergeant, you drive that car across the road. Leave it in the clearing in front of the trailer. Never mind if it gets stuck in the snow. I want it off the road."

De Gier took the shotgun, released the chamber's spring latch, and made the shells jump into his hand.

"Right, you guys, who owns the wreck?"

Another man stepped forward. "Me, sheriff."

"Got forty bucks?"

"Got a check, sheriff."

"Write it out. I'll radio for a tow truck. Make the check payable to the sheriff's department and we'll pay the truck. Check better be good."

"It's good."

The man wrote the check, and the sheriff pocketed it. The sergeant came back.

"Let's go."

They drove back at a reasonable speed.

"You did well, Jim."

"Got him nicely, didn't I? But it wasn't a fair fight. Too much beer in the man. And I was all there, I didn't have to watch the others. Good thing you came along. I couldn't have taken them all, and Bernie would have taken too long to get here and Bob is home and Bert has his eggs to worry about. He was thirty miles out anyway. So tell me what else happened at Madelin's."

De Gier took the raccoon tail from his coat pocket and showed it. He told the story that went with the tail.

"Shit," the sheriff said. "So that's why the tail wasn't hanging in your face. I was wondering what had happened to it. But that's homicide, sergeant. You might have called me. You saw him get away you say?"

"Yes, on snowshoes. The rifle was strapped to his back. He was taking his time. He knew nobody would go after him."

"Good shot," the sheriff said. "If he missed on purpose. Could have been the fox. He shot a man through the hair once, from a fair distance. The bullet went straight through and didn't even nip the man's head. We couldn't prove it was the fox, but it was the fox all right. Maybe it was the fox now. You remember the time?"

"Eight-forty."

"We can check his alibi. And Albert's alibi, and Tom's. It couldn't have been Madelin, could it? She's a good shot too."

"No. I saw her while the gunman was getting away in the woods."

The cruiser stopped in front of Robert's Market. The sheriff got out, opened the rear door, and let the three men out. Leroux groaned.

"Cuffs too tight, Leroux?"

"Yes."

"They'll be off in a minute. I'll be holding you for the night. You had your warning. You're in trouble now."

The cruiser shot off, a little too quickly, and the rear wheels spun in the road.

"Well," the sheriff said softly. "This thing is getting out of hand, sergeant. They're making fun of us. First the trick with the door. Then you get shot at. But you are me—you are part of my outfit now. I'll have to get busy or I'll never get anything done again. You're still with me?"

"I am."

"You don't have to be. You don't live here. You live a long way off. There's no reason why you should get yourself killed here."

"It's all right," de Gier said. "I am enjoying it, I think."

"You should so far. She was a good lay, was she?"

"Yes."

"I haven't had the pleasure, but I believe you. Maybe I'll have it later, but I'll have to get in her way. You sure got yourself in her way."

They reached the jailhouse and Bernie came out and took the prisoner. The sheriff made coffee while de Gier cleaned and polished the shotgun with a piece of cloth he had found in the cruiser.

Bernie came back from the jail and held his mug under the coffee machine.

"We're sure busy these days, Jim."

"We sure are, Bernie."

"I've been thinking today. You want to hear, Jim?"

"Yes."

"About Cape Orca, Jim. Five people died, right, and one ran away, right?"

"Sure, Bernie."

"I know who killed one of them. The fox did. Old Paul Rance drank himself to death and he was singing and carrying on when he croaked, and the fox was with him. I know that for sure. Liquor was poison for old Paul and the fox fed it to him, by the half gallon. Right, that's one murder and there's nothing we can do about it. Captain Schwartz ran away because the fox paid a friendly call. That isn't homicide, but it's something else that ain't right. Terrorism or something. Young Albert made me rip my cruiser to pieces. That's terrorism again. Right?"

"Let's say you're right, Bernie. Then what?"

"So maybe we should do something, Jim. We're the law, we got power. Let's make sure we cripple them before they do something else, like take a shot at us."

The sheriff held up his mug. "I'll have coffee too, Bernie, and maybe the sergeant would like some. Somebody shot the tail off his hat tonight."

Bernie dropped his mug. It broke.

"I want to hear about that, Jim."

"It was the sergeant's hat, Bernie."

"Sergeant?"

De Gier looked up from his cleaning. "As Jim says, Bernie, I stood on Madelin Astrinsky's driveway, halfway between the Dodge and the front door, and *whap*. The tail is in the cruiser. The hat is on the hook over there."

"You see who did it?"

"Something in the woods. A silhouette, black, maybe six feet high, on snowshoes. It went away."

Bernie stared at the shards near his feet. He looked up again. "That's right, you're a cop too. You tell us what you saw, not what you think you saw. But I'll tell you what you saw, you saw the BMF gang. They knew you were on your way to Madelin's because you said so on the radio. The fox and young Albert and Tom were listening in Robert's Market. The CB radio is under the counter. Or maybe you were set up from the start. Madelin is bad too. One of the boys, or all of them, got in a car and raced over to Madelin's while you were talking to us under the elm trees. The fox has snowshoes in his jeep. We've got to cripple them, Jim. They'll have us next. I don't know about you, but I'm not going to have myself shot at."

Bernie's voice had become shrill.

"Coffee, Bernie."

"Yeah, coffee." He took the sheriff's mug and got two more from the shelf.

"Here you are, Jim. Here you are, sergeant. When did it happen, sergeant?"

"Eight-forty."

"Okay, can I go around and check alibis, Jim?"

"Sure, Bernie."

"And can I run them in?"

"On what charges?"

Bernie sat down. "Theft. I've had complaints about the fox and Albert stealing lumber off people's land. Vague complaints, but I can shake the complainers and get good complaints. Theft is a crime, and that's all we have on them now. All the other stuff is nothing. You won't find that boat either, Jim. I had the Coast Guard on the phone just now. Your friend is on leave, and he'll be away for a while. I can't get the game wardens to cooperate either because they're mad at me about old Bill Thompson's dog and the ten sixty-fours."

"I'll find the boat, Bernie, or the sergeant will. Madelin has a little Cessna, in excellent repair. How about phoning your girlfriend and asking her to fly you over the bay tomorrow, sergeant? The number is in the book. I'll look it up for you."

The sergeant phoned. The call didn't take long. He put the phone down. "Sure, Jim. I suggested that the commissaris come too. He might like a chance to get away from his sister. She says tomorrow morning ten o'clock is fine. It'll be a clear day."

Bernie had been moving the shards of his mug with his foot. "I'll check the alibis tomorrow morning, Jim. What are you going to do? Maybe we should get them from all sides at once."

The sheriff got up. "I'm going to my room to think. Sometimes I come up with something if I think long enough. There's Carl Davidson's death, the guy who froze in the woods. Some time ago I ran into an Indian who was telling me about Carl. They used to go out hiking together. I could go and find that Indian tomorrow. He'll be in the reserve. Sergeant?"

De Gier woke up. He had drifted away. The horse of death had floated through his dream, brushing the snow with its hoofs. It had been ridden by Madelin, in her long purple skirt. "Yes," he said. "Yes, Jim."

"Go to bed, sergeant. You've had a long day. I'll wake you for breakfast. We'll have eggs. I'll make an omelet. How about asking your chief to come out for breakfast?" He looked at his watch. "It's close to midnight. You think I can still phone him?"

De Gier was on his way to the door. "Yes. I am sure he would like to come out."

"Okay. We'll have a good long breakfast and go through the case with him. I can use some advice it seems."

Bernie's round red head turned away from the sink where he was washing the mugs. "You got terrorists in Amsterdam, sergeant?"

"Yes."

"What do you do with them?"

"We bring them in, if we have arrestable charges against them."

"I say you should shoot them, by accident like. Lots of people get shot in the woods, especially now, in the hunting season. Old Jones got shot through the head two years ago. That was the season too. If you shoot them first they can't shoot you afterward, can they?"

"We don't have woods in Amsterdam, Bernie."

"Europe is soft," Bernie said. "That's why we had to come out twice to help you people."

"Calm down, Bernie," the sheriff said quietly. "Calm down. We've got to get proof and we're going to get proof. And when we have it we'll arrest them and give them to the judge."

"Maybe you're soft too, Jim," Bernie said and turned back to the sink.

11

"Very good of you, sheriff," the commissaris said and feasted his eyes on the table offering a profusion of choice in a strange assortment of bowls and covered-up dishes. "Can I look?"

"Go ahead, sir."

The commissaris lifted lids. "Sausages, mmm! Bacon, a-ha! An omelet, splendid! The sergeant was telling me about your home-baked bread. Is that it?"

"Yes, sir."

"Came out very well, didn't it? Looks like the bread I buy from the Jewish baker on Sundays. Still warm, just like yours. You know, sheriff, the Dutch have never learned that breakfast is the one important meal in the day. We try to get by on stale bread that never had any taste in the first place, and maybe some jam, and a cup of weak tea. And sometimes porridge, bah! Disgusting, absolutely. My sister has retained the habit, of course."

"Go ahead, sir. It'll get cold."

The sergeant cut bread and the sheriff served. The commissaris began to eat.

"Amazing," the commissaris said some time later. "I didn't know I could eat that much. The stew was delicious. Lamb stew, wasn't it?"

"Yes, sir, a dog got the lamb and we got the dog. The lamb was our prize. The subject gave it to us. I had it slaughtered and we kept it in the freezer. It's about finished now, but we'll have a deer next. The pay is poor, but we still manage to live well, thanks to the prisoners mostly. They keep the greenhouse going, and we have clams from the beach and there's a vegetable garden. The old sheriff was very good at organizing, and I'm planning to continue the tradition. The deputies are married and have their own homes, but I have to live in the jailhouse."

The meal was over and an old man came from the jail to clear the table. He poured more coffee.

"Shall I do the dishes now, sheriff?"

"No, later. I'll call you, Mac."

The old man nodded and went back into the jail. The heavy door closed behind him.

"What is he in for, sheriff?"

"For nothing in particular, sir. We picked him up because he was drunk and wandering around. He didn't want to go home. Mac lives by himself and he's out of firewood. I don't have too many prisoners just now. When I get some I'll make them cut a few cords for Mac. Then he'll want to go home again. He's one of the town drunks, okay for the first two weeks of the month, but when they drink their way through the welfare check they become a nuisance."

"And Mac makes himself useful here?"

"Oh yes, he likes being told what to do, like most of us. In a way that's why you're here, sir. To tell me what to do. The sergeant may have told you that homicide isn't really the sheriff's business, but it seems we've got ourselves into the situation now and I'll have to go on."

"But you are doing very well, sheriff. *We* aren't, I am afraid. We must be a burden to you, what with our inexperience and clumsiness. The Dodge is stuck on the estate again. We had to go back and fetch the station wagon and it isn't even snowing."

"I am not doing so well, sir, and I feel guilty about having given so little protection to the sergeant. My trouble is that I'm new too and the deputies aren't trained for this type of investigation. My chief deputy is showing signs of panic already, and the other two are young, converted rowdies who were hired because of their availability. They are good at fistfights and racing around with the siren going, but this thing is quite beyond their capacities."

The commissaris cleaned his mouth with his handkerchief and lit a cigar. "A homicide investigation has simple rules, sheriff, and I am sure you know them all. Name the suspects and question them and sniff about for information. Follow up any clue and try to fit it into a theory. If a clue doesn't fit, discard the theory. As I happened to be here I've taken the opportunity to talk to some of the people who seem to be involved with Cape Orca. That location is the center of it all, don't you agree?"

"Yes, sir."

"So who do we have? My dear sister, Suzanne, who prattles on and on but has never really lived there and knows nothing. Even so she did manage to tell me something last night. I'll bring that up later. Then there is Mrs. Wash and her gentleman-servant, Reggie. Then we have Michael Astrinsky, and last but not least Jeremy, the friendly hermit. The BMF gang is in and out of the whole unfortunate business too, but they are posing certain problems. I can't fit them in at all. Can you, sheriff?"

"They do consider the cape their private property, sir."

The commissaris raised a thin finger. "True. That's the part I can fully understand. When I was a boy I grew up in a small town near some woods. The woods were private property, but the owner lived somewhere else and he never showed up. I knew every tree in those woods. I even named some of them. There was the camel, for instance, a tree with an enormous branch growing a few feet above the ground. I would sit on that branch for hours and have all sorts of adventures. And there was another tree, a log really, quite dead, that was the rhinoceros. The rhinoceros was my dearest friend for many years. It was a strangely shaped log, very fat, resting on broken-off branches and with a big sort of head. It really looked like a rhino. It took me into the jungle. I fought black warriors who attacked from all sides. It was great, sheriff, absolutely great!"

The sheriff grinned.

"You understand that sort of thing?"

"Yes, sir."

"Good. But then the woods were sold and cut down, and I hated the men working there. I saw the camel and the rhino die and disappear. The rhino was just burned. The wood was too punky to serve any useful purpose. It was very sad. I was ten years old then, but I would have killed the laborers if I had been able to. The BMF gang may have similar feelings about their cape, and when the retired people came and built their homes and spoiled the landscape . . ."

"We know the gang got rid of two of the occupants, sir."

"Yes, but there may have been other reasons. The sergeant has reported fully to me. Captain Schwartz was a Nazi, and Nazi ideas will provoke strong reactions in many minds. Paul Rance was a dying man, miserably alive because of medical care. Some people believe that the old should be allowed to die, happily if possible. I've met the fox once and I must say I was rather impressed by him."

The sheriff nodded. "He is very much together, sir."

The commissaris looked surprised. "Together?"

The sheriff gestured. "Well organized, sir, practical, a tight person, no holes."

"Ah, I see. Together, eh? That's a good word."

"And immoral," de Gier said. "He suggested to his girlfriend that she work in a porno studio at two hundred dollars a day. He killed a man in a provoked gang fight. He left the corpse of his own friend in a New York slum street. He likes to experiment."

"What?" the sheriff asked. "Did Madelin tell you all that? Is she the girlfriend who was supposed to do the porno work?"

"Yes."

The sheriff shook his head. "Madelin isn't the fox's girlfriend. I've seen them together but not in that way. I know she has lovers, university students who come up for the weekend. Her father has been complaining about that. But Madelin is on her own."

"Her car registration is BMF ZERO," de Gier said.

The commissaris waved his cigar excitedly. The sheriff smiled. The commissaris looked very neat in his old-fashioned three-piece suit, carefully knotted tie, and gold watchchain.

"There we have it!" the commissaris said. "The inconsistency that has been bothering me. Or fascinating me. First it was the name of the gang and their insistence on adding 'bad' to the other word. And now Madelin stresses the mystery by adding 'zero.' Zero means nothing. We have been suspecting all along, and so we should perhaps, that the motive behind the killings was greed. Confucius, I believe, once said that ordinary man acts because he thinks his act will be profitable; the superior man, however, acts because he thinks his act is right. But what on earth is 'right'? I've often been tempted to think that right equals nothing. Perhaps 'nothing' is the ultimate wisdom. Now zero means absolute nothing and the idea it symbolizes is a void, an absolute void." He looked up. "I am sorry, am I talking rubbish?"

"No, sir," the sheriff said. "I am not qualified to say so, but I don't think you are. I remember that zero did strange things to equations. I saw that when I was try-to get some credits in mathematics. Please go on, sir."

"Exactly. So perhaps, but this is far out of course, far out, I picked up that expression here, an Americanism no doubt. As I was saying, it could be that the BMF gang has hit on the idea that 'nothing' is an interesting concept. They might be motivated in conducting experiments for no acceptable reason at all, certainly not for profit. The sergeant told me this morning what Madelin gave him in the way of information. The business about the deed and so forth. But I also saw something else. Something in the way the sergeant was set up— that's a correct expression, isn't it?—set up for the rendezvous and perhaps for the warning shot in her driveway. Then there is the painting of death in the room where she seduced him. All these details. Very clever, and immoral perhaps, as the sergeant suggested. Amoral perhaps, no morals at all. Yes?"

"Yes, sir. Perhaps."

"Of course, just a theory, no certainty here at all. But perhaps we can imagine that the gang murdered all these people as another experiment, as a macabre joke, to prove to themselves, or to us, to authority, that immoral behavior is just as valid, or acceptable, as moral behavior."

"Yes," the sheriff said. "It's possible, and it would be my luck to turn across that sort of thing in Woodcock County, Maine. An intellectual gang. Both the fox and Albert have degrees and Madelin has a super-degree and is still studying. And Tom is an original, and an ingenious, as they say here. I saw him in the public library the other day. He was taking out the complete works of Edgar Allan Poe and a manual on jungle warfare."

"Ingenious intellectuals, sheriff. Well, you won't be bored. Neither will the gang be bored. Which may be a good thing. Organized life in what we call civilized countries can be very boring. All adventure has gone, even the holidays are without surprises, programmed into every possible detail. So the adventurous, the unusual, the creative, the originals will try to make things happen and, expectably, may break the law in the process."

The sheriff grinned. The commissaris suddenly looked sad. "So, as I was saying, this gang will stop at nothing, or try to go beyond nothing. That would be an almost mystic endeavor. But I am probably carried away by my own rambling mind. The gang is also friendly, helpful even. The fox got our cars unstuck. There was chanting and flute playing in Robert's Market. And lovemaking in the Astrinsky parlor. Facts hard to rhyme with a bullet snipping off the tail on the sergeant's hat."

"So they may go free after all, sir?"

"Possibly."

The sheriff cleared his throat. "When you mentioned the suspects just now you included your sister's name, sir. Suzanne Opdijk."

"Yes indeed. I mentioned her first. I would consider her a good suspect in the case of her husband's death. I've listened to her for hours on end, and it is quite obvious that she couldn't stand Opdijk. He was stronger than she. He dominated Suzanne, frustrated her. He controlled the money, drove the car, got about, was sociable and happy in his way, while she had to stay home and try to live in a dream. She didn't want the dream, she wanted the reality that was shadowed in her dream. All she wanted was to go back to Holland. Opdijk wouldn't even discuss that possibility. So one day he is standing on the ice, close to the cliff, and she goes out and pushes him. Not at all unlikely. I am sure she can be vicious when cornered and she must have felt very cornered. But if she did push him she will never admit to having done so and we would have to produce witnesses. No witnesses have come forward."

"But she's your sister, sir."

"If we create justice we must make it universal. There can't be exceptions. She is my sister but she is still a prime suspect, but only in the case of Opdijk's death. I can't see her sneaking around the other houses and taking plastic foam out of a boat, or firing a rifle, or enticing a man to go out into the woods with her. But she did have a motive to kill her husband, a very strong motive I would say."

"Yes, sir, and Janet Wash?"

The commissaris looked at the tip of his cigar. "Well, why not? She owns the rest of Cape Orca and she may have wanted to own all of it, although she didn't seem to be that type of woman to me. She was complaining that the upkeep of the house and the land gave her too much work. She is an old woman in spite of her beauty. I could suspect her more easily if she were young, in the strength of her life."

"Reggie?"

The commissaris nodded. "There's an inconsistency there too. A young man spending all his time in the service of an older woman. Would he be well paid, do you think, sheriff?"

The sheriff shook his head. "I don't know. I can't check with the bank, although I might try. I know the manager, not too well though. But Reggie doesn't strike me as being very interested in money. The few times I've met him he only talked trees and shrubs. He's a dedicated gardener. The azalea gardens he made are beautiful. Even I can see that, and I know some of the men who work on the Wash's property in summer, Leroux, for instance. I have him in jail now. They all say that Reggie has done good work on the cape."

"But he was a guerrilla fighter in Vietnam. Perhaps he likes violence. Did Reggie make that sort of impression on you, sergeant?"

"No, sir. He seemed very quiet and well behaved."

"Jeremy," the sheriff said.

"Jeremy is a hermit and he doesn't like people bustling about. He shifted his cabin to the other side of the island. He may also be a violent man since he carries a revolver and has a rifle in his cabin. Not an ordinary rifle—I saw quite a big clip on it."

"That island is a fortress, sir. I've sailed around it. Jeremy's dogs followed my boat, running along the island's shore. The raven was out, and even the seals seemed interested in my movements."

"Paranoid?" de Gier asked.

"Yes, but perhaps he has a reason to be paranoid."

"The man is not insane," the commissaris said quietly. "I wouldn't even call him a dreamer. A practical man who has reasons behind whatever he does. Good reasons."

"That leaves us with Michael Astrinsky, sir."

"Another prime suspect, sheriff. And he left for the Bahamas the minute he saw the sergeant and myself sniffing about."

The sheriff got up. "I did some thinking last night, sir. About Astrinsky among others." He checked his watch.

"I'll phone Beth. She has a little traveling agency, sells tickets for Enterprise Airlines from her restaurant. I'll give her a ring."

He dialed. "Beth?

"Sheriff here. Listen, Beth, you sold a ticket to Astrinsky the other day. Where to?

"Boston? Open return? Good. What's that?"

The sheriff found a pad and a pencil. "Yes. Thank you, Beth.

"Michael Astrinsky didn't go to the Bahamas. He's in Boston. Beth booked him into the Fosterhouse Hotel."

"A lie," the commissaris said. "Lies are what we have been looking for. Can I trouble you for another cup of coffee, sheriff?"

The sheriff poured and the commissaris stirred his cup triumphantly. "You did excellent thinking last night, sheriff. Can you come up with a reason why Astrinsky would have lied about the destination of his trip?"

"Yes, sir. Astrinsky is holding the land he bought from the murdered people's estates for a third party. Madelin told the sergeant as much, although her information wasn't definite. But you and the sergeant had marched into his office, introducing yourselves as police officers. I would deduct, from his behavior and the information his daughter supplied, plus the facts the cape is giving us, that Astrinsky is no longer interested in protecting the real owner of the land. He knows that we can find out whose name the deeds are now registered in. I obtained that information yesterday from the town clerk. The name on the deeds is Michael Astrinsky. But if Astrinsky forces the real owner to register the deeds, then Astrinsky is cleared, not all the way but part of the way. His behavior is still suspicious. He may not be the killer, but maybe he's working with the killer."

"We know where Astrinsky is, sheriff. If you like I can go to Boston, or the sergeant can go. The sergeant has some experience in following people. He can shave off his mustache and wear different clothes."

"My mustache?" De Gier asked.

"Why not, sergeant. Your trip was financed by the exchange fund. Shaving your mustache off would be a way to show your appreciation for the fund."

The sheriff stared at the wall. He got up, and felt a knot in the paneling.

"What do you think, sheriff?"

"It would be a long shot, sir. Astrinsky has probably seen the third party already. But perhaps he'll see him again. I don't want to waste your or the sergeant's time."

The commissaris got up too. "You can think about it, sheriff. I confess that I didn't want to get into this case at first, but its many aspects have been changing my mind. I'm certainly quite willing now. And the sergeant has his duty to consider, and the police fund that has been financed by taxpapers' money. Your taxpayers and ours. Let's be off, sergeant. Madelin will be waiting for us. Perhaps we can find that unfortunate lady's boat."

The sheriff hadn't been listening. "You mentioned that your sister had given you some information, sir."

"Ah yes. It may be nothing, but there is a lie involved, so it could possibly be of interest. When the sergeant and I had drinks at the Wash mansion Mrs. Wash told us that Reggie had overturned her station wagon some time ago. But my sister tells a different story altogether. She claims that she was in her garden when she saw Jeremy coming ashore, accompanied by a dog. At about the same time she saw the Wash station wagon driving along with Janet Wash at the wheel. She didn't see anybody else in the car. The trees obscured her view, but she heard a commotion and went to the end of her garden to get a better look. There had been an accident. I asked Suzanne to take me to the exact place from where she had seen the accident and she also walked me to the spot where the event took place. There's some considerable distance so she can't have had a really close look, and as I said, there are a lot of trees in the way. What happened was that the wagon slipped and careened off the road. It turned over several times until it was stopped by some alders. Suzanne did see that Jeremy ran to the wreck and helped Janet to free herself. There seemed to be nothing wrong with Janet. And Suzanne, being what she is, remembered that she had a roast in the oven and returned to the safety of her home."

The sheriff thought. "I see, sir. I see the lie. Reggie wasn't involved. Right. But I don't see that the lie fits in with any of our possible theories. Perhaps Janet didn't want to admit to being a bad driver and blamed Reggie. Was Reggie present when Janet told you that *he* had wrecked the car?"

"Yes, sheriff."

The sheriff scratched his chin. "A strange relationship indeed."

"Very," the commissaris said brightly. "Thank you for a truly marvelous breakfast, sheriff. I won't forget that lamb stew."

The sheriff smiled. "You're welcome, sir. Come again. Any time."

12

The small plane dropped a few feet and steadied itself shakily. The commissaris smoked his cigar and watched the sea gulls, white specks above the open ocean. De Gier was studying the point of Cape Orca, approaching rapidly.

"Once more," Madelin said. "Monotonous, isn't it? Like plowing a field. On and on, and back, and on and on."

"No matter," the commissaris said. "I am enjoying it." He looked back at the airplane's tail, a flimsy fin, probably made out of plastic. A toy plane, but it performed well.

De Gier pointed. "That must be the fox and his friends." They saw three black dots, busy with a tree in a white clearing. The flat motorboat had been anchored to the ice off the cape.

"And there's Janet," Madelin said, pushing the small two-handled gadget that steered the plane. "Behind the garage. And Reggie is splitting wood. She's supervising him I guess. Let's see what Jeremy is doing." The plane banked and reached the bay.

"Marvelous," the commissaris said. Madelin had pushed the throttle back and was circling. They saw Jeremy's house. It looked like a bird feeder. The bird was present too. It flew a hundred feet below the Cessna's wheels.

"He is playing with his dogs," de Gier said. "There they are, all three of them."

The plane headed out toward the ocean. "We can't go on for too long, gentlemen. There's more snow due. We've been at it for nearly two hours. I'm afraid the search is useless. Three dogs you said?"

"Yes, three."

"There should be four of them."

"Three," the commissaris said. "We saw only three when we were on the island."

"There are four. Osiris and Isis, the parents, and Seth and Ra, the children. But you're right. Last time I was on the island I didn't see Osiris. Osiris is the best of them all. Jeremy always takes him when he goes to town. Shall we continue the search?"

The commissaris shook his head. "No, we can't go on forever. Look, there's Suzanne's garden. I saw Suzanne too, but she just went back into the house. Would you do me a favor, Madelin?"

"Certainly."

"The sergeant tells me that you buzzed Opdijk once when he was fishing off his shore. Would you mind repeating that performance?"

"You'll have to fasten your seat belt. You too, sergeant."

The latches clicked.

"Ready?"

The commissaris was rubbing his hands. He bit his cigar.

"Ready."

The plane lost height rapidly and the Opdijk house and grounds grew. De Gier forced himself to keep his eyes open. The trees behind the cliffs rushed the small airplane. He saw the white bulge that was Opdijk's boat parked upside-down behind the cliffs. Then the engine roared and there was nothing but pale blue sky and clouds.

The commissaris was laughing. "Excellent. You must have given him the fright of his life. Thank you." He turned around. "How did you like that, sergeant?"

"Fine," de Gier said and tried to smile. He had looked away as the plane shot up, convinced that they were about to hit the pines on the Opdijk grounds. But while his head was turned away in fear he had seen something.

"I think I saw an orange spot, sir. Over there, near those rocks with the broken pack ice around them."

"Good," Madelin said. The plane found the rocks. There was a definite orange spot. "Could be the boat," Madelin said. "Could be something else. There are a lot of empty plastic containers floating about. I suppose the big factory vessels throw them out, the Japanese and Russian fishing fleets that rob our seas empty. They're soap containers I believe, and some of the floats the lobstermen use are orange. Let's check again. I'll fly as low and slow as I can."

The commissaris and de Gier peered down. The orange spot, pushed up by the ice, was clearly visible. Madelin made the plane circle the rocks. "Yes, I know Mary's boat. That should be it. Eleven feet long, bright orange. The current must have brought it back, but it took its time. But it's caught by the ice. The sheriff will have to get at it with a pick. Shall we go back now?"

"One more favor, Madelin. Please circle Jeremy's Island before you return to the town's airstrip. Would you do that?"

The commissaris giggled when they saw the raven take off and wheel up in defiance and the dogs running on the path between Jeremy's cabin and the shore on the cape's side. "God must feel like this, high and comfortable, puffing on his cigar while the puny beings he created run about and get through their lives. Yes, a divine experience. I must really try to get on a Dutch police plane when we get back, sergeant. We'll watch the lawbreakers from above and wiggle our fingers at them. Tsk, tsk. Don't do this, don't do that!"

"It won't be very effective, sir."

"No, but it will give us a powerful feeling. Soaring while they grovel. What's Jeremy carrying there, a sign?"

"Yes, sir, a board on a stick. Could be a sign."

"He is propping it up between some rocks."

"Probably a KEEP OFF sign," Madelin said. "If I buzz it we can see what it says."

"Wait for him to get away."

She looked at the clouds. They were closer and lower, but most of the sky was still clear. "All right, we'll fly over the cape again and come back. We'll give him a few minutes." The fox and his helpers were rolling logs toward their boat. Reggie was still splitting wood. Janet came out of the house carrying a tray. "Coffee time. That reminds me, I brought a thermos. Would you pour, sergeant?"

De Gier poured three plastic mugs of steaming coffee while the plane followed the coastline, revealing clusters of small islands, long thin peninsulas of evergreen woods and patches of what appeared to be dry sticks, birches mostly, and everywhere the white ice, sometimes broken up into twisted patterns by the currents and the tides. They sipped the coffee and gazed at the desolate but majestic scene.

"Hold on to your mugs. I'll have to go over the hills, and there may be air pockets." But the plane flew on quietly, controlled by the light, adjusting touch of Madelin's fingers. The commissaris looked at the girl's hands and at the small triangular face with the dark eyes smiling back at him. He wondered what she had been like when she was with the sergeant and was amazed that he didn't feel the slightest twinge of jealousy. He was really getting old. He wondered whether the absence of desire was just due to the gradual ebbing away of his life force or whether he had reached some other level, where the mind indulges in abstractions rather than in actual activity. He shook his head sadly. The possibility wasn't encouraging.

The plane flew toward the sea and continued its swing, leveling out slowly. The cape was in view again and Jeremy's Island beyond the cape. They could see the sign standing by itself on the island's bare ledge. Jeremy, escorted by the three Dobermans, was halfway between his cabin and the sign.

"Down we go." The commissaris glanced at the

speedometer. Over a hundred miles an hour and going up. Then he looked at the sign. There were big white letters on a dark background: BEWARE THE BEAR.

Madelin laughed. "Bear! Jeremy has no bear."

"Bear?" the commissaris asked. "There are bears here, aren't there?"

"Certainly, but they'll all be asleep now, hibernating in their caves. Sure we have bears, big black bears, up to five hundred pounds, over five hundred pounds sometimes."

"And Jeremy never had a bear?"

"No. A bear would be hard to keep on the island. It would swim ashore. And bears are sexy. They become bad-tempered when they don't have a mate. To keep two bears, and their pups, would be a major undertaking."

"It rhymes," de Gier said. "Maybe he likes poetry. Beware the bear. Take care, take care."

"A joke," the commissaris said. "That's nice. To make a sign and carry it for a long distance, and set it between rocks, and go home again. That's the way to live to have time to play."

"He is fun," Madelin said. "He spent months last year building a pile of firewood. He had a lot of twisted logs and he stacked and restacked them, and made all sorts of weird shapes, and then he got some cow skulls from a farmer and stuck them on, and he had driftwood on top of the pile. It became a gigantic structure. He was using a ladder in the end. I used to fly out specially to follow the pile's changing manifestations. He even took the whole stack down again and rebuilt it because he wanted the moon to light it up from a certain angle. I came out at night to see the final effect. It was gruesome. The three skulls stared and caught the moonlight, and the driftwood was like manes on a lion, a prehistoric, three-headed lion."

"We didn't see that," de Gier said.

"No, it was firewood, and when the winter came he ripped it all apart and sawed it into foot-and-a-half logs for his cookstove."

"Good," the commissaris said. "He didn't take photographs?"

"No. He just likes to play around. But there's a lot of sense in what he does. Only it takes time to understand what he means, and he never likes to explain."

The plane was landing. The sheriff's cruiser was parked next to the corrugated iron hangar.

The sheriff helped the commissaris down. "Have a good flight, sir?"

"Very. Beautiful land, sheriff, and sea."

"Did you find the boat?"

"Yes, the sergeant saw it when we were ready to give up."

"Near the rocks on the southeast side of the point of the cape, sheriff," Madelin said. "Here." She showed him a map.

"I'll go out this afternoon. Can I have a word with you, sir?"

He guided the commissaris by the elbow in the direction of the airfield's office while Madelin and the sergeant pushed the plane into the hangar. The sheriff looked over his shoulder.

"I didn't want to talk in Madelin's presence. This has to do with her father. I know she doesn't seem to like him much, but still . . . I ran into the town clerk this morning and he told me he had a special-delivery letter from Boston, sent by a company called Boston Better Holdings. The envelope contained all the deeds of the dead people's property, except Opdijk's, of course, and the letter asked the clerk to register them. I checked the dates of sale. Michael Astrinsky sold the various properties to Boston Better Holdings, in each case about a week after he bought them. Astrinsky made no profit on the deals, so I imagine he worked on a percentage paid to him by the sellers."

"You have the address of this Boston company, sheriff?"

"Yes, sir. 73 Varsity Street. I've lived in Boston. Varsity Street is a slummy alley, not too far from the Beacon Hill area. I drew a map for you. Perhaps you'd like to go there, you and the sergeant, and speak to the president. He signed the letter. His name is James D. Symons."

"Very good, sheriff. I suppose we should go as soon as possible."

"Yes, sir. That's why I came out to the strip. I booked the two of you on the afternoon flight of Enterprise Airlines. I spoke to their pilot on the radio. The weather is deteriorating but he's coming in all the same. He'll be here in about an hour and a half. I thought we might go back and pick up your and the sergeant's luggage. I've also booked you into the Fosterhouse Hotel, the same hotel where Astrinsky is staying. But I can cancel the bookings if you want to go later, or not at all. This is my job, but I can't get away from Jameson. Or the sergeant could go by himself if you prefer."

"No, no, we'll go, sheriff. Let's get the sergeant."

The sheriff looked at the hangar. "He'll come, sir. We can wait in the cruiser."

Madelin had opened de Gier's coat and pressed herself against him. "Kiss me, sergeant."

Yes, de Gier thought, and he bent down a little. His arms were around the girl. He tried to match Madelin's passion, but he was back in the full-page ad again, advertising bourbon nationwide.

She got out of the coat.

"I don't turn you on, do I?"

"Yes," he said, "but I've just been flying. I don't fly so often. It was quite an experience."

"Flying has nothing to do with it, sergeant. But it doesn't matter. I'll stop bothering you. Will you be leaving soon?"

"When the commissaris goes."

She stamped her foot. "And I've been helping you find that damned boat. Do you know that I've been *helping* you, sergeant? And I'm not on your side. You're in another gang, the pig gang."

"Beware the pig," de Gier said. "Beware the *bear*. What would Jeremy mean by *bear?*"

"I don't know."

"But you are helping me."

"I don't care what Jeremy means by *bear*."

"You said that whatever he does makes sense."

Her hand stung his face and he rubbed his cheek. She was walking away, her body very small in the open hangar doors.

"Bear," de Gier said. The cruiser began to bark, then stopped abruptly. When he came out of the hangar Madelin's car was spinning around. It broke its spin and came at him. He stopped. She missed him by a foot and he turned to see her speed down the lane in the direction of Jameson. He shook his head. Madelin's car was veering from side to side, crunching against the lane's snowbanks.

"Bear," he said. "What the hell. And the bears are all asleep now. What bear doesn't sleep in winter?"

13

"Clouds," the commissaris said. He was lying back on a double seat and talking to no one in particular. De Gier was in another double seat, two rows ahead. They had the plane to themselves. The commissaris watched the grayness streaked with dull yellow on the other side of his window. De Gier heard the commissaris mumble and came over.

"Sir?"

"Look at that, sergeant. Cotton wool, dirty cotton wool, just what I have in my brain now. We are moving, but it doesn't seem we have reached any definite point in our investigation so far."

"The sheriff should be with that boat in the ice now, sir. If there's no plastic foam in it we know we are dealing with murder."

The commissaris smiled tiredly. "Yes, our one and only possible clue, the probable absence of plastic foam. I suppose that any mathematician can accuse me of wild guessing. Just because the sun rises on four consecutive days I say it rises forever. The gang chased the Nazi captain away and saw to it that old Mr. Rance drank himself to death. I have ignored those facts because they are in my way, and they are in my way because I don't want to suspect that fox boy and your friend Madelin. But I really enjoy suspecting Suzanne, just because I don't like her cooking. What do you think, sergeant? Am I being subjective because I am always like that, or is the change of scenery a possible cause?"

"The sun, sir. You said the sun rose four times. Four people died of accidents and we assume murder, but so far we only see the possibility of proving one murder."

"True, sergeant." The commissaris sighed. "If there is no plastic foam in the boat the sun has risen once. I cannot deduce that the other three deaths are due to murder because the fourth is." He sat up. "You did check on the dates of the deaths, didn't you, sergeant?"

De Gier produced his notebook. "Jones died first, then Mary Brewer, then Schwartz left, then Davidson died, then Paul Rance, then Opdijk. The intervals are irregular. All deaths occurred within a span of three years."

The airplane drilled through the cloud cover and the sun shone into the windows on the commissaris' side.

"Light! At last. Light is objective. It shines on us all. And how subjective am I, or how illogical? You know, sergeant, I don't really think I have been reasoning illogically. My thinking may be hazy, but I have been in criminal situations so often that I am sure my subconscious reacts correctly. I somehow don't want to suspect the BMF gang. Every time I think about them my mind blocks."

"The fox was serious when he suggested that Madelin spend some time in a porno studio in New York, sir. Just because the gang was out of money."

"And you have no sympathy with pimps, I know. I've seen you react to them before. Remember the doorman of that elegant brothel when we were trying to trap the Arab? The man was just teasing you and you frothed at the mouth. He-he."

De Gier was standing next to the commissaris' seat. He scratched his bottom.

"And Madelin never did work in that porno studio. Did you ever see any porno movies, sergeant?"

"Yes, sir."

"Were you pushed into the cinema? Was your visit part of an investigation?"

"No, sir."

"He-he."

"Yes, sir. Did *you* ever see any porno movies, sir?"

The commissaris sat up and fished around in his pockets for his cigars. "No, sergeant. I don't want to admit it, but the truth is that I felt shy. Old men always sneak into porno cinemas and I didn't want to join the doddering crowd. I may also have been frightened of being disappointed. I don't think that type of art attracts the right producers. I didn't want to see good material badly used. But I have seen some good scenes in regular movies. I remember seeing a girl, or a full-grown woman rather, a really beautiful woman, undress herself on one of those enormous revolving discs in a window of a store selling motorcars. There was only one spotlight in the window, and the disc turned slowly so you could see her in the shadows. Then there was a flash of direct light but too quick for you to take it all in, and then she moved into the half light again, darker and darker, almost completely dark, and then there was a pale light again, growing stronger. Now *that* was done by a good producer. Splendid, sergeant. I often revive that scene, especially when I am in pain. I can see the woman go around, sometimes for as much as several minutes, and as I have the type of mind that can only concentrate on one subject at a time the pain is completely absent."

De Gier grinned. The commissaris looked out the window. The plane seemed to be resting on the clouds and the clouds stretched endlessly in all directions. "I hope the pilot knows how to go through that mess again. As you were saying, if the sheriff finds no plastic foam we have murder. Murder of Mary Brewer. But we still don't know who. Our suspects are having their games with us. We haven't rattled the BMF gang. On the contrary, Madelin has been going out of her way to help. And Jeremy . . . ha! He gave us the tip about the boat and then sat back on his island and smirked. Do you know why I think he gave us that tip? Not to be of help at all but to see what we would do. Like he watches his seals in the surf around his island. He didn't want us to give up, for then the show would be over. The BMF gang may be doing the same. And Suzanne just mumbles through her house and wraps her porcelain dollies in tissue paper. She has unwrapped them all again now because she can't bear to be without them. The crates won't arrive for a few days. And Janet Wash plays lady in the castle and Reggie plays . . . what does he play, sergeant?"

"I think he plays son, sir. If we go into his past we'll probably find that his mother left him when he was quite small. Or perhaps she died early."

"Right, perhaps he plays son. I see, yes, that's not a bad assumption, sergeant. We might ask the sheriff to check."

One of the pilots came into the cabin. "We have almost arrived, gentlemen. You can fasten your seat belts."

"But still, we must have rattled them somewhat, sergeant," the commissaris said as they walked through the hall of Boston's airport. "We arrived like two pebbles thrown into a very calm pond. I wonder if the sheriff would have done anything if we hadn't arrived. But I may be underestimating the man. On the other hand, what could he have done? Sheriffs are elected and have to watch their popularity. Fishing in murky waters has never made anybody popular. I know that from experience. I was threatened with a transfer once because I reopened a file. What a file that was. Corruption, bah. This should be more interesting."

He stopped and poked about in the thick hall carpet. "I like this case in a way, perhaps because the setting is so good. Do you like the case, sergeant?"

"Yes, sir, I like the case. There's no crowd around us this time. In Amsterdam I get tired of the jostling and the traffic. I liked the chase last night when the sheriff raced out to an accident. They have good sirens on the cruisers here."

The commissaris began to walk again, slowly, then stopped and pushed a door marked NI. The door wouldn't give way. "You are subjective too. That chase wasn't even connected with Cape Orca. What's the matter with this door, sergeant?"

"It says IN, sir, but the lettering is on the other side."

"That's right. I want to go in, into the city."

"You want to go out of the airport, sir."

The commissaris stepped back and look at the two letters again. "Out? Ah yes."

A taxi arrived, as they stepped into the cold wind, and a window opened. They looked into the gray face of a young man. The face was narrow, half hidden in long dirty hair. The driver's eyes sat in the face as if two blobs of pink paint had been thrown into a lump of decaying plastic. De Gier stepped back.

"To the city?"

The commissaris was getting into the cab. "Come, sergeant. Yes, driver. Fosterhouse Hotel."

The cab moved before de Gier had closed the door. It dived into a long tunnel and became part of a row of speeding vehicles, glued together, almost colorless, in the tunnel's pale light. The driver turned his face. "What hotel you say?"

"Fosterhouse."

De Gier shuddered. There had been no life at all in the pink eyes. A junkie, in charge of a car speeding in a tunnel. This would be death proper. He thought of Adjutant Grijpstra, who often compared death to a tunnel. A long dark tunnel, endless, and a phantom to show the way. What way? There was only one way. He looked over his shoulder. They were followed by a dented limousine caked with mud and wet dirty snow. An old woman steered the car. Behind the limousine loomed the high cabin of a truck. De Gier couldn't see the driver's face, just the fingers holding the wheel. The tunnel rumbled. Perhaps it would cave in. He forced himself to listen to the commissaris.

"What were you doing in the hangar when the sheriff and I were waiting for you, sergeant?"

"The girl wanted me to kiss her, sir."

"Did you kiss her?"

"Yes, sir."

"So why did she almost run you over when she left?"

"I don't know, sir. I did my best."

"She is an attractive girl, sergeant."

De Gier heard himself tell the commissaris about the full-page advertisement. The old man listened. "Yes. I think I know that feeling. I have it too here. We play roles in these people's minds and it makes us mechanical. We are not used to being manipulated, sergeant. It never dawned on the gang that you could have refused to go to the Astrinsky house. You couldn't have, they were right. *A*, the girl is attractive, and, *B*, the enemy was opening up. So you ran along and got shot at and seduced. Perhaps you would have liked to seduce the girl, but they turned the tables on you, the way Jeremy did with me. It's a one-sided game. They know the country, the undercurrents." He poked the sergeant's chest. The tunnel was still stretching away.

"But there is more to it, sergeant. Where did I hear the word 'experiment'?"

The sergeant was staring into the tunnel. No light ahead at all.

"Sergeant?"

"Yes, sir. I said that. Madelin told me that the gang experiments."

"Quite. On us, but also on themselves. That trip to New York, for instance. I'll have to talk to that fox— listen to him rather. Talking won't do any good. Ah, finally. I thought that tunnel would never end. Have you noticed the driver's face?"

"Yes, sir. Drugs."

"He has been sneezing and wheezing. Needs his next shot. Let's hope the hotel isn't far."

It wasn't far. The taxi honked its way through the traffic, ruthlessly pushing other cars out of the way, even scratching a compact's fender. The compact beeped, but the cabdriver didn't look around. They had got to a park, surrounded by tall buildings, some of them half alight so that they appeared to be tottering crazily. The cab turned abruptly and the commissaris fell against de Gier. The driver braked hard.

"Fosterhouse Hotel."

De Gier paid. The driver didn't check the amount and dropped the folded bills into an open tin at his side. The hotel was black and shiny. A costumed, unsmiling doorman took the two overnight bags from de Gier's hands. The man's chin had sunk away in a frilled collar, and his high boots were spattered with mud. An impeccable clerk waited behind a plastic-topped desk.

"Credit card?"

"No."

"How will you pay?"

"In cash."

"Please pay now." The clerk's mouth was a slit in his perfectly shaved face. His eyes were cold.

De Gier wandered away. The costumes seemed part of the hotel's trademark. Bellboys and waitresses moved about in caps and bonnets and riding breeches and long skirts. He supposed the clothes would fit in with the city's history. Amsterdam had also dressed its servants up when the city celebrated its seven-hundredth birthday. He remembered arresting a waiter dressed in a black corduroy fisherman's suit, with bulging trousers and a short jacket sparkling with silver buttons. The charge was rape. The suspect had gone free. The victim hadn't impressed the public prosecutor. She had gone to his office in hot pants, bikini top, a scarf. No witnesses, since the event had taken place in the privacy of the lady's own room.

"Right, sergeant. The clerk was good enough to take my money. Coming up? Our room is on the top floor, with a view of the park."

De Gier played with the television set while the commissaris checked the room's bath and shower. He turned the switch. A lady with a distressing overbite smiling over a bar of soap. Two young men in shiny jackets pulling the strings of their guitars while a tape-recorded audience applauded at set intervals. An actor whom he remembered having seen as a tough cop in a movie in Amsterdam advertising a new brand of popcorn, smiling from the corner of his mouth, exactly as he had done in the film. An old man playing the violin. A puppet dancing.

He was about to switch the machine off when the commissaris came out of the bathroom. "Hold it, sergeant." They watched the puppet together. It was very good. It never showed his feet. The dance was all in the hands. But then German troops suddenly appeared, in black and white, marching and singing. An advertisement for a book about World War II.

"Switch it off, sergeant. We have seen that in color. This room is fine and there is an abundance of hot water. I can have a long bath later on. According to that helpful clerk downstairs the good restaurants are all on the other side of the park. Be my guest, sergeant."

It wasn't six o'clock yet, and the park was crowded in spite of the cold. Old men sat on benches, peering at newspapers under streetlights, well-dressed office employees walked briskly, eager to get home, a group of children raced about laughing and yelling. Their shrill voices brightened the winding paths under the protective silence of dark trees.

The commissaris stopped. A Christmas carol, sung by a pure female voice, was piped through hidden loudspeakers. De Gier put out a hand and nudged the old man into motion again.

"Beautiful," the commissaris said, but the song was torn apart by police sirens and the sudden growl of traffic released by a changing stoplight. The park ended, and they found themselves in dark streets, which funneled the icy wind. Store windows displayed girlie magazines, thrown about haphazardly between dust and grains of mouse poison. Young men in padded coats and woolen hats pulled over their ears shouted from open doors, "It's hootchy-cootchy time, gentlemen. It comes off, all of it comes off, on the *inside*. The new show is beginning right *now!* College girls only, gentlemen. A dollar and a half for any drink." The commissaris limped on, small and helpless in his hooded army coat. A patrol car raced past, stopped halfway on the sidewalk, and two policemen ran into an alley. They came back dragging a man by the hands. The man was pushed into the cruiser and the car roared away.

A girl clicked past on high heels. She stopped and smiled. "Combat Zone all right tonight?"

"Pardon, miss?" de Gier asked.

"You're not from here, are you? That's what we call this district. The Combat Zone. Anything I can do for you, gentlemen? I work in a good bar, just around the corner. It's still happy hour. Drinks are half price now."

"No, miss. We're looking for a Chinese restaurant."

"Another block. Have a good time now."

"Pleasant girl," the commissaris said.

"She would have taken our last penny, sir. That sort of bar sucks you in and throws you out the moment you're broke."

"I know, sergeant, but she wasn't rough when we refused. That's something."

The stores had changed. They were Chinese now and displayed food, mostly red carcasses of birds hanging side by side above constellations of cans that looked as if they could fall over any moment. They came to an intersection where policemen, dressed in long orange plastic coats, were attempting to sort out the traffic. A woman on their side of the street suddenly yelled, turning away from her escort, a big, well-dressed man.

"Bitch!" the man shouted and slapped the woman's face. She staggered and began to fall, but the man grabbed her by the collar of her coat and yanked her upright again. He swore at her in a guttural language with four-letter English words thrown in. He raised his arm again and de Gier stepped forward, but the commissaris held on to the sergeant's sleeve. Two of the orange-coated policemen walked up to the man.

"Mister!"

"You know what she just told me, officer?"

The commissaris pushed de Gier toward the nearest restaurant. The sergeant looked over his shoulder. He could only see the coats of the policemen. The woman was whimpering.

"Not our business, sergeant."

"What would that woman have said to the man, sir?"

The commissaris' long teeth reflected the street's garish light. "That she prefers the man's best friend to the man. Love, sergeant, the cause of much violence. Let's go in."

When they walked through the park again their mood had improved. Fortified by a six-course meal, they hardly noticed the looming trees, reaching down threateningly, and they almost casually avoided staggering drunks and shuffling junkies. It was dark now and the young lady singing Christmas carols was coming to the end of her program. The police sirens hadn't. They tore at the chanting voice and blotted out most of the twittering of a flock of starlings shifting from tree to tree. The commissaris plodded on with the sergeant striding at his side.

"Coffee," the commissaris said, "and then to bed, but we should make an effort to waylay Astrinsky, although I don't really feel like work."

De Gier spotted Astrinsky a few minutes later in the hotel's coffee shop and pointed him out to the commissaris. The commissaris sat down at the next table and smiled at his suspect.

"Good evening, Mr. Astrinsky. How are you tonight?"

Astrinsky lowered his magazine. It took a few seconds before he recognized the man who greeted him. He dropped the magazine and got up. When his elbow hit his coffee cup it fell off the table.

"You!" The word was both an exclamation and an acknowledgment.

"Yes, you remember? Suzanne Opdijk's brother. You remember Sergeant de Gier too?"

"Yes."

"Have you been in touch with Jameson at all lately, Mr. Astrinsky?"

"No. Why?"

"Perhaps you should go back. All sorts of things have been happening. Mary Brewer's boat was found, and the sheriff is very active. You knew Mary Brewer, didn't you?"

"Yes." Astrinsky's eyes stared. His half glasses had slid to the end of his fleshy nose, and his hands were crumpling the magazine.

"Of course you remember her. You bought her house. Ah!" The commissaris' little fist hit the table. "That's right. I knew there was something I wanted to discuss with you. Suzanne's house! You offered me thirty thousand, but after you left so suddenly I asked another realtor, a friend of the sheriff's, wasn't he, sergeant?"

The sergeant nodded helpfully.

"Right. I asked this realtor to appraise the property, and he came up with a figure three times as high. Are you sure you didn't miscalculate, Mr. Astrinsky? Suzanne thinks very highly of you. You were a good friend of my brother-in-law's, but I don't think she should give the property away just because you are a friend."

Astrinsky's mouth gaped briefly and closed with a snap.

"Perhaps we can look into the proposition again sometime. The sergeant and I will be flying back tomorrow morning on that nice airplane. But weren't you supposed to be in the Bahamas?"

"I'll see you tomorrow," Astrinsky said. "I've had a long day. Good night."

"Good night, Mr. Astrinsky."

"Well, how do you feel about our investigation now?" the commissaris asked when he switched off the light. The sergeant grunted sleepily. "Something is moving, don't you think?" The sergeant grunted twice. "What was that, Rinus?" But the sergeant had nodded off and no longer heard the creaking of the sheets, while the commissaris was moving about finding comfort for his aching legs and hips.

The dream was amazingly clear. Events passed quickly and he couldn't remember them all afterward, but it seemed that the case had been solved and the New York police general, accompanied by other dignitaries, was shaking his hand. He was being offered a commission and he accepted and found himself in uniform. The uniform was crisp and white, with very long trousers and a tight tunic. And a cap of course. A naval uniform—he was now a seaman. His assignment seemed most logical. He was being posted to a battleship in Rotterdam harbor. The battleship was American of course, the flagship of a combined fleet, and he was to be a liaison officer. He was being whistled aboard, with men standing at attention everywhere. And then he was being shown around. He was in a fast-moving motorboat, cutting through the murky water of the port, and he saw various warships, of different nationalities. They each had a purpose and a specialty. Gradually the ships were becoming smaller. The last ship was no more than a small boat, a twenty-foot wooden vessel like he had seen on the Maine coast. The explaining voice next to his ear dropped to a whisper. "Swimdogs," the voice said. "A secret weapon. See them?" He saw the animals, but they were seals, the seals of Jeremy's Island. There were dozens of them, swimming leisurely around their floating base. He saw their intelligent eyes and long silver whiskers. The voice was giving him more details. The animals were highly trained and equipped with electronic gear.

But then he was back on the battleship again, alone in his luxurious quarters, smoking and thinking. Something was worrying him. He couldn't be in the American navy because he was Dutch. He would need permission, the queen's permission. The scene changed at once. He was now in the state police jet, landing on the lawn in front of the queen's castle. Dutch military police, in parade uniforms with bearskin hats and curved sabers, greeted him smartly and marched him to the main building. The queen waited for him on a low couch and inclined her head as he stood stiffly, stating his name and former rank. He also stated his new rank and apologized for not asking for her approval before. His clipped phrases came out neatly. He was staring at the ground but raised his eyes when the queen answered.

"Permission granted."

"Thank you, ma'am."

He turned on his heels and marched out. He had seen the queen's face. Madelin's face, but mellowed and dignified, Madelin's beauty softened with the grace of royalty.

So far so good, but the terror of the dream came at the end. He was back in Rotterdam port, in the water this time, struggling, being dragged down by the weight of his uniform and boots. The seals came for him, but they changed as they approached. The round, smooth faces grew hairy protuberances; the eyes receded and were slanted and cruel. Their coloring changed too. They were black on top and white underneath.

He woke up because the commissaris was shaking him by the shoulder. The commissaris had switched on his bedside light.

"Rinus!"

"Sir?"

"You were dreaming. Do you remember your dream?"

De Gier told him what he remembered, and the commissaris nodded, smiled, and lit a cigar, puffing peacefully.

"That's it?"

"Yes, sir. There may be more, but it is all fading out now. The meeting with the queen was very important, and the end."

"Do you know what orcas look like, sergeant?"

"Not really, sir. The sheriff described them to me, but I wasn't paying too much attention at the time. Black and white. Large. Dangerous."

"They are of the whale family, sergeant, with smooth faces. Not hairy or lumpy. But we will meet them I think, or rather their human counterparts."

"We'll be fighting them, sir."

"Yes," the commissaris said gently.

14

"But that's not the firm we are trying to locate," the commissaris said, stooping to read the clumsily written sign hanging askew just inside the entrance of the long dark corridor: SYMONS TOY AND NOVELTY COMPANY, IMPORT AND EXPORT. "This is some wholesale company. Ah, here we are." He adjusted his glasses and peered at the business card that had been fastened to the sign's corner with two thumbtacks: BOSTON BETTER HOLDINGS, JAMES D. SYMONS, PRESIDENT. "So we did come to the right address after all." He straightened up. "Symons. Same name, must be the same man. A versatile businessman, our Mr. Symons. But to judge from the sign his wholesale business must be the more important of the two. Amazing. Let's become acquainted with him."

A dirty bulb further along the corridor seemed to be the ramshackle building's only illumination. The commissaris limped ahead slowly, tapping the cracked floor with his cane.

They climbed a flight of stairs and faced a door that had been painted pink a long time ago. The commissaris knocked.

"Welcome, gentlemen. The door is open."

The voice was gravelly, and the words teetered off into a squeaky cough.

They went in. There were shelves and tables loaded with cartons. Part of the floor had been used for a display of miniature electric trains, but two locomotives

had hit each other head-on and a disorderly heap of
railway carriages was gathering dust between a tin
station and a mountain overgrown with faded plastic
evergreens. A torn mask, presiding over a row of other
smaller masks, stared at them from the rear wall. They
all depicted the same old female face, toothless, pimpled,
wrinkled. The faces were green, the string wigs orange.
They smiled from drooling, wormlike lips and the eyes,
made of cut glass, were glittering with insane delight.

De Gier stopped and studied the array.

"Yes, gentlemen? The masks are of interest, are
they? I only have the one model left, in various sizes,
and as I can't offer a selection I will discount them, of
course. But I think I should start off by showing you my
new items. This box, for instance, a most profitable
proposition, and there will be immediate delivery for
limited quantities."

The commissaris and de Gier turned to face Mr.
Symons. They saw a fairly young and fairly well-dressed
man with red-rimmed eyes. He had walked across the
room so that the masks stared over his shoulders and
his own face became part of the display of demented
creativity.

"Look at this box, gentlemen. Here, let me open it.
What do you see? Little plastic building blocks, nothing
new, Germany has been marketing them for years, good
steady line, the kiddies love it, and at every Christmas
and birthday party everybody in the family gives the
little dears additional boxes so that the *wunderkinder*
can build bigger cranes and tractors and trucks and
what have you. Bread and butter line, right? But expensive and not too much margin. The Krauts have patented
the stuff and they can call the cards. A-ha! But this
box doesn't come from Germany, gentlemen, it comes
from Taiwan, and the price is half of what you are used
to paying. You've been happy to pay the German
prices so far, so how happy will you be when you pay
the Taiwan prices that are half of what the Krauts have
been daring to ask? How happy will you be? I ask again,
and the answer comes to mind immediately. You will

be *doubly* happy. A moneymaker, gentlemen, sell it for ten percent less than the German stuff and it will shoot across the counter. And the quality is excellent. Beautiful stuff, gentlemen, I've a thousand boxes in stock and more on the way, delivery early next year. Well? What do you say, gentlemen?"

"Interesting, Mr. Symons," the commissaris said, "but you must be mistaking us for somebody else."

Symons smiled politely. "Yes? You aren't from the Total Toys chain stores?" He checked his watch. "Ten o'clock, they said they would be here at ten-thirty. I thought you had come early. Never mind, gentlemen, you can buy my Taiwan boxes too. I'm not reserving them for anybody special, first come first served."

"No, Mr. Symons. We are not in the toy business."

Symons' smile hardened, then disappeared. "No? You wouldn't want to sell *me* anything, would you? I'm not buying these days. I'm clearing my stocks for a while. The times are hard, gentlemen, and the competition is tough and capital—need I mention capital?—is scarce."

"The Boston Better Holdings Company," the commissaris said. "We've come to see that company, and you are its president I believe."

Symons walked to the back of the room and sat down under a tattered wire mobile dangling small cardboard hands from its rusted extremities. The hands had long, bent fingernails and pointed in different directions as the draft in the room moved the mobile. Symons waved at two low chairs. "Sit down, gentlemen. That company has been so dormant for so long that I had almost forgotten its existence, but it's true that I am its honored president. What would be your interest? The company owns this building and pays me a flimsy wage for serving as its janitor. You wouldn't want to buy the building, would you? That would be good news indeed. Do the insurance companies want to build another sky-poker? Can I tell my shareholders that fortune is smiling at last?"

—"No, sir. We are not after Boston property. We are after a property called Cape Orca on the Maine coast."

Symons shook his head. "Tell me another, sir. Nobody knows where Cape Orca is. I know where Cape Orca is, but I am a most exceptional man, widely read and widely traveled. You would be a foreigner, sir, am I right?"

"From Amsterdam, the Netherlands."

"Exactly, so how would you have come across Cape Orca, a little splinter of the large solid block that is the U, S, *and* A?"

"I will tell you," the commissaris said. "My sister owns a house and some land on Cape Orca. Her husband died recently, and she asked me to come out and liquidate her estate. It so happens that I am interested in her property myself, as an investment. I have some surplus capital in the Netherlands, waiting to be invested in a country where taxes are still payable. I like Cape Orca—I think it could be developed profitably—but I want more than just my sister's few acres. I walked around the cape a bit and noticed that there are some empty houses, some of them wrecked or burned. If I buy I would buy the whole strip. The town clerk was good enough to inform me that the properties were registered in the name of a Mr. Astrinsky, but Mr. Astrinsky wasn't around when I went to look for him. He is traveling I believe. But yesterday morning I ran into the Jameson town clerk again and he told me that he had just found out that your company now owns the properties. And as I had some business in Boston anyway I thought I might see you. The shore strip would be for sale, wouldn't it?"

Mr. Symons had been listening while he played with the contents of the Taiwan box. He had also opened and closed the drawer of his desk a few times.

"Yes," he said. "I see. Well . . . How about a small drink to start the day properly, gentlemen? You are talking big business, and I always find that a small drink heightens my powers of perception. Some fine whiskey perhaps? I happen to have a bottle on tap and if you reach out to that shelf on your right you'll find three clean glasses."

"Surely!" the commissaris said. "That would be a splendid idea indeed, sir."

"But it'll have to be a small one. I'll have those sharpies from Total Toys here in a minute and I really must convert my junk into greenbacks. It'll be a miracle, but miracles have come my way before, the Lord is good and must be blessed from time to time, although a good kick into his divine ass can be recommended too sometimes. One of my pet theories, it has a lot of details and twists and turns, but we don't have the time to discuss it fully now. Here we are, gentlemen, three of the best, your very good health!"

"Now," Symons said a few seconds later. "Now, about Cape Orca. It so happens that the shareholders of Boston Better Holdings did discuss their interest in Cape Orca recently. They have been holding the land for a while now, but I only sent in the deeds a few days ago, for registration. The properties were bought for development, of course, but the shareholders are old, and hard to prod into activity. That's why nothing has been done. Now if you were willing to pay a price . . ."

"Yes," the commissaris said, "the price. What would be the price?"

Symons held up a hand with three rings, each with a different-colored stone. The hand dropped by its own weight, grabbed the bottle on its way, and poured a little more whiskey into its owner's glass.

"Of course. You need to know a price. But I have no price, not today. There are several shareholders, and I'll have to round them up and make them talk sense. The effort will take time. You have some time, sir?"

"A few days."

"And where can I reach you?"

"In Cape Orca. I am going back to my sister's house this afternoon. She has a telephone."

Symons got up. "Very well, sir. Let me write the

number and your name down and you'll hear from me. Within a few days, no doubt about that."

"Another front, sir," the sergeant said as they walked back to the hotel.

"Yes, sergeant. If he hadn't been drinking he would have betrayed himself easily, but the alcohol kept his mind steady and made him come up with a good enough answer. He'll be telephoning Astrinsky now, trying to find out who we are. And Astrinsky will tell him. Symons won't be overworried. On the contrary, he might be pleased. Our visit may have given him an opportunity for blackmail. Symons knows who the real owner is behind Cape Orca. He may be able to charge money for keeping the name a secret."

"We can find out, sir. There'll be a chamber of commerce here. Boston Better Holdings will be registered, and the name or names of its owners should be on file."

It took a while to find the chamber of commerce, and it took longer for the clerk to give them the required file. De Gier and the commissaris both smiled at the same time. "Bahama Better Holdings Company," the commissaris read. "How's that, sergeant? Do you want to fly to the Bahamas?"

"And find another company behind *that* one, sir?"

"Very likely. But there will be an end to the maze, sergeant. If we keep at it we'll find our way out."

"The Bahamas are British I believe, sir, or independent by now. It might be a bit of a job to trace the shareholders. We might telephone the Dutch consul on the islands."

"No, sergeant. If we do that we have to go through Amsterdam headquarters, and the chief constable isn't even aware that we are involved in an investigation. We should also remember that our boss is the sheriff of Woodcock County, Maine, USA. The investigation isn't ours at all. We are free-lance detectives employed by the Jameson sheriff's department."

De Gier grinned. "Are we, sir?"

"Of course."

"But your sister wants the right price for her house, sir."

The commissaris' voice dropped to a hissing whisper. "Really, sergeant. That's private business. If the sheriff had shown no interest in Cape Orca I would have advised Suzanne to take her thirty thousand and get out while the going is good. But it so happens that the sheriff *is* interested and we can bring him some positive information now. Astrinsky is shaken and Boston Better Holdings is a front. That Mr. Symons is a bad egg, not a very bad egg though. He is too weak to be evil. Just rotten. Yes, I think we can advise the sheriff to push a little further."

"Where do you think Astrinsky stands, sir?"

The commissaris waved his cane. "Astrinsky? Either a middleman or a true criminal. I would think that he is a middleman. I can't understand yet why Astrinsky consented to play the game in the first place. He isn't courageous by any means. I wonder what the connection between Astrinsky and the wanted party is. Just greed?"

"Half the people I have arrested were breaking the law to make money, sir."

"Yes, sergeant. But the desire to make money is a symptom of all sorts of emotional disturbances—greed is only one of them. Mr. Astrinsky, yes, hmmm . . . I would like to think that his part in the game is a little more complicated than it seems to us now. Not just greed. I would be disappointed if we uncovered nothing else. The stories his daughter told you are fascinating. She should be an unusual girl. And if that assumption is true, her father might have more depth than we have given him credit for."

They had to cross the park again to reach the hotel, and the commissaris walked slowly, stopping every now and then to study the trees. Most trees were adorned with small name plates, and the commissaris mumbled the Latin words, following the English classifications. Three men with long black beards sheltered under an impressive oak. They eyeballed the commissaris solemnly and greeted him by holding up three identical flat, unlabeled bottles.

"One, two, *hop!*" the tallest man said, and the three bottles pierced the three beards.

De Gier nudged the commissaris' arm. "Let's go, sir. When they have swallowed that they'll be looking for trouble."

The commissaris quickened his step. "No more trouble, sergeant, no more than is strictly due to us. You're right."

But they ran into a little more trouble before the day was over. There were other passengers on the plane to Jameson: several hunters and Michael Astrinsky. Astrinsky raised a hand when he boarded but made no effort to start a conversation. The commissaris dozed and de Gier smoked and looked out the window. Nothing but clouds, nothing happened, they didn't even hit any air pockets.

When the plane landed the cruiser was waiting. The sheriff didn't smile when the commissaris limped up to him.

"Good to see you, sir. I was waiting for you. I've just come back from the scene of a crime. Bob and Bert are still there. I think I'll have to call in the state police for sure now. Bernie got himself shot in the head this morning, on a road that goes nowhere, north of Cape Orca. His head is almost off. The weapon was a shotgun, fired from close quarters. Perhaps you'd like to have a look at his corpse before I sound the alarm and call in the supercops. You might see something we've missed."

15

"The snow," the sheriff said. "It does help to cover it all up."

Nearly two feet of snow had transformed Bernie's cruiser into an indeterminate, sparkling white shape in a curve of the narrow road.

"The engine was still running when we arrived this morning."

The commissaris was studying a disturbed area at the side of the road. "You found the chief deputy's corpse over here, sheriff?"

"Yes, sir. Albert thought there was still a chance that Bernie might be alive, so he moved the body. And tampered with the evidence, of course."

"Albert?"

"He telephoned from a house further along, a few miles from here on the way to town. I came out at once. Albert was here when I arrived."

"Did Albert have anything to do with this?"

"He said he was driving along in his little truck, saw the cruiser, stopped, and found Bernie's body."

"Did you arrest Albert?"

"He's in the jailhouse now. I don't know what charges to bring against him yet. I'm just holding him. But Albert is in trouble all right. Bernie had been looking for him, after having checked Tom's alibi. Tom was in town when the sergeant was shot at. Old Beth swears he was in her restaurant around eight-thirty the day before yesterday, and her daughter says so too. But nobody could find Albert, and Albert has a sign on the door of his cabin: OUT HUNTING. So Bernie went on looking for Albert and then Albert finds Bernie and Bernie is dead."

"And the fox?"

"I am holding the fox too, sir. He can't explain his movements either. He's very vague about where he has been. Bernie must have got himself shot early this morning. The fox says he was wandering around in Cape Orca looking for dead pines. Nobody saw him and he saw nobody. He could have been anywhere."

The commissaris walked over to Bernie's cruiser. Its passenger door was open and a shotgun had slipped between the front seat and the wheel.

"Bernie's gun?"

"Yes, sir. We found an empty shell. Bernie shot something, or at something."

"Did Albert have a shotgun in his truck?"

"Yes."

"Had he fired it recently?"

"Yes, sir, he was out hunting. He had a goose in the car and some ducks."

"Can you identify the ammunition?"

The sheriff spread his hands. "Everybody here buys his ammo from Robert's Market. Tom only stocks one brand. This must be BMF business, sir. Bernie was after the gang and the gang shot him. That Albert reported finding the body is an example of their style. It would be just like them to find their own victim!"

The two young deputies standing next to the dead man's cruiser nodded grimly.

"Did you have a chance to check out that boat in the bay, sheriff?"

"Yes. We couldn't get it out. It was frozen into the ice. I smashed some of the ice with a pickax. Jeremy was right. Not an ounce of plastic foam in the boat and the bulkheads had been replaced neatly. When Mary Brewer went sailing that day she thought her boat couldn't sink, but it sank like a brick and the current must have moved it to the rocks, very slowly. It may have taken months."

"Did the gang see you go out to the boat? How did you get to it?"

"They may have seen me. I rowed a dory across the open channel and then pushed it over the ice for a bit until I got to open water again, and I rowed the last few hundred feet. A man pushing a boat over the ice is visible for miles. I'm surprised they didn't have a crack at me with a rifle."

"Yes," the commissaris said thoughtfully and took a cigar from his pocket. The sheriff struck a match. The commissaris puffed. "But so many patterns have been moving around here. The BMF gang is only one of them. The obvious doesn't always point at the truth. Have you dug about in the snow at all, sheriff?"

"Yes, sir, there's a lot of blood. In two places. Around where Bernie's corpse was, of course, and in another place, some five feet further down. Perhaps he walked a few steps, like a chicken that has lost its head, staggered about I mean."

"Where is the corpse?"

"In the back of the cruiser. We wrapped it in blankets."

The commissaris poked at the snow with his cane.

"Do you have any ideas, sir?"

"No, sheriff, only abstractions. I have no facts to make the abstractions concrete. Is there anything you can tell me about Bernie? I only knew him as a pleasant fat man, and that is by hearsay. The sergeant described him to me."

"Fat," one of the deputies said. "Bernie was sure fat. It was worrying him. He burst out of two uniforms and he had to pay for new ones. He was getting close to two hundred and fifty pounds. That isn't fat anymore, that's obese."

"Was he worried about losing his job?"

The sheriff nodded. "He may have been. I'd talked to him about his physical problem. He'd been getting a little sleepy lately. He would drop off a lot, even on patrol. Can't have a sleeper next to me in the cruiser."

"Any other problems?"

"The dog," the sheriff said slowly. "The damned dog. Bob, where does Bill Thompson live, the old farmer whose dog was causing all the ten sixty-four's. Doesn't Bill live at the end of Blueberry Neck Road?"

"That's right, sheriff."

"This is Blueberry Neck Road!" the sheriff shouted. "It goes to the sea and stops. Bill's farm is three miles from this spot. His dog was killing the deer in these woods right here!"

"Bernie has been after that dog, sheriff," the deputy said. "He was talking to us about it."

The sheriff was rubbing his chin furiously. "So maybe he got the dog. That would explain the blood. And then somebody got *him.*"

"I know Bill Thompson, sheriff," the deputy called Bob said. "Bill has two shotguns and two deer rifles and a couple of wooden boxes full of shells and cartridges. His house and his barn are on a hill. He would have some hand guns too."

Bob walked over to his car, next to the sheriff's. "Shall I call the state cops, sheriff? We'll need more men to take that house. Maybe it's not a house right now. Maybe it's a bunker."

"No. No, wait, Bob. We can handle this. You and Bert get in your cruisers. Follow me, but stay out of sight. Lock Bernie's car. You gentlemen can come with me if you like."

"Hell," the sheriff said a little later. "I think I can see it now. Old Bill must have been driving his Ford truck with the dog sitting next to him. A big short-haired brown dog, friendly enough when he hasn't got the smell of deer in his nose. Bill's buddy. The two of them are driving along quietly, on their way home probably, and Bernie comes zooming along after them. Bernie switches on his lights and plays his siren and old Bill pulls up. Bernie stops behind the Ford and takes out his shotgun. Maybe he talked to Bill, maybe he didn't, but he must have got the dog out of the truck. He probably just opened the dog's door and called him. Dog jumps into the road and Bernie shoots him straight in the eyes. Bang. Dead dog. Bernie's temper has been bad lately. He was polite enough to me, but he hadn't forgotten my remarks about his big belly and his fat bum. And the BMF gang got him scared. And the game wardens had been after him about Bill's dog. So he meant to do something, for a change. But Bill doesn't know about Bernie's troubles, and cares less. All Bill hears is a bang, and all he sees is his buddy dead on the snow at the side of the road. So Bill reaches over, grabs the old sixteen-gauge that's hooked up against the roof of his truck's cabin, slips in a shell, and pokes it out of the open door. *Wham!* Another corpse in the road, but this time it's Bernie. And Bill picks up his dog and carries him into the truck and drives off, and the snow falls and falls and blots everything out. Albert says Bernie was completely snowed under when he got to the scene."

"Yes," de Gier said. "That sounds fine. What's Bill Thompson like?"

"Old. Eighty and some I should think. And quiet. He still farms and he still fishes and he still hunts. A proud old man who doesn't cash his social security checks. He won't take money from the welfare people either, not even if they put it on his kitchen table. He pushes it back at them. In summer he sells fish off his truck. I've bought them for the jailhouse. He's got the fish spread on crushed ice and his price is about half of what we pay elsewhere, and then we have to drive forty miles."

"A nice old man?"

"Not nice. He isn't friendly. He says what he has to say and goes home again. I think he really can't stand people, like a lot of us around here. But he is a good man and I don't want to shoot him up. I know what my deputies want to do. Call the state cops, and the sheriff from the next county and his men, and get everybody in position around Bill's house. They'll yell at Bill a few times and order him to come out with his hands over his head, and if he doesn't they'll blast his house from all sides at once."

"I see," the commissaris said. "Your suspect won't be the sort of man who likes to be yelled at. But he might listen if talked to."

"I'll talk to him," the sheriff said. "And I'll go alone." He stopped the cruiser well away from the house and parked it behind two imposing maples. He pressed a button and picked up the microphone. The house and the barn looked pretty and restful under their loads of glistening snow. A black battered pickup truck stood next to a tractor with a snow-blade attached. The sheriff picked up his microphone and activated the loudspeaker on the cruiser's top.

"Bill," the sheriff said quietly. "I know you're in there. Listen to me."

The hill echoed and the sheriff adjusted the loudspeaker's volume.

"This is the sheriff speaking, Bill. I'll be coming out of the cruiser in a minute. I'll have a gun, but I won't use it. I'm going to walk up your driveway and you can shoot me if you like, but I advise you not to do that. You've killed my chief deputy. Maybe you were right, maybe you were not right. I'm going to ask you to come with me and the judge will hear your case."

The sheriff released the button on the microphone and looked at the house. There was no movement. He pressed the button again. "I'm coming now, Bill. I won't put a hand on you. I'm going to ask you to accompany me."

The commissaris looked around. Bob's and Bert's cruisers had stopped at a safe distance. The two deputies stood in the road. They couldn't be seen from the house; neither could their cars.

The sheriff sighed and opened his door. The commissaris and de Gier watched his small straight figure walk up the driveway. The short walk took a long time. The sheriff stopped next to the black truck, crossed his hands behind his back, and waited. De Gier looked at his watch. Thirty seconds passed. Then the door of the house opened and a tall man in a dark floppy hat and a long gray coat stepped out and walked up to the sheriff. He walked with a stoop and supported himself on a stick. The sheriff turned and began to walk back to the cruiser. The tall silent shape followed him after a slight hesitation.

The commissaris touched de Gier's hand. They both got out of the cruiser.

"All clear?" Bob asked.

"Yes," the commissaris said. "Mr. Thompson is coming quietly. Can you give us a lift back?"

16

The commissaris, the sheriff, and the sergeant thanked Beth and said they didn't want any more coffee. They had drunk three mugs each, they had eaten her home-made ice cream, and the ice cream was still settling on her stew and the many fresh rolls served with it.

"Just let us sit here and enjoy your stove's heat and tell me how much money you want of me. You're a good cook, Beth."

The commissaris and the sergeant agreed. Beth smiled. She began to clear the table, and the three men waited and smoked.

"So that was all," the sheriff said when Beth was clattering her pots and pans again. "You've told a few stories and I've told some of mine. The fox and Albert are free. Everybody is free except old Bill. The state cops took him, but they promised to treat him good. Leroux is out on bail and Astrinsky is home. All I have in jail now is the old man who doesn't want to go home because he's still out of firewood. I might get him some, but then I won't have anyone to do chores."

"No prisoners," the commissaris said. "But there seems no shortage of suspects."

"Sure. We now know that Mary Brewer was mur-dered. We also know that Carl Davidson was murdered. When you were away I spoke to that old Indian I told you about who sometimes accompanied Carl when he was wandering in the woods. He says that Carl froze to death because he didn't have any matches. He also says that Carl always carried matches. Carl was a careful man who wouldn't forget a necessity. He doesn't think that Carl got lost, but if he had got lost he would have found a tree and set it alight. The Indian taught him that trick. Indians don't bother to cut wood when they have to make camp in a hurry. They find a dead hollow tree and make it burn. A good-sized tree burns all night. They sleep fifteen feet away, and they don't sleep too deeply since the tree may fall over. The tree makes a strange sound when it burns. The air roars up and the tree becomes a flute. *Whoooo, whooo,* the Indian said. But Carl was found frozen in the snow. The Indian says somebody was out in the woods with Carl that day. Our suspect stole Carl's matches and ran away."

"If the Indian knew the victim so well he may have a suspicion. Did he mention a suspect?"

The sheriff shook his head. "Indians don't name names, sir, and the locals don't either. Everybody for himself. They'll help up to a point. It's quite something that the Indian says he thinks Carl Davidson was killed. I tried to press a little further, but he just smiled and drank his beer. White man's business, not his. He went back to the reserve. He wouldn't sign a statement. He says he can't write."

"Can he write?"

"Sure he can write."

"Good," the commissaris said. "But we are getting the same sort of information. Everything tells us that we are dealing with crime, but nothing so far points to any specific person."

The sheriff began to fill in a check. He looked up. "But I don't want to stop now, sir. The case is moving."

"It is, sheriff. Can I make some suggestions?"

"Please."

"I would like you to authorize me to pay another visit to Jeremy's Island. There's something there. The sergeant and I saw three dogs, but when Madelin flew us around the island she said that Jeremy has four dogs and that he takes one dog ashore with him if he goes shopping."

"That's right. Osiris, a big black Doberman. It stays close to Jeremy."

"Osiris is the missing dog. And you remember that Janet Wash told me a lie about the accident with her wagon and that my sister saw Jeremy helping her out of the overturned car? Maybe it all means nothing, but another visit to Jeremy would do no harm. He has not been helpful, apart from mentioning Mary Brewer's boat. I can tell him that his suspicion was proved by your investigation of the boat, and I can ask him about the accident and the missing dog."

"Sure, go ahead. Do you want to take the sergeant?"

"Yes."

"Fine. Anything else you would like to do, sir?"

"Yes, I would like to see the fox."

"Right. I have something in mind too. Leroux is free on bail, but the charge against him is assaulting an officer. I can still withdraw the charge. If I don't he'll be fined a lot of money, and he has no money. He has a wife and two kids. Leroux has lived here all his life. He has worked with the fox. They've been out logging together. He has also worked on the Cape Orca estate. Reggie employs him as a gardener in the summer. The BMF gang members have also worked on the estate. You can't see it now, but that estate is very beautiful. Reggie has planted an azalea garden, there are big lawns sloping down to the sea on the north side, there is a little forest of white pines that he keeps clean, there's a wildflower reserve with little bridges and ponds. He can't take care of all that by himself so he gets help, and Leroux is usually in charge of the help. Leroux has worked for Jeremy too when the hermit's cabin was shifted to the other side of the island. And Astrinsky has employed Leroux. Leroux is a handyman, but right now he is out of work. It so happens that I know a man in the county who has bought a lot of used chain saws and other machines, lawnmowers, little tractors, and so forth, that he is repairing and rebuilding for resale. He asked me if I knew of somebody who could help him. Leroux knows that type of work, and I can bring the two together and get Leroux a job for the rest of the winter. But I'll do nothing if he doesn't give me information. I want to know everything he knows about all our suspects, no matter how trivial or far-fetched."

"Good," the commissaris said and suppressed a yawn. "Tomorrow?"

"Tomorrow, sir. How are you planning to get to the island? The channel froze yesterday. A boat can't get through now, and you can't walk over either because the current is breaking up the ice again."

"A plane," the commissaris said and smiled. "I am getting used to flying in small planes. You think you can persuade Madelin to take us out again tomorrow, sergeant?"

"There'll be snow on Jeremy's airstrip too, sir, I think. I'll ask Madelin and let you know."

"The Astrinsky plane can be fitted with skis."

The sheriff gave his check to Beth. "That was a very good meal indeed, Beth."

The woman smiled.

"What do you think, Beth," the sheriff asked suddenly. "You've lived here all your life. Do you think we're doing the right thing? What about all these dead people on Cape Orca. Should we just let them be dead?"

Beth's smile faded slowly. "I don't know, sheriff. I've been wondering. I've been a free woman all my life. I don't hold with uniforms and stiff hats and those big cars you and the deputies scream around in. But I don't hold with the black cloud over Cape Orca either. It's been there long enough now. Maybe it should be pushed away."

"What do you know about the cloud, Beth?"

The woman was walking back to her wood range. She opened its lid and threw in a log.

"What do you know, Beth?"

She turned around. "There'll be more snow tonight, sheriff. I wish it was rain. Rain is easier to shovel than snow."

17

The Cessna's short wide skis skidded over the loose snow of Jeremy's airstrip. The flight had been flawless, up to the last few moments, when a crosswind grabbed the plane so that it approached the strip like a rag thrown by a tired charwoman. But it managed to straighten out at the final split second. The commissaris didn't know—he had closed his eyes. The plane would roll over and the cabin would crush. He was waiting. But there was only the roar of the engine and the sharp hiss of the skis. He opened his eyes and tried to smile. So much for his death wish. He had so often told himself that he would like to die in an accident. He looked at his hands, clutching his knees, and ordered them to release the safety belt. They obeyed, but they took their time.

"Well done," the commissaris said. "Well done, Madelin."

The sergeant breathed out sharply. De Gier's eyes had been closed too, and he had remembered the skeleton riding its black steed in Madelin's dining room. A different scene but of the same quality.

"I'm sorry," Madelin shouted over the engine's din. "Did I give you a fright? That wind came so suddenly. I wasn't expecting it."

"You did," the sergeant said and put a hand under the commissaris' elbow. The commissaris was clambering out of the small door, looking down into the long snouts and cold eyes of Jeremy's Dobermans. The three dogs growled softly. The raven swooped from a pine behind the cabin and fluttered to the plane's wing.

Jeremy himself came striding up.

"Morning, Madelin. You're bringing unexpected visitors. Shame on you, you're breaking the code." But he smiled as he helped the commissaris down and told the dogs to go away. "Don't we have a lovely climate here? Snow all night while we're tucked away under our comforters and a bright sky awaiting in the morning. You've had breakfast? You can share mine if you don't mind celery soup, and I'm not quite out of coffee, I believe. Are you bringing me news from the mainland, or have you thought of more questions?"

The dogs were nuzzling his boots and he spoke to them sharply. They turned, one after another, and trotted away to the woods. "That's right. Go back to your squirrel catching." He pointed. "That's what they do these days. A big squirrel out there keeps them amused. He'll come down and chatter from a stump and only jump for cover when they're just about on top of him. Once he's in the pines he's worth watching. A ten-foot leap from tree to tree is nothing to him. It's marvelous to see his silhouette against the rising sun. I'm sure he knows that he'll be nothing but a bit of bloody fur when those devils get hold of him. Would you follow me? The cabin is good and warm. Out here the wind will rip your noses off."

"I am sorry to disturb you again, sir," the commissaris said as he settled himself close to the cookstove and ate his celery soup. "But we are coming to the end of our business here and are collecting some last answers to some last questions."

Jeremy frowned. The commissaris smiled. He pointed at his bowl with his spoon. "Excellent soup, sir. I must tell my wife. She makes it too, but she forgets to put in the fried bread."

Jeremy smiled back. "Looks like duckweed. But tastes better, I hope. You have questions? Ask away, but perhaps I won't answer. A bad answer spoils a

good question. Some questions should be permitted to
live on."

The commissaris put his bowl down and glanced at
Madelin. There was a vacant chair, so it wasn't necessary for the girl to sit with the sergeant on his small
bench. Her thigh was pressed against his. The sergeant
was smoking and staring at the floor. He didn't appear
to be at ease.

"Some time ago," the commissaris said, "about a
week ago I believe, Janet Wash rolled her station wagon
off a Cape Orca road. The car nearly went over the
cliff but was stopped and held by some alder trees. I
was told you were there and helped the lady out of her
car's wreck."

"That's right. Very clumsy of Janet. She should know
how to drive on an icy road by now, but down she went.
She wasn't hurt, fortunately, and the car was insured.
No harm done."

"Some harm was done, sir. It seems to me the wagon
killed your dog Osiris. You must have been upset since
you love your animals. Osiris was your favorite, wasn't
he? He was the dog who accompanied you to town,
and you never allow the other dogs to leave the island.
What did you do with his corpse?"

"Ah," Jeremy said and fussed with his pipe. "True.
He was my favorite dog. But he died, by accident as it
turned out. He just happened to get into the station
wagon's way, and the car was out of control by then.
The corpse, you say. I took him back to the island and
burned him at the end of the airstrip. Couldn't bury
him, the ground was frozen. But he had a proper fare-
well. I burned him at sunset and the other dogs attended.
So did the raven. I had wanted the seals to come too,
but they're frightened of the dogs. They did watch from
afar, however."

The commissaris' pale almost transparent eyes rested
on Jeremy's face. The hermit was having some trouble
with his pipe.

"Mrs. Wash must have been troubled about the accident, sir. You weren't hurt in any way? Were you standing next to Osiris when the wagon hit him?"

Jeremy got up and collected the empty bowls. He poured coffee and distributed the mugs. He sat down again. Madelin's thigh was no longer pressing against de Gier's. The sergeant was staring at the suspect. There was no expression in his eyes. Jeremy's silence became oppressive. Madelin crossed and recrossed her legs.

"Yes," Jeremy said finally. "I jumped out of the car's way. Any further questions?"

The commissaris smiled pleasantly. "I said I was sorry to disturb you. But I am curious, and perhaps my curiosity can help to dispel the black cloud over Cape Orca. That expression isn't mine. Beth gave it to me last night when we were having dinner at her restaurant."

"Beth!" Jeremy said gruffly. "There's a meddling woman for you. She doesn't like the idea of me living here by myself and insists on giving me things for free. Ice cream and stuff. Excellent ice cream for sure, but I'm not asking for favors. I am always giving her things in return. Potatoes, vegetables when I have them. I don't like to feel grateful. It's like feeling guilty." He suddenly blew into his pipe, and smoke and sparks filled his corner of the cabin. A spark smoldered on the rug, but Jeremy didn't move. The sergeant stretched a long leg and stamped it out. Jeremy turned to the commissaris. "You know what I mean?"

There was too much intensity in the question to let it go. The commissaris bowed forward a little as if to acknowledge the seriousness of the moment. "Yes."

"Good."

The commissaris sat back and puffed peacefully on his cigar. "One last point, sir. You told me when we came here for the first time that you bought your island from an agency that has since left the town of Jameson. The owner, you said, was a gambler and in urgent need of money."

Jeremy looked into his pipe. "Yes, I said that. Would you want the name of that guy?"

"I would."

The raven tapped on the window. Jeremy got up, opened the window, waited for the bird to hop onto his arm, and closed it again. He turned around. "I don't recall the name now. Something with a y in it. I have it on the tip of my tongue. The island's deed has the name, but to find that bit of paper would be a major undertaking." He waved at some cartons stacked in the back of the cabin. "Might take all day. Ah, it has come back to me. Reynolds! Yes, sir. That's the fellow, or was. Probably's blown his brains out by now. Gamblers usually do."

Jeremy walked them back to the plane, followed by his dogs at a respectable distance. When they passed the woods the squirrel made a brief appearance, balanced precariously on the tip of a branch and chattering furiously at the dogs. The Dobermans snarled and jumped. The squirrel honked, a long deep sound like a blast from a saxophone. Then its mood changed and it chirped, turned, and disappeared into the pine needles.

Madelin laughed. "He's very much like you, Jeremy."

"Not quite," Jeremy said, "but he's learning."

He shook the commissaris' hand and nodded at de Gier. "Thank you for coming, gentlemen. I hope I haven't disappointed you."

18

The Opdijks' station wagon ground slowly ahead, whining in first gear. The commissaris was driving. De Gier sat huddled in his fur-lined coat.

"You look like a polar traveler, sergeant, an unhappy polar traveler. Aren't the hounds pulling the sleigh fast enough? The sawmill should be at the end of this road. We'll arrive in a minute."

The sergeant blew some thin smoke out of the collar of Opdijk's garment. "I am not unhappy, sir, I am trying to figure out what we were doing on the island. Jeremy gave you no answers; he only confirmed that his dog died. You surmised that correctly, I should have thought of the possibility, but I didn't. I have been thinking about little else than the Cape Orca murders. The dead dog seems no part of them. You think Janet Wash ran the dog down on purpose, sir?"

"Here we are, sergeant. There's smoke coming out of that big shed. Our friend is in."

"And he didn't give you the correct name of the gambler. I'm sure he was only play-acting, yet you seemed pleased enough with his answer, or nonanswer."

"Out," the commissaris said and opened his door. "You've been my student long enough, sergeant. Why ask if you can find out by using the brain you keep in that handsome head of yours? The answers are clear enough. I can see them, so why shouldn't you? I haven't been hiding any of the information that came my way, and I trust you have given me all of yours. The encounter we had on the island was the result of an attack based on our combined knowledge. Good day, sir. I hope you can spare us a little of your valuable time."

The fox was waiting for them on the path to his shed. Albert had come out of the shed too, carrying some boards that he lowered carefully onto the trailer attached to the fox's jeep. The fox shook hands.

"We've met before," the sergeant said. "You pulled us out of the snow."

The fox grinned. "We've met a number of times, sergeant, directly and indirectly. We made you as welcome as we could, circumstances and existing limitations providing. Will you be leaving soon?"

"I think so."

"A pity. I was thinking of making you an honorary member of my organization, such as it is these days. Would you and your friend come in? The mill isn't too comfortable, but it'll be a little warmer than out here. I have two barrel stoves going, but one wall is open so that we can pull the saw logs in. Most of the heat goes straight out again. Albert, you're coming in too?"

Albert came, smiled at de Gier, and shook the commissaris' hand. "I hear you're a police commissioner from Europe."

"I was," the commissaris said, "and very likely I'll be one again, but here I am trying my hand at being a private detective."

"You find the activity worthwhile?"

"Yes, thank you, very."

The fox took his woolen hat off and poured coffee from a jug standing on a hot plate in a corner of the mill. Most of the shed was taken up by an old truck engine powering a circular saw and the machinery required to maneuver the logs into position. The engine was going, forcing them to shout, and the fox switched it off. "Drop of brandy in your coffee? It's nasty day. A bit of brandy makes a difference."

"Thank you."

They raised their mugs and sipped. The fox dug about in his curly hair, which had flattened under his hat; only the two tufts near his ears stood up. His long face with the tilted eyes looked expectantly at the commissaris.

"You deserve your name," the commissaris said.

"I hope so. I've spent some time observing the way a fox lives. There are several around here, and they hunt close to the mill sometimes. Yesterday one of them got my rooster. I saw him coming and shouted, but he never wavered. He knows I won't shoot him, so he comes by daylight. The neighbor's chickens disappeared during the night. The fox opened the latch of the barn door."

Albert laughed. "Don't exaggerate. Your stories are getting too good. A fox doesn't open a latch, the raccoons do that."

"Excuse me," the commissaris said. "What's a raccoon again? Some sort of bear?"

"Yes, they look like bears, but I don't know if they belong to the bear family. They're small. Here, the sergeant's hat is made of a raccoon skin."

"Ah yes. I had forgotten. Go on with your story please."

"Story? Oh, the fox getting at my neighbor's chickens with the help of a raccoon, that's right. The fox must have gotten a raccoon to open the latch of the barn door for him, and then he shared the chickens with his friend afterward. A fox is a leader, of course. He initiates the action, delegates what he can't do himself, and shares the benefits." The fox laughed. "Some animals are smart. Do you know what we call policemen in the States, gentlemen?"

The commissaris shook his head.

. "Pigs. All of us have qualities of animals. So have the police. The police like to wallow in dirt, and they'll gobble up anything that falls on the side. They get fat and eventually they get slaughtered, but there are always new pigs. Pigs are very fertile."

The commissaris sipped his coffee.

"You don't agree, sir?"

"Perhaps. Your statement is a little too general I

think. Tell me, Mr. Fox, when you started your gang, the BMF gang I believe it is called, what sort of a gang was it? In its initial stage I mean."

The fox looked at Albert. "What were we like, Albert?"

"Like we are now. I don't think we've changed much. But the trimmings were different. I remember I had a black leather jacket with a white skull and bones painted on the back and I wore a chain round my neck. I used to like to wear dark glasses and I tried to ride a motorcycle, but I wasn't very good at it then. I fell off a couple of times. You had some special army helmet, and Tom and Gérard and the others sported little leather caps. We would ride our motorcycles in formation, and we sometimes went to Bangor and the Canadian cities and drank a lot of beer and we had some good fights."

"Hell's Angels," the commissaris said and smiled. "We have them in Amsterdam. It's a popular type of manifestation. Must have been with us for twenty years, longer maybe. The black leather clothes and the dark glasses are universal properties of that type of gang. You know what they always reminded me of?"

"No."

"Of us, of the police, of the strong arm of the police. A darker more romantic version but essentially the same. That hypothesis was confirmed later when I learned that the beatniks, the flower people, the hippies, and their latter-day varieties use Hell's Angels to do police work at their rallies. I watched young men with bare chests and black leather jackets and the other customary paraphernalia, the SS helmets and so forth, ride their motorcycles to keep the thoroughfares open. I even saw them beat up offenders, youngsters who climbed fences or got annoyingly drunk. A most interesting discovery. Rebels have rules and appoint police to enforce their rules. It is true that the police terrorize and are aggressive, but it is also true that the police keep order. Humanity, in whatever society, has an inborn need for order. It cannot function in anarchy."

The fox had been listening carefully. He toasted the commissaris with his mug.

"Do you agree, Mr. Fox?"

The tilting eyes gleamed. "You are talking about humanity."

"I am, sir."

"But perhaps humanity doesn't matter so much," the fox said. "Perhaps we overemphasize our importance. I've spent time in the woods, the wild woods. There weren't any humans about. All I saw were trees and plants and animals and insects. The woods are quiet and beautiful, and there's no police force. There are no rules, no morals. I don't see jack rabbits riding cruisers, or jays in stiff hats, or squirrels hanging around in helicopters to see if everything is the way they think it should be. It's the way it should be without any interference at all."

The commissaris held up his mug.

"More coffee, more brandy, or both?"

"More brandy. Thank you. Very good brandy. Did you stop to think what would happen if humanity ignored its rules, starting tomorrow, for instance?"

"Yes," the fox said. "There would be anarchy, as you said just now. A terrific mess. Just like the woods would be if you suddenly drove a million animals into one area. The clever and the strong would eat the stupid and the weak. There would be an orgy of killing, but not for too long. Disaster would change into balance. In a few years the woods would be quiet and beautiful again."

The fox sipped from his enamel mug. "And if there were no interference from us, if the superrace, the humans, would have the grace to disappear, the beauty of the woods would spread. The trees would push over the cities, very quickly, more quickly than you would expect. There's a road in the back of this sawmill. It was a first-grade hardtopped road two years ago, but when it was short-circuited by the new highway and forgotten, the woods moved in and covered it up. There are cedars growing through the broken tar now, and moss and wildflowers between the cedars' roots. Two years. In ten years New York City would be overgrown. I would like to be a witness to that process."

"You would be among the dead, Mr. Fox."

The fox nodded. "I would be. But would that matter?"

The commissaris' eyes twinkled briefly. He had remembered the plane landing on Jeremy's Island and recalled his fear. "It wouldn't matter to you, would it, Mr. Fox?"

The fox smiled back. "Oh, it would undoubtedly. I scare easy, but we are discussing a theory. The point is that my death, which would be part of the extinction of our species, may not be all that important."

The commissaris drank his brandy. De Gier moved uneasily. There was no breakthrough yet. He wished the commissaris would reach out more openly and wondered whether he could help.

The fox had moved too, but the commissaris sat very quietly, his whole attitude suggesting that he was very much at ease and had nothing in mind. Except sipping a little more brandy perhaps.

The fox tugged at his hair. "You came to ask questions? I hear you visited Jeremy earlier on today."

The commissaris looked over the rim of his mug. "News travels quickly in Woodcock County, Mr. Fox."

The fox shrugged. "I have a CB radio in my jeep. I heard Madelin talk to the old guy who runs the airstrip. You asked Jeremy questions?"

"Yes."

"Did he answer?"

"In a way."

The fox jumped up, clapped his hands, laughed, and sat down again. "In a way!"

De Gier laughed too. It was done now. He got up, stretched, and wandered over to Albert, who reached for the brandy bottle. Albert grinned back at him and poured. The fox was still talking.

"Jeremy is my local sage. I used to go over to the island and I would ask him questions, but he never answered. He would talk about other things instead, different things altogether. Tell me stories, jokes, anything. But he never seemed to hear what I asked. Then later, maybe the next day, I would think about what he had said and find that he *had* answered. Very funny, and annoying too. He plays around, and very seriously, once you get a feeling as to what he is doing. But go ahead, you can ask *me* questions now. I may want to try to imitate Jeremy's method, but I won't be as good at it as he is."

"You try, and I'll try," the commissaris said good-humoredly.

The fox was on his feet again. "One moment, before you go ahead I want to ask a question too. How does your quest go? Can you point at anyone yet?"

The commissaris shook his head. "I am a foreign visitor to your great country, Mr. Fox. I wouldn't point a finger at anyone, but your sheriff will I think, and I would imagine that we don't have to wait long now."

"You hear that, Albert?" the fox asked. *"My* sheriff. *Your* sheriff too. Our public servant, if only he would remember."

"Oh, he does, Mr. Fox. I have had the pleasure of being able to observe the sheriff, and so has the sergeant here. We are quite impressed. And so should you be. To consider authority as the enemy isn't always wise, and perhaps even . . . yes . . . childish. But no matter. It is my turn now, and here is my question. How did you manage to send off Captain Schwartz? I believe you admitted being instrumental in his departure, but I didn't hear how you forced him to remove himself, and I am interested."

The fox ran his fingers over a freshly cut board. "Okay, if you want to know I'll tell you, but you'll only get my side of the experiment. You should ask the captain too. But then his side might be confused. They say he's crazy, which, unfortunately, may be true. If it is true my experiment is all balled up. I was hoping that he'd turn out to be intelligent."

"He wasn't?"

"Perhaps not. But he *was* a Nazi, and still is I'm sure. I did some reading at college about what the Nazis call their philosophy. There was a lot of hog-wash in their literature, but they also talked about the right of the strong, which interested me, of course. Like what I saw in the woods—the clever and the strong eat the stupid and the weak. The superrace. And when you have a superrace you have an underrace. You can either destroy or use the underrace. But the Nazi books were too crude somehow. They said something, but they didn't say it right. And I knew I couldn't just learn from books, I would have to find some direct learning, mouth-to-mouth stuff, and do some experimenting. And here was a real-life Nazi, an officer. I had another angle too. My father was shot by the Nazis. According to what I've been told, he was caught by an SS patrol and the Germans didn't feel like being bothered by prisoners that day. Maybe they were short of man-power or maybe they didn't have time, I don't know. Anyway, they lined up their catch and machine-gunned them from the rear."

The fox was on his feet, talking almost eagerly.

"Yes?"

"So here we have Captain Schwartz. It was only afterward that I found out that he'd never been a fight-ing man. He was only a clerk captain, doing paper-work behind the lines in Korea. Rather a mousy man, but all I had. And he does walk around in a U.S. uniform with the proper insignia taken off and replaced by a red armband with a black swastika. He has a portrait of Hitler in his hall, and he plays records of German war songs. I went to see him and took a hand gun, a Magnum, a heavy gun. He wouldn't let me in, but I kicked the door out of his hands and let myself in. He went for the telephone, but I beat him to it and threw the telephone through his window. The window was closed. There was a bit of a mess. I wanted to show him that I was the stronger party, you see."

"Obviously."

The fox grinned. "Quite."

"Did you manhandle the captain?"

"No, that wasn't necessary. I sat down and made him sit down opposite me, and I asked him about his philosophy and about what he was trying to do. He didn't answer. Then I put my gun on the table. I told him I would leave the room and that he could shoot me in the back. I even cocked the gun for him as it has a heavy trigger. I also told him that if he didn't shoot me, I would come back into the room again to collect my gun. I didn't say I would kill him or harm him in any way."

"You're still with us, Mr. Fox."

"Sure. He did nothing. The experiment fell flat. He wouldn't even answer the simplest questions."

"You had some revenge, Mr. Fox. Did you tell him about what happened to your father?"

"No. I didn't have revenge in mind. But you're right in a way. It was good to see him fidget and listen to his teeth chatter. He left Cape Orca the next day. His son or somebody came and sold the house."

"Thank you," the commissaris said. "Very good of you to confide in me."

"Confide?" the fox asked. "I did more than that. You are working for the sheriff and I've just made a confession. According to local rules my behavior was criminal. You can have me arrested."

The commissaris put his mug down and nodded when Albert held up the bottle. "Just a drop, please. No, Mr. Fox. There's no call for your suggestion. If you hadn't known that I wouldn't pass on your information you wouldn't have given it to me. But I'd like to know a little more. Madelin told the sergeant and the sergeant told me that you took your disciples, or fellow students, to a slum in New York once and fought a local gang. One of your mates got a knife in his chest and died. You yourself knifed and killed a member of the opposing gang. Is that correct?"

"That's correct."

"Why did you go that far?"

The fox took a moment and grinned slyly. "Go all

the way to New York, you mean? But what else could I do? We're out in the sticks here, on the edge of the country. Canada starts across the hills and it's all sticks up there too, for hundreds of miles. We're backward country people. Some of us read books and so did I, but books are theory. I learned how to saw lumber from books, but I couldn't cut a board properly until an old sawyer came along and taught me. In New York we could be shown what our thoughts look like in action."

"Gérard died."

"He didn't have to go to New York. It was his decision. Mine was my own. I could have died too, but the knife flew his way."

"The suggestion was yours."

"Yes, oh yes."

"Here's my question. Do you have any feelings about your friend's death now?"

"No."

"No feelings at all?"

"If I have any I have good feelings. Gérard tried. So did we. We are still trying. There are more people out here trying. Jeremy. Madelin. Tom of Robert's Market. And a few others, out in the woods, or on the islands. Not too many fortunately, we don't want to crowd each other. I've been back to New York since the gang fight. I hung around and looked at people. I spent a lot of time, days on end, mostly in the subway stations. I must have seen a million people. And none of them seemed alive. They were all very busy, running in circles, like the chipmunk my mother had in a cage. I let him out and he ran into the woods, but he ran in circles. He was crazy. A raccoon got him, a slow old raccoon. The chipmunk was a good meal for the raccoon, his last meal, for my neighbor bashed his head in with the butt of his gun. The raccoon wasn't worth a shell."

The commissaris nodded solemnly. "Yes, Mr. Fox. Thank you very much. For the brandy and your good words." The commissaris got up. The sergeant followed suit.

"You don't want to know about who I killed on Cape Orca?"

"I know who you killed, Mr. Fox."

"Who?"

"An old man by the name of Rance. Paul Rance."

"Yes, I did."

"I think I can see why you killed him. And you got rid of Captain Schwartz."

"I didn't kill any of the others?"

"No, Mr. Fox."

The fox and Albert were operating the mill again when the station wagon drove away.

"We've been very clever, sergeant," the commissaris said and shifted the car into second gear. "But we are still nowhere. To know the suspect's identity is one thing, to lay charges, as the sheriff says, is another. I'll have to think of a plan, and it should be better than the plan that has occurred to me. I don't like that plan at all, but it may be our only possibility."

"You might tell me what you have in mind, sir."

The commissaris stared ahead.

"Sir?"

A thin hand patted the sergeant's knee. "Find your own answers, sergeant. You have the training and you have the intelligence."

"When will it be, sir?"

"Tomorrow I think. Shall I drop you off at the jailhouse?"

"Yes, sir. I think I'll be going for a drive."

"The snooping and searching are over, sergeant."

"Just a drive, sir. The landscape is beautiful, and we may be leaving soon."

The wagon followed a long row of full-grown cedars. A flock of startlingly blue birds wheeled toward them. The bay glittered on the horizon, and the sun was setting behind a snow-covered hill, bright orange in its last low rays.

"Yes," the commissaris said. "I wonder where Mr. Fox will go from here."

"Will he have to go much further, sir?"

"I would think so, sergeant, but he is on the right track. A dangerous track though. Let's hope he won't die too soon or lose his mind."

"Are you on that track, sir?"

The commissaris grinned. "Didn't you know, Rinus? And so are you. You've been on it for some time. You should recognize the view. The track leads uphill. Uphill tracks usually offer good views after a while."

19

The blue Dodge was parked at the side of the road leading into Cape Orca. De Gier sat behind the wheel. He was mumbling to himself in a reassuring manner. It was cold in the car and the BMF brandy had worn off. He had a slight headache and a slight thirst.

"It is not *really* complicated," he said in a sudden loud voice. "It just *seems* complicated. They have told the truth but not all of the truth. *He* knows by now, and I should know. Point is that I don't, not quite. No."

He stubbed out his cigarette, lit another, then cleaned the windshield with his free hand. He had a clear view of the bay and the white expanse helped to steady his thoughts. Surely the commissaris had worked out the solution. But only after he had seen the BMF gang and after he had spoken with Jeremy. De Gier was ready to disregard the BMF gang. The householders of Cape Orca's shore had been removed out of greed. Somebody wanted their land and their houses, but only to destroy them. The prime interest had been for the land, and still was. Counting in the island. Jeremy knew his island was wanted, for he had gone to a great deal of trouble to protect himself. The island was a fortress and its owner walked about armed, accompanied by fierce dogs and an all-seeing bird. Jeremy was friendly with the BMF gang, another point to consider. And the gang, although quite prepared to kill, would only kill if violence fitted into their experiments. The fox

had turned out to be a curious man, not a greedy man.
The behavior of a group is determined by the behavior
of its leader. Albert, Tom, and Madelin were individ-
ualists but also active members of the gang. De Gier
sighed. He was pleased that Madelin could be dis-
carded as a suspect for a number of reasons. What reasons? But he shook his head and forced his mind to return to its original subject. The murders. Madelin was
out.

So who was in? Not Jeremy—the man was on the defensive. But there might be a motive in his case. Jeremy fancied himself a hermit, and hermits don't like
neighbors who sail around the bay and operate chain
saws and make themselves obnoxious in a number of
irritating ways. But would Jeremy, the not unfriendly
hermit, kill his neighbors? No.

"Right," de Gier said pleasantly. Very good. Not
Jeremy. Besides, Jeremy was a victim himself. Janet
Wash, not Reggie, had steered the station wagon in
such an aggressive manner that Osiris, the hermit's com-
panion at that moment and his most ferocious dog, had
attacked the wagon and got himself killed in the process.

De Gier's fist banged the steering wheel. But why,
oh why, oh triple why, had Jeremy assisted the lady in
escaping from her car wreck and why hadn't he denounced her to the sheriff? If she tried to kill him once
she might try to kill him again, and Jeremy, although
an original man, a negative original man, didn't seem
to be interested in getting killed. And why had Janet
said that Reggie drove the car?

Just a minute, not everything at once. He had a
headache, he was tired, and he wasn't particularly
clever. Easy does it. Nice short connecting lines, lines
he could control. What, for instance, was the exact relationship between Janet Wash and Reggie. The man
was her servant, her retainer, but there might be more
to it. If Janet was the guilty party, not only in the attempted murder of Jeremy but also in the completed
murders of her neighbors, she wouldn't have committed

her crimes herself. She was, after all, a lady, an elderly lady, some sixty years old. Reggie has better qualifications. An ex-Vietnam warrior, highly trained. Had she paid him? No, surely not. Reggie might be a killer, but not a paid killer. A gentleman. So what then? Was he her lover?

De Gier had met several gigolos, and consulted his memory. Gigolos don't split wood—they wouldn't even grow an azalea garden. They might water the azaleas on a sunny afternoon, but that would be all. Five minutes with the watering can and back to the porch and a Tom Collins, to be sucked through a straw.

The lady and her knight in shining armor. More like it. And a touch of mother-and-son. Sick, undoubtedly, but not sexy sick. A platonic relationship with the knight/son protecting and serving the lady/mother. Taking the blame for the station wagon accident so that the bad men can't harm the exalted female deity.

De Gier's mouth sagged. Was he exaggerating? Maybe he was, so what the hell. He wasn't a psychiatrist, he was only a police detective. He could simplify as long as he didn't slip from the track.

But why had Jeremy protected the lady? Out of his originality? His contrariness? Gamesmanship?

The island's squirrel jumped through de Gier's headache and he winced. Jeremy had said something about the squirrel. It provided sport for the dogs—voluntarily. Jeremy had also claimed that he had gone beyond the squirrel, and Jeremy liked to speak in riddles, or answer in riddles. So said the fox.

His thoughts broke. For god's sake, a zoo, a whole zoo, and he was in the middle of it. A squirrel, dogs, a fox, seals, a raven, a raccoon.

Patiently he tried again. The raccoon was in this too. His own hat, minus tail. A raccoon, a small type of bear. A washbear, the Dutch name. Raccoons wash their food before they eat it. They had discussed raccoons, alias washbears, with Jeremy during their first visit to the island.

De Gier sat up and grinned stupidly. BEWARE THE

BEAR. BEWARE THE WASH BEAR. Jeremy, the hermit
known for exceptional behavior, carting a sign about,
and that's what the sign said. Beware the bear, beware
the wash, beware Janet Wash.

This discovery blocked all further thinking for a
while, and he stared at the bay and the island. But once
again he tried. So Jeremy *had* denounced the lady of
the mansion to the authorities, in his own spectacular
manner. By carrying a sign. No wonder the commissaris had been in such a good mood afterward, smiling
and chatting and burbling in spite of his pain, for he
was limping badly these days, his rheumatism aggra-
vated by the cold.

So what puzzles were left? Why would Reggie kill on
behalf of his employer? All right, some nuttiness there.
Why would Jeremy help his would-be killer out of her
car?

Love, according to the commissaris, causes most violence. De Gier agreed. Tested police knowledge. Lovers
and loved ones are first-class suspects. Now Janet
wanted the island—he was getting ahead of himself
again, but he could sort the next puzzle a little later.
Why would Janet want all that *land?* There could be
no other motivation—she didn't want her neighbors'
homes because she had them destroyed. Back to Jeremy
now.

Jeremy loves Janet. No, past tense: Jeremy loved
Janet, and the other way around too. They were of
the same age and Janet's husband had been a cripple
in a wheelchair. She might have taken a lover. She was
still a beautiful woman at sixty so she would have been
stunning at forty. Jeremy had been on his island for
twenty years. Very good, an illicit affair, a small boat
rowed between island and shore. Charming, really. He
looked at the bay, an ideal spot for a love affair. And
when the general died, his widow proposed to Jeremy
or expected to be proposed to, but nothing doing. Jeremy preferred to be a hermit.

So now Janet had a double motive; she wanted revenge and she wanted the island. She told Reggie to

kill Jeremy and Jeremy changed his island into a fortress. Perhaps Jeremy enjoyed the situation, like the squirrel enjoys being chased by the dogs. And if that were true the BEWARE THE BEAR sign had been to warn the commissaris and himself, the sergeant. Jeremy didn't want innocents to suffer. Good old Jeremy.

De Gier sighed and scratched around in his curls. The headache was still getting worse, so was his thirst. Very well, on with it. The final puzzle: Why did Janet want all that property? Why did she buy it through the realtor Astrinsky, Boston Better Holdings, and finally Bahama Better Holdings? Where did Mr. Symons fit in?

He had come to a full stop for lack of data. Even computers can't conclude if they haven't been fed properly. But the commissaris had managed to extricate himself from the case's traps and claimed to be ready for a finale. So where had he, Detective Sergeant Rinus de Gier of Amsterdam's homicide squad, gone wrong?

Were there any other open leads?

His hand moved to the car key when he finally remembered.

Jeremy had *not* told them for sure who he had bought his island from. He had mentioned a name, Reynolds. But he hadn't proved his statement. The name would be on the island's deed and the deed was supposed to be in one of Jeremy's cartons and Jeremy wouldn't look through his cartons. But there would be a copy of the deed in the town clerk's office.

De Gier started the car. He found the Jameson town office, a one-story brick building next to the jailhouse. The clerk turned out to be helpful and talkative.

"Jeremy's Island?" . . . "Certainly" . . . "Had an inquiry about the island this morning" . . . "Old gentleman came in, with an accent, same as yours" . . . "Dutch accent, is it?" The clerk had Dutch ancestors. He had been to Holland. Lovely country. De Gier became frantic and knew he couldn't show his state of mind. He thought about a variety of subjects while the clerk prattled on. The clerk came to the end of his journey through the Netherlands and began to discuss the shortcomings of his stove. "Might as well paint it red, look at it now, bright red but still no heat. If I painted it it would save a lot of firewood, eh? Hahahaha."

"Hahahaha," de Gier said.

"Now what was it you wanted?"

"The name of the man who owned Jeremy's Island before Jeremy bought it."

"That's right," the clerk said. "Man by the name of Symons. Symons the gambler we used to call him. Brother of Janet Wash. Janet was called Symons before she married the general."

"Ah," de Gier said.

"You know Janet Wash?"

"Yes."

"Nice lady. But not her brother James. He got half the estate, part of the cape, and the island, and he sold it all and split. Left his wife and his son, James the Third. He's bad too. James the First was fine, a Yankee skipper, made his fortune in the China trade in the time of the big clippers."

"What happened to James the Second?" de Gier asked.

The clerk looked sad. "Got himself killed I hear, in the bad country, the country where they do the gambling."

"And what happened to James the Third?"

The clerk held up a finger. "Trouble here. All sorts of trouble, so he left town." He held up a second finger. "Went to Bangor, more trouble." Third finger. "To Portland, same again." Fourth finger. "To Boston, more of the same but he's holding out I hear. Buddy of mine ran into him in the street. Had a drink with him. Young James does a lot of drinking."

"I see," de Gier said. "Thank you, you've been very helpful."

*   *   *

The Dodge took him back to Cape Orca. He was whistling. "Straight, No Chaser." When he had whistled enough, he sang. "Cannon*ball*."

So he had his answers, the same answers as the commissaris had found. The picture was complete, more or less. He still wanted to know why Jeremy had helped Janet out of her car, although he could surmise an answer. Jeremy had said that he had gone beyond the behavior of the squirrel. The squirrel, when cornered, would try to bite the dogs, but the squirrel was an animal, with a limited program imprinted into its small brain. Jeremy considered himself to be an advanced human. And he very likely was too. Jeremy might be prepared to fight Reggie and therefore carried arms, but he wouldn't fight a lady who, once upon a time, had been his mistress. If she wanted to try to kill him, fine, but he wouldn't be violent in return. The fox had described the hermit as a sage. Perhaps he was. And the commissaris had got on very well with Jeremy. The commissaris was a sage too, full of tricks, but tricks of an elevated and superb order. Such as turning the other cheek, *without losing out*. That was the superb part of the trick: the commissaris never lost out, not so far anyway, and de Gier had spent many years watching his chief move about, sneak about. "But there is sneaking," de Gier said aloud, "and *sneaking*."

And Symons, young Symons the Third had been able to get out of trouble, time and again, because his Aunt Janet helped him. Like now, for she had made him the manager of her holding companies, and paid him a wage.

There was still Astrinsky, of course, but de Gier refused to think about Astrinsky. The realtor would fit in later. Right now he had a headache and he had thought enough. The car picked up speed as his foot came down. One last look at Cape Orca and he would drive back to the jailhouse and enjoy supper and have an early night. The commissaris would be coming in the morning and they would have a grand counsel. A sign flashed past, a square yellow sign on a white stick. There was one word on the sign: HILL.

"Too fast," de Gier said and touched the brake gently. The car was skidding. He pressed the brake hard and the car turned around, then around again. De Gier sang. The theme of "Straight, No Chaser." He hummed it over and over as the car made several full turns. He saw the tree coming and he felt the car turn over. For a few seconds the Dodge rode on the edge of its roof, then fell on its side and rested against the tree. De Gier stopped humming. He turned the key and the engine cut off. It was quiet on the road. A bird screamed further down in a ravine. He could hear a brook gurgle under the ice.

"Shit!" de Gier said. He used the English word. It seemed more appropriate than its Dutch translation. He was upside-down, held by the safety belt. He began to move about carefully and managed to unlock the belt. The driver's door was closed, probably forever, but the passenger door still worked.

He walked down the rest of the hill until he saw a light shimmering through the snow-covered evergreens. He found a path leading to a cabin. He knocked on the door.

"Come in."

"Ah, it's you," Reggie said. "Out for a walk?"

"I just busted the sheriff's department's brand-new Dodge," de Gier said.

"You did?"

"I did."

"Well, come in. An open door is the last thing we want at this time of the year. You aren't worried about the car, are you? That car is insured. Who cares about a police car anyway? To them a car is just wheels. If the wheels go they get other wheels. They waste the taxpayer's money, we pay them to waste it, and everybody is happy. Sit down. Drink?"

"Yes," de Gier said. He knew he should have refused. The fox's brandy was still in his blood. He shouldn't have driven the Dodge. He thought of the excuses. The commissaris had played along with the fox, accepted the suspect's brandy to make him talk. De Gier had played along with the commissaris, but he also liked to drink. He could have left the brandy in the enamel mug. He could have pretended to drink, taken little sips, spat some back. But he had drunk it all. Technically he had caused a total loss while under the influence, although he would never be charged. Technically the insurance company wouldn't have to pay, but it would.

Reggie poured bourbon, a big glass. "On the rocks?"

"Please."

"What are you driving around the cape for? It's dark."

"Lost my way. I was trying to get out."

Reggie grinned. He looked the perfect country gentleman, in his tweed jacket and sturdy trousers. The cabin was rough but comfortable. The fire in the big fieldstone fireplace crackled. The cabin's paneling was old, showing the dull shine of pine that has matured for a hundred years, a deep orange, almost reddish, shine. There were good thick rugs on the floor, and the low bed in the rear of the cabin was covered with sheepskins. The only decorations, hanging from hooks on the low, handhewn tamarack beams, were tools and weapons. A rifle, a shotgun, a bow and arrows, a crossbow, several axes with delicately curved handles, a machete in a gray green canvas sheath, a blowpipe.

De Gier pointed at the blowpipe. "A trophy from the jungle?"

"Sure. The mountain people use them in Vietnam. They tried to teach me, but the poison worried me. I did better with the bow and arrows. The crossbow is American. I've used it on the woodchucks a few times, but it can't beat my squirrel rifle. Come here. I'll show you my real trophies."

De Gier got up and looked out a side window. The view was a small yard with a high fence around it. Reggie picked up a flashlight and pressed it against the glass. "See?"

De Gier saw a tableau made out of barn boards, framed neatly by weathered two-by-fours. The tableau grinned at him out of many small dark eyes. Small skulls, white in the light of the torch.

"Count them."

Rows of ten, five down. Five full rows and the sixth row had only four skulls.

"Fifty-four of the little bastards, and room for another forty-six. When I fill it up I'll start a new one."

De Gier felt Reggie breathing next to him. Reggie's breath was short and sharp, the breath of a man in anger, or in heat.

"Took me a few years to catch fifty-four of them, but I'm getting clever at it now. Woodchucks are the worst threat on the estate. They tunnel and dig, interfere with the roots, and eat the shoots. I had to start the azalea gardens twice over. You hear that? *Twice.* They ate all the little plants. They would sit up and whistle at me. I swear they even waved their filthy little paws. I always shoot them in the chest. Doesn't do to damage the skull. I need the skulls. But I don't have too much time, and they get busy when I'm busy. In the spring when the garden needs my time. But I get them all the same. Now they rest. They're in their holes, fast asleep. If I know where the holes are I can dynamite them out, but I don't want to do that. I need their skulls. Dynamite blows them to bits, and the bits are deep down in the earth. Another drink?"

"Sure," de Gier said. "Please."

Reggie poured the drink and pulled out the drawer of a bureau next to his bed. "Here, this is the map. See?"

He was whispering hoarsely. His finger pointed at certain areas. The map showed Cape Orca and Jeremy's Island. It had been drawn by hand, very carefully, and colored in several shades of green and brown. Its different hieroglyphics indicated trees and plants and grass. Reggie was explaining, still in the same hoarse whisper, "This isn't a garden, this is an *estate.* Not as big as the estate the Rockefellers donated to Maine further down the coast, but more beautiful. More love has gone into it, more work. *My* love. Here are the azalea gardens. I know every plant. There are the cedar trees, and here is the white pine reserve. I've cleaned the reserve myself, I do it every year. I rake and rake, and when I don't want to disturb the pine needles I go down on my hands and knees and I crawl around with a plastic pail and I fill the pail with twigs. The reserve needs a golden carpet and the needles are gold when the sun touches them. And it needs clean moss so that the gold shows up better. I rake the moss with a bamboo comb and sometimes with my fingers. The white pine reserve covers an acre. It takes me weeks to go through it. A few weeks, every spring. The others won't do it. They don't care, they're clumsy. Leroux is good, but only when he can mow the lawn and sit on a tractor. Some of the local girls are good at picking the dead leaves off the azaleas. But they don't see details. And they don't care about the woodchucks destroying their work. They think the woodchucks are cute. *Cute.* The bloody little bastards. They are bastards, you hear? With their big gnawing teeth and their sharp beady eyes. They never miss a shoot or a bud. There are others. The geese eat the rhododendron flowers, pick them off. They rob an eight-foot bush in a few minutes. They'll jump for the high buds, but I shot the geese a long time ago, every single one of them. The geese are big and clumsy. The woodchucks are quick, and their colors blend with the landscape. Another forty-six and then another hundred. I'll kill them all."

The hoarse whisper had become a hiss. "You hear me?"

"Yes," de Gier said.

Reggie's voice became calmer, but his breathing was still disturbed. He had switched off the torch and was warming his back at the fire. "Sit down, be my guest. Yes, the woodchucks. I can't stand them. Janet hates them too. Tell me, where did your accident happen?"

"Not too far from here."

"Did you go off the road?"

"No, a tree stopped me."

"Didn't damage the tree, did you?" The voice dropped down again. Reggie's eyes were bloodshot and vicious. His hands moved nervously, and his lips trembled. De Gier was working out a defense. He didn't feel too sure that he could use strategy. He had drunk too much to react quickly. He would have to be alert to determine the point where Reggie would become violent. De Gier moved under a beam that held an ax resting on two pegs. He should be able to swing the back of the ax against the man's temple, but the cabin was small and cramped. If he missed, Reggie would run him down.

"Hello? You there, Reggie?"

Reggie breathed in deeply and seemed to make an effort to control himself. He walked to the door. "Evening, Madelin. A sociable evening indeed. Come in. Have you visited Janet? She said she was having an early night tonight."

"No, Reggie, I've come for the sergeant. I saw his car. Are you all right, sergeant?"

"Yes, I am fine. The car isn't."

"No. I've just had a look at it. I'm glad you aren't hurt. The sheriff has been trying to raise you on the radio. I heard him on my CB. But you didn't answer."

De Gier put his glass down. "Thank you, Reggie, but I'll have to go now."

"You fool," Madelin said. "That was the last place in the world you should have gone to. Did you drink a lot?"

"Yes."

"Was he drinking with you?"

"Yes."

"He always goes bananas when he drinks unless Janet is around. Did he show you his skulls?"

"Yes."

"Did you notice anything?"

"Yes, he began to speak in a funny whispering way and his breathing became heavy and torturous."

"I know. He did that once when I was in his cabin, but Albert and Tom were with me and he doesn't see us as a threat. He's psychotic. Maybe all professional soldiers are, but Reggie is *very* psychotic. You know what he specialized in when he was in Vietnam?"

They were in Madelin's car, almost out of the estate. De Gier was glad he didn't have to watch the road. It was snowing heavily and the wind drove the snowflakes into the windscreen. The car was going dead slow. When it skidded, just as they reached the main road, Madelin let go of the wheel. "That's what you should have done, sergeant. But you were going fast I suppose. If you let go of the wheel the car will steady itself again. Did you slam on the brakes?"

"Yes."

"It's hard not to slam the brakes on when you're in a skid, but when you do the car becomes a sleigh and you lose all control."

"Yes," de Gier said. "I am an idiot. What did Reggie do in Vietnam?"

"He told me once, at a cocktail party at Janet's place. He and his buddies, four of them in all, sought out Vietcong camps. They would arm themselves with knives, a small mortar, and light machine guns. Reggie would kill the guard. It was very important to kill the guard. If he couldn't do it they would go back into the jungle again and call the whole thing off. But if Reggie could get his knife into the guard the four men would spread out and fire their machine guns, at a height of about a foot, horizontally. They would strafe and spray until they were out of ammunition. The Vietcong slept a foot off the ground. Next they would lob mortar shells into the camp. And then they would run off and meet in some prearranged place. His buddies got killed and Reggie trained new buddies and went on. He survived and then the war was over. Now it's woodchucks."

"And retired old people on the Cape Orca shore."

"Indeed, sergeant."

Madelin laughed. "No. You had to find out. But you stumbled into it, didn't you? You *crashed* into it."

"I did."

"You don't have some clever excuse? Why don't you tell me that you knew all along and that your accident tonight was a clever ruse."

"No, I was just blundering along."

She stopped the car. "I love you, sergeant. You're forty-one years old, you need half glasses to read small print, and you're not intelligent. Kiss me."

She waited for him to make the move. He did. He was a little slow. His neck hurt.

"Hmmmm," Madelin said. "That was good. Do it again."

"No."

"Please."

"No."

"I want to feel your teeth."

He sat back. "My teeth?"

"Yes," Madelin said. "You have nice teeth, but they do protrude a little. That's why I was so worried when I saw the wreck of the Dodge and the lights of Reggie's cabin."

"For God's sake," de Gier said and felt his teeth. "You don't mean that I look like a woodchuck, do you? I've never seen a woodchuck. Some sort of rodent?"

She let herself fall over sideways, twisted, and looked up from his lap. "Yes. Some sort of rodent. Big and handsome. With wide shoulders and curly brown hair and a big beautiful mustache. Not so clever but very genuine. I love you, sergeant."

20

"I am sorry," the sheriff said, "but I'll have to take you out for breakfast. The old man in jail doesn't feel well, and I'm low on energy myself. We really have a need for a matron. I wish I had the courage to tell that to the selectmen. Do you mind going out for breakfast?"

De Gier was facing the mirror and had just raised his upper lip. "A rodent!" he muttered. "The girl is quite mad. My teeth aren't *that* long. And they don't protrude *that* much!"

"Pardon?" the sheriff asked, settling himself a little more comfortably on the sergeant's bed.

"Nothing, just muttering."

The sheriff watched the sergeant manipulate his can of shaving cream. "You aren't doing that right, you know. Don't you have ready-made foam in Europe?"

"We do," de Gier said, "but I've never used it."

The sheriff sat up. "Don't just take a quarter of an inch. Go on, let it whoosh out. Be a devil! You're in America now, plaster it all over your face. Go on!"

The sergeant shaved and the sheriff watched as he continued, "Do you know why I'm low on energy? No? I'll tell you. I'm weak because I used my brain all night, a most unusual activity these days. I haven't used my brain since I left the university."

De Gier wiped his face clean and turned around. "University?"

"Sure. I have lots of qualifications. I'm the most overqualified official this county has ever hired. I could be a real cop in a real city, but I haven't learned to be ambitious yet. The splendor of the big time frightens me. Or maybe the big assholes taking care of big crime haven't impressed me. They don't take care of crime anyway, they just find ways of living with it, or off it. Anyway, I thought last night. With some success, I think. I know it all now, or most of it. What I don't know doesn't matter. You've figured it out too, haven't you?"

De Gier was splashing on the after shave. "No. I can't fit in Astrinsky. Madelin goes free, you agree to that point?"

The sheriff smiled, then giggled. "Of course, can't haul in my colleague's girl friend, can I? You spent some time with her last night again?"

"Not too much. She gave me a lift back here. I am very sorry about the Dodge, Jim."

"That's okay. The tow truck should be on its way to collect the wreck now. I didn't want to bother you last night. You looked a little tired and beat-up. Did the accident have anything to do with the investigation?"

"No, just with my bad driving."

The sheriff shrugged. "The Dodge was a good car, but that model is too small for police work out here. I should be able to screw a better replacement out of the authorities. Don't give it another thought, sergeant. We need good wheels. The hell with their penny-pinching. So what did you turn up last night?"

"Same as what you turned up. You spoke to Leroux, didn't you?"

"I sure did. We can discuss it all a little later. Your chief should be here any minute now. Why don't we go down?"

De Gier was adjusting his silk scarf. He got it right, but then it slipped down too far. He clicked his tongue irritably and started all over again. The sheriff watched him patiently.

"Are you done now? It looks very elegant like that."

The commissaris' station wagon turned into the yard as the sheriff and de Gier came out of the jailhouse.

"Morning," the commissaris said. "How good of you to ask me again. I forgot to tell Suzanne and she was boiling porridge, but I got away. Same sort of porridge my mother used to make."

"You didn't care for your mother's porridge, sir?"

"Didn't care?" the commissaris asked in a high voice. "Yagh! Aren't we going in, sheriff?"

"No, sir. I thought I'd take the two of you out to Beth's. She knows we're coming. I telephoned."

The commissaris stopped frowning. "Beth's! Good!" He rubbed his mittens together. "Ha!"

Beth served and the three men ate. There were home-fried potatoes and sausages and three eggs each.

"How do you like the eggs?" Beth asked. "Don't they taste funny?"

"Taste good," the sheriff said. "Fine," de Gier said. "Excellent," the commissaris said. "Why, Beth?"

Beth made a face. "Duck eggs. I bought them from Bert. He came around hawking them. Robert's Market has been out of eggs ever since the truck turned over, so Bert can ask a price. I told him he was overcharging, and I asked him whether he had anything to do with the egg truck going off the road. He didn't like that. He slammed the door when he left. Look."

The sheriff glanced at the door. The glass in it was cracked.

"Have it repaired, Beth. Then order more eggs and don't pay. If Bert gets disturbed tell him to talk to me. Bert hasn't got a sense of humor yet. Maybe you and I can teach him a little."

Beth laughed, poured more coffee, and walked back to her stove.

"Now," the sheriff said, wiping his mouth, "I spoke to Leroux yesterday. Or maybe I should say that I listened to him. He didn't sing like a canary, but he certainly chirped like a chickadee. He didn't have much choice of course. I was holding the ax and his head was on the block. I explained that to him and he agreed in the end. And now he has a job for the rest of the winter so he doesn't lose out."

"What did you learn, sheriff?"

"Most everything I wanted to learn. Leroux is a proper local. He knows all the concerned parties and he knows how they tie in together. He isn't a stupid man by any means. He doesn't only feel the undercurrents, he can describe what they've been doing and how they're working at this particular moment. He did some nice evasive footwork when it came to pointing the finger, but he did intimate who could perhaps have had something to do with what. And he won't testify, if he does he'll have to leave the county—maybe even the state."

"You have conclusions?" de Gier asked.

"Yes. They're the right conclusions too."

"Can we hear them, Jim?"

"My privilege, gentlemen."

The sheriff spoke for quite a while, and his guests nodded and said the right words at the right moments.

"So there you are," the sheriff said at the end. "All the facts. All the bits and pieces fit and the picture shows a corpse in every square. It's a horrible picture and I should have completed it earlier, but I wasn't experienced enough. It's the first time I have created and used an informer. The technique is new to me. Leroux gave me the facts, but the connections and deductions are mine. How does it sound to you, sir? Does it tally with what you've been thinking?"

"Beautifully," the commissaris said. "What about you, sergeant?"

"Yes, sir. I worked it out after I left you yesterday afternoon. I saw the town clerk, as you did, and found that young Symons is related to Janet Wash. I would agree with the sheriff that our drunken Bostonian friend probably knows nothing about the murders. He hasn't been anywhere near Jameson for the last five years."

The sheriff's uniform creaked as he stretched. "And we also know why young Symons' father, Symons the Second, couldn't sell to his sister Janet. She would have nothing to do with him anymore. If he telephoned her she banged the phone down, and when he wrote she returned the letters unopened. Black sheep, bah bah! But that was silly of her. He was only trying to sell her his share of the Cape Orca land, and she could have bought the land with the general's money. And a lot of people would still be alive today. However, Symons the Second lost patience and sold the land to an agency, and the agency cut it into parcels and sold the parcels to whoever wanted them. Meanwhile Janet stayed in her huff. Perhaps she didn't care so much at that stage. It was only when houses were built and people began to mill about that she realized what she had lost."

"And Astrinsky?" the commissaris asked.

The sheriff smiled coldly. "That's a different kettle of fish altogether, sir. A kettle I'd like to keep my hands out of. Land deals are often linked with corruption. There are persistent rumors in the state that some high official tipped off Astrinsky about a land deal, the sale of a large tract of virgin forest. Astrinsky bought the land cheap from the state and sold at some huge profit to a commercial party, a paper mill or a sawmill. Some of the profit found its way back to the official. All parties were supposed to be happy. But other officials, who got nothing, got wise and threatened to raise a stink. And they were brought to heel by a snort from very high up. General Wash was a super big shot, with friends and relations in the government. I would say that Astrinsky ran to the general and was saved in the nick of time. Janet knew what her husband had done for Astrinsky; one hand washes the other. But I'm not getting into any of that, sir. I'm only a minisheriff in a minicounty in a corner of nowhere. As I explained to the sergeant this morning, I am not ambitious, and not suicidal either."

The commissaris nodded. "I see. So Astrinsky covered up for Janet and probably made no profit. He is a suspect, but not a prime subject. I've met and studied the man twice, and I don't believe that he would have followed Davidson into the woods and stolen his matches, or that he would have ripped the plastic foam out of Mary Brewer's boat and replaced the bulkheads, or that he would have sneaked up on his friend and fellow Crustacean Opdijk and pushed him over the cliff. Leroux said Astrinsky was not a sporty type at all. Did Astrinsky ever do any boating?"

"No, sir. He headed the prize committee whenever there was a race, and he delivered the speech, but he was never seen on the water."

The commissaris waved his coffee spoon. "Away with him then. Now it's the sergeant's turn, I think. De Gier, what happened after you left the town clerk's office?"

"I drove back to the cape, sir. I shouldn't have because the snow was getting worse, but I wanted to be on the actual territory where the crimes had taken place while I thought of my possible conclusions. All I managed to do was wreck the sheriff's Dodge and stumble into Reggie's cabin. Reggie offered drinks and had too many himself. The alcohol released whatever is torturing him and his behavior became notably bizarre. He wasn't just drunk."

The commissaris' hands kneaded his thighs while he listened to the rest of the tale. "I see. So Madelin saved you in a way. You're sure that he would have become violent?"

"Yes, sir. I was just another woodchuck to him."

"So the man isn't right in the head. No murderer is, of course. Janet must be very odd too to go to such immense trouble to obtain some land. The taboo on killing is the heaviest rule our systems of justice apply, and she broke the taboo so easily. But only because her own insanity linked up with Reggie's. A little like Hitler meeting Himmler. Hitler painted post cards and Himmler raised chickens, I believe. Together they caused the holocaust. Janet and Reggie never even gave their victims a chance. They were picked off one by one, at the lady's convenience." He looked at the sheriff. "Perhaps the sergeant was right when he told me in Boston that your scene, your peacetime scene that is, is somewhat rougher than what we are used to."

"Scene," the sheriff said. "Yes, sir, it's rough. But it

goes with the mood of the country. We haven't been civilized very long and we still acknowledge every man's right to carry arms. And we have strict ideas about property, exaggerated ideas perhaps, so they can be perverted easily. It's lawful here to shoot a burglar through the head."

The commissaris felt his impeccably shaved chin. "Yes, another type of society altogether perhaps. I saw a license plate on a car yesterday, not from this state I think. It had a slogan printed into the metal: LIVE FREE OR DIE. I was most impressed. I hope you don't think I was criticizing. We've gone too soft on our side of the ocean. The big wars started in Europe and when we choked on our viciousness we had to yell for help, which you provided, thank heaven. Still, I would hate to see the people of Amsterdam wear six guns on their belts."

"*Our* license plates just say VACATIONLAND, sir." The sheriff had sharpened a match and was poking it around between his strong teeth. He took the match out of his mouth and studied it. "We are still where we were, gentlemen. I don't see that there's anything we can do now. We may have managed to reconstruct the various events, but there's no proof. There are no witnesses. Jeremy saw Janet drive her car at him, but he'll never say so in court—he won't even say so to us. If I remember my lessons correctly we should now start to work on our remaining suspects—interrogate them, manipulate them, and so forth. Given time they may break down and not only confess but produce sufficient circumstantial evidence so that we won't look foolish in court. This state has some very smart lawyers. At this point the D.A. wouldn't even bother to listen to me."

"We could get at Reggie," de Gier said.

"We could, and he would tell us about his woodchucks and azaleas and white pine reserve while he basks in Janet's motherly warmth. We might try to keep Janet away from him and pour him full of bourbon, but I'm not sure whether the D.A. would like that. And I wouldn't even try Janet. She'd wave the general's medals at me and telephone Washington. We're quite stuck, gentlemen. We know what happened and that's *it*."

"Perhaps not."

"You have an idea, sir?"

"Yes," the commissaris said. "I made an appointment with Janet, but I'll cancel it if you don't approve. The appointment is for this afternoon, for tea and cookies, just her and me."

"You think she will tell the truth, sir?"

"If suitably provoked, yes. I plan to approach her from a different angle. I've no authority here so I can be, eh, nasty."

The sheriff carried his match to Beth's stove and opened one of its many lids. He dropped the match onto the glowing coals and watched it flare and crumble. The lid fell back with a clang.

"The interview will have to be witnessed somehow, sir. Can't you take the sergeant?"

"No, because she'll have to talk freely. I was thinking that we could use some mechanical means perhaps."

"Radio," the sheriff said. "I don't have a bugging device, but the state cops do. Their nearest barracks are too far to drive to and be back on time, but there's an airstrip. I think I'll have the pleasure of Madelin's company this time, if the sergeant doesn't mind of course."

The sheriff grinned at the sergeant and the commissaris smiled paternally. De Gier didn't notice; he was studying the tabletop.

"And how will this equipment work, sheriff?"

"It'll be a small microphone, sir, hidden under the lapel of your jacket. The transmitter is very small too. It won't make a bulge. I'll receive you via my cruiser's radio and I have another radio for the sergeant. He could carry it about with him. The state cops will have to provide me with a tape recorder too."

"Splendid. Yes. Now if you could park your cruiser somewhere near the mansion and the sergeant could make himself inconspicuous on the grounds nearby I would feel reasonably safe, I imagine."

The sergeant had gotten up. "I don't like the plan at all. Reggie will be loose and he is crazy. If he feels that you are antagonizing Janet . . ."

"A small risk, Rinus," the commissaris said. "I've taken small risks before. So have you."

The sheriff cleared his throat. "Perhaps the sergeant is right. You're not exactly a fighting man, if you'll excuse me being frank."

"I may have other skills, sheriff. And than you and Beth for a very good breakfast. You did me a true favor. You saved me from Suzanne's porridge."

21

Janet Wash dropped her long graceful hands to her lap and sat up a little straighter. Her tongue found a small morsel of chocolate-covered cookie that hadn't quite crunched yet. She pushed it between her teeth, chewed, and swallowed. Her eyelashes fluttered down and swept up.

"No," she said. "I don't believe it. You'll have to tell me again, my little man. Are you trying to *blackmail* me?"

The commissaris stirred his tea. He didn't want to look at his hostess. Her pose and general acting were quite good, of course, but any performance that contains too many repetitions tends to become monotonous. His eyes wandered about and studied his surroundings. The porch was vast, equaling the combined floor space of the entire first story of Suzanne's house. Its furniture was all cane, old and gracious. There were simple chairs and elaborate couches, blossoming out into great ovals and side wings, thickly padded and upholstered. in linen. The linen was richly embroidered, by Chinese artists probably, in the days that James D. Symons' tea clippers waited for their cargoes in the harbors of Canton and Hong Kong. The porch was well heated by tall woodstoves. He counted three, each with its own supply of logs, split neatly, stacked meticulously. Reggie's handiwork no doubt. Whatever Reggie did he did well.

"So," the icy delicate voice said. "Let's go through all this again. You claim that you know that I murdered all these people, or had them murdered. Now what were their names again? I forget so easily when I am not interested. Jones, you said? And Davidson? And that ridiculous Brewer woman who tried so hard to be the arty, sporty type? And good old Pete Opdijk? I do remember *his* name. He always tried to stay for dinner when he was only invited for a drink. And such a crushing bore. Now, that's what you said, wasn't it? I did murder all these people?"

"That's right, madam."

"Well, *really*. Wasn't it clever of you to have found out. And wasn't it clever of you not to want to tell anybody but me. Now why was that again?"

The commissaris folded his hands on the silver handle of his cane and rested his chin on top of them.

"Ah yes. How superbly intelligent! You went all the way to Boston to talk to my nephew, young Jimmy. And Jimmy Symons manages my holding companies. Well, that much is true. I do own the family's land again. But I bought the land quite legally you know."

The commissaris shook his head patiently.

"Didn't I buy it?"

"At give-away prices, madam."

She snorted. "What nonsense. You said that before. You suggested that I contrived and schemed and managed to use Michael Astrinsky so that he would buy me the vacated land, and the miserable hovels on the land, for next to nothing."

"That's correct, madam."

"More tea?"

"Oh yes, please."

"More tea you will have. I'll pour it into your cup, not into your face as you deserve. We must remember our manners. Here you are."

Janet poured and the commissaris sipped.

"A most delicate taste," he said pleasantly. "Not at all like Suzanne's tea."

She clapped her hands. "Taste? You dare to use that word? My God! And you have the bad taste to tell me that I am a criminal but that you'll forget that fact if I pay a hundred thousand for Suzanne's bourgeois monstrosity!"

"That would be the proper market value of Suzanne's very comfortable home, madam. If you want her land you should pay the price. And I promise you that once I have the check, Suzanne and the sergeant and I will leave and that I will not pass my information to the sheriff. The sheriff is an ambitious young man, but he hasn't made a name for himself yet. With my, and the sergeant's, help he can take you to court and obtain your conviction. It will be a good start for his career."

Janet tucked her legs under her long skirt. She lit a cigarette and blew smoke into the split leaves of a large potted palm. "What garbage. I will call your bluff. Astrinsky, my little slave, ever faithful because he remembers before I remind him, will renew his offer of thirty thousand and you will be glad to take it. What else can you do? There are no other buyers."

The commissaris bowed his small head. "Very well, madam. You leave me no option. I can prove what Reggie did to Mary Brewer's boat. He was seen by several local young men and I was lucky enough to find them. I can also produce a witness who saw what Reggie did to Mr. Davidson. Reggie, when questioned properly, will implicate you. You will lose your house, all your land, and your liberty. But you shouldn't blame me. I offered a choice."

Janet laughed. A harsh, not altogether artificial tinkle of high notes. "Bluff, my dear sir. But you do not know who and what I am. I can trace my ancestors for many generations and I have friends in high places, and I am a Yankee. Yankees have dealt with the Dutch before, here and in the Far East where my forefathers made their fortune. Whenever we compete with the Dutch we win, because we call their bluff and refuse to make a deal. It was we who coined such expressions as "double Dutch," "to go Dutch," and "a Dutch treat.""

"Really?" the commissaris asked politely.

* * *

The sheriff grinned. He started the cruiser and reversed a few feet to get the sun out of his eyes. He switched the engine off. The cruiser was parked in the dip of a path leading to the Wash mansion. It was out of sight of the house, but close enough. No more than two thousand feet from the front porch. The sheriff settled back and adjusted the volume of his radio.

"So?" Janet asked. "You've heard all I have to say. Isn't it time you took yourself away?"

"You also tried to kill Jeremy," the commissaris said. "And this time you made the effort yourself. Wasn't Reggie available that day?"

De Gier was also in the sun, but he couldn't move out of its glaring light. The sergeant was perched on a rock behind the mansion's back porch. He had to be careful to stay out of Janet's sight—and out of Reggie's sight. He hadn't seen Reggie when he'd left the sheriff's cruiser and made his way through the cedar bushes along the shore. He had heard Reggie. The man was splitting wood somewhere close by. He couldn't hear him now.

"Reggie," Janet said. "Certainly he was available."

"Didn't he try, Mrs. Wash?"

Janet sat up a little straighter. "Yes, once. He made it to the island but was stopped by the dogs. Jeremy let him go. Our hermit can be a perfect idiot at times. He hasn't been learned from his animals. Animals kill what they catch."

"I see. But why did you say that Reggie was driving your car when the accident happened? You were at the wheel, weren't you? Suzanne saw you."

"Suzanne!" Janet waved the name away as if it were an insect. "I said Reggie was at the wheel because Reggie should have been at the wheel. But Reggie still thinks of excuses whenever I mention Jeremy. I believe Reggie likes the man." She laughed shortly. "But

Reggie will listen to me. I am not giving in. Not to you either. You know that now, don't you?"

The commissaris muttered his agreement. "Indeed. How did you manage to find such a good man, Mrs. Wash?"

Janet giggled. "Through a magazine. One of the day laborers once left a magazine and I looked through it. It was called *The Mercenary,* and it was filled with stories about tough men and what they had done in the wars and what they were doing now in private armies, serving sheiks and princes in out-of-the-way places. There were some advertisements too, and one of them caught my attention. It went something like this: *Vietnam veteran. Light weapons and unarmed combat. Guerrilla operations specialist. Officer rank. Interested in country work of any description. Serious offers only. Details. Reggie.* And a telephone number. I telephoned, we had a nice chat, and he flew in the next day. He has never left."

The sheriff was still listening. De Gier wasn't. He had moved to the edge of his rock when he heard the snow crackle and he was crouching down near his radio, although there was little point in being furtive. Reggie was only a few yards away, on the next rock.

"Hello," Reggie said.

"Hello."

"Listening to the radio, are you? Who is she talking to? To your friend the commissioner?"

"She is."

"She is talking a lot, isn't she? Your friend is very clever. But you are not. You are in my way, sergeant."

De Gier got up and slipped out of his heavy coat. "Can I choose my own accident?"

"No. The others couldn't either. Your body will go into the bay, and it will stay in the bay."

De Gier flexed his muscles and controlled his breathing. Reggie wasn't armed. "Do a good job this time, Reggie. Mary Brewer's corpse was found. So was her boat. You've been careless with the evidence."

Reggie grinned. "You're a fool, sergeant. I gave you fair warning when I shot the tail off your hat. I should have shot you in the chest, but Janet told me to be subtle. She should have listened to me. It doesn't do to be subtle with woodchucks."

Reggie jumped and de Gier fell over sideways, extending a leg for the big man to trip over. Reggie fell but rolled over and came again.

"Madam," the commissaris pleaded. "I do advise you to take my proposition seriously. You can still save yourself a lot of really bad trouble."

He leaned a little further forward and his cane slipped out of the rug. He pulled it back with too much force, and the handle came up and knocked the microphone from under his lapel. The microphone fell and dangled on its cord. Janet stared at it. Then she stopped staring, got up slowly, and snatched. The commissaris thought she aimed for the microphone and brought up a defensive hand. But Janet had grabbed his cane and raised it.

"Help!" the commissaris said quietly.

"Shit," the sheriff said. He started the cruiser and moved his automatic shift. The rear wheels of the cruiser spun on the ice in the dip of the path. "SHIT!" the sheriff shouted and got out of the car and began to run toward the house.

When Reggie came again de Gier was more careful. He had left his rock and jumped down onto the ledge, where the beach met the bay. Reggie rushed straight at the sergeant, pretending to aim for his chest but brought up his hand at the last moment, with two stiff fingers pointed at de Gier's eyes. De Gier moved his head, grabbed Reggie's sleeves, and pushed him to the side, pivoting Reggie's body on his own leg. The sergeant's flat hand came down as Reggie slipped off his leg. The hand crushed Reggie's nose. De Gier stepped back. Reggie fell but jumped up and came again. His punch made contact, but the sergeant veered with it and grabbed Reggie's wrist. The sergeant didn't use the restraint he had been taught by his instructors. His fingers pressed on, and Reggie's wrist snapped back and broke. Reggie staggered back until his heels found some support against the rock. He pushed himself off the rock with his good arm and kicked. De Gier swayed slightly, waited for Reggie's foot to reach the top of its curve, caught the foot and pushed it up. Reggie's other foot slipped on the ice and he smashed back against the rock, hitting it with the back of his skull. He crumpled and slid down. Reggie's eyes broke as de Gier bent down to peer into his face.

De Gier ran too. He reached the porch when the sheriff reached the front door. They found the commissaris behind one of the woodstoves, legs wide apart, ready to jump one way or another. Janet was on the other side of the stove, brandishing the cane. The commissaris had lost his glasses, and he bled from a cut on his cheek.

The sergeant grabbed the cane and twisted it out of Janet's hand. Janet screamed and went on screaming until the sheriff slapped her face. The sheriff pushed her roughly into a chair. De Gier picked up the commissaris' glasses and gave them to his chief. "Sorry, sir. Reggie found me on the beach and we fought. I killed him."

"You killed him?" Janet screamed. The sheriff raised his hand. "Shut up."

Janet's eyes opened wide and closed. "Little men," she mumbled. "Little men. Reggie was right. They are like woodchucks, tunneling and prying. Destroying what others try to build. How can we kill them all when there are so many? Reggie got some, but there are too many left. And only me on this side. Only me."

She began to cry.

"I killed him," de Gier said quietly to a potted palm. "I've never killed a man before."

The commissaris limped to the sergeant, leaning on his stick. He put a hand on de Gier's sleeve.

"Rinus."

De Gier's eyes had closed. He turned toward the commissaris, but his legs were giving way. His hands grabbed the palm and pulled it to the floor. His knees buckled and he fell with the palm.

22

De Gier had been asleep, but a squirrel gliding down the steep roof had waked him up, and he now struggled to stay awake. An almost unnaturally white light was streaming through a small pane of glass set in the whitewashed ceiling, and sharp shadows played on the wall at the foot of the bed. A branch of a pine danced slowly on the plaster, each needle exactly silhouetted. The squirrel came back, its tiny feet pattering and scratching on the frozen snow. The night was so quiet that he could hear its silence. The sergeant's stomach glowed, and his skin was pleasantly warm and alive.

"Ah . . ." This was very good indeed. His whispered exclamation faded away in the large room.

"What?"

"Nothing, a squirrel."

The girl snuggled into his arm. "Go to sleep, Rinus. You have a long trip ahead of you."

"Yes. I am asleep."

She sat up. "You are not. Okay, I'll be awake with you. Would you like some tea?"

"No thank you."

Her finger followed his mustache. "You still don't want me to do anything for you, do you? You're not alone now. I'll go down and make tea and bring it back. I bought some Dutch cheese in the city and crackers. We can have a midnight snack."

He looked at his watch. "It isn't midnight."

"Oh, don't be so difficult. Are you pleased to go back?"

"A little."

"Will you miss me?"

He stroked her hair. He wanted her to go back to sleep. He wanted to look at the flowing pine needles on the wall.

"I can come over to Amsterdam. Would you like me to stay with you for a while?"

A cloud passed the moon and the needles became blurred, then disappeared. He sat up and lit a cigarette. She took it away from him and he lit another.

"Madelin," he said patiently. "Don't come to Amsterdam. And if you do, do not come to see me. Perhaps I am a romantic figure to you here, but it is different over there. I live in an apartment the size of this bedroom, and it is divided into two rooms, a hall, a kitchen, and a shower. My balcony is two feet square and its only decoration right now will be a concrete flowerpot the size of a bucket, filled with gray mud."

"In the spring," she said. "I'll come in the spring."

"In the spring the place will still be too small. I have no furniture but a bed and one chair. My table is a board that hinges off the wall. If Tabriz is in the kitchen I have to wait for her to get out before I can go in."

Her breast touched his arm. "Who is Tabriz?"

"A nine-pound cat that looks as if she weighs twenty pounds, but the difference is hair. She has seven main colors and a thousand shades in between. The colors don't blend, and her one eye looks the wrong way. She is the ugliest cat you've ever seen."

"I like cats."

De Gier turned on his side and put the tip of his finger on the girl's small straight nose. He pressed lightly and it flattened out a little. "Madelin. I am a sergeant in the Amsterdam Municipal Police. I earn tuppence halfpenny a month, and the halfpenny is kept by the police for a fund. I don't have a car but ride a bicycle that is so decrepit it won't hold a passenger. I use public transport and spend an hour each day waiting for the bus and the streetcar. Even the patrolcar I drive is dented. I am a plainclothes cop and when I walk around the city I am just another shadow."

"Do you mind?"

"No. I don't mind."

If you do you can stay here. I'd like you to stay here. Father will retire and I don't plan to run the business. Real estate is easy."

"No."

"You could be about all day. We'll have a clerk to take care of the paperwork. The busy season only lasts a few months. The rest of the year you'll be free to wander and read and do whatever you like. The fox wasn't joking when he said that he wants to make you an honorary member. You could join some of our experiments, or think up your own and we would join you. The sheriff likes you."

De Gier laughed. "Will you make him a member too?"

"Why not?"

"No."

She giggled. "You don't want the job because you dislike my father. But he did help. He gave your commissioner a check for sixty-five thousand dollars yesterday. Maybe you don't like him, but the business is worthwhile, a small but profitable line. He's always saying that, and he's right."

De Gier grunted. "The house was appraised at ninety, and the commissaris threw in the car."

She shrugged. "Yes, under ideal circumstances, but the cape has a bad name now. It won't be so easy to talk anybody into living there."

She lay down and pulled the blanket up to her chin. "Sixty-five wasn't a bad price. Your commissaris drove a hard bargain, and if father hadn't felt guilty he wouldn't have given in. He'll be lucky if he can sell at that price. Did I tell you that I have news of Janet?"

"No."

"I spoke to a psychiatrist who works at the state mental hospital. Psychiatrists aren't suppose to discuss their patients, but he's a good friend. Janet is behaving very crazily, and there's no doubt that she'll be declared incurably insane and moved to a private clinic in Massachusetts. Shame."

"Shame? That horrible woman?"

"I was thinking about your commissioner. The cut on his cheek still shows. It must have been an awful scene when she was chasing him around her porch. Good thing you were around."

"He would have got away. He's been chased before. Even by a bulldozer. He's always been able to outwit the enemy."

"Did he outwit the bulldozer?"

"He had some help," de Gier admitted.

"You?"

"No. Another bulldozer."

"Tell me."

"Not now, Madelin. I am almost asleep. Let's stay this way."

She bit his ear and he squeaked with pain.

"So you do hurt, do you? In spite of all your damned cool. Is there nothing I can do for you? Don't you have some secret wish I can fulfill?"

He looked at the telephone on the floor near the bed. "Yes, I do have a wish."

"I'll do it." She was sitting up again and her hair brushed into his face.

"I'd like to make a phone call to Amsterdam."

She sighed. "Go ahead. The Dutch are a stolid, small-minded race. Isn't that what Janet told your commissaris?"

De Gier had finished dialing.

"Police headquarters."

"Hello, dear."

"Is that you, sergeant?" the female constable asked. "I haven't heard your voice in weeks. Are you in the building?"

"No, I am outside. Can you put me through to Adjutant Grijpstra please?"

"Sure. Bring me a candy bar when you come in. Bitter sweet. I'll pay you."

"Tomorrow. I can't come in today."

"Don't forget. I'll connect you now."

"Grijpstra," a deep voice said gruffly.

"Morning. Have you had coffee yet?"

"De Gier! Where are you?"

"Jameson, Maine, U.S.A."

"Still there? When will you be back? How is the commissaris? You've been away two full weeks, you know. What's keeping you?"

"We'll be back tomorrow. The commissaris is reasonably well. He was limping badly, but he has spent the last few days in his sister's bath."

"So what have *you* been doing?"

"Waiting mostly. It took him a while to sell his sister's house. Couldn't get the right price, but it's all done now. I helped pack the chinaware yesterday, Mrs. Opdijk has a collection, including some truly marvelous items. You should have been here; it was a job you would have cherished. There was a pink rooster and some guinea pigs with hats on, and a snuffbox with an angel on top, holding a flag, and two porcelain frogs singing to each other on a green shell and . . ."

"Who's paying for this call?"

Madelin grabbed the phone. "Hello?"

"Yes."

"Do you speak English?"

"A little," Grijpstra said and sighed. "A little, miss. What can I do for you? Are you with the sergeant?"

"I am very much with the sergeant. Who are you, sir?"

"Detective Adjutant Grijpstra, Amsterdam police headquarters. Are you in any trouble?"

"I should hope not." Madelin giggled. Grijpstra peered into his telephone, studying the giggle. It was low, self-conscious, and somewhat seductive.

"I'll give you back to the sergeant now."

"Grijpstra?" de Gier asked nervously.

"Still here. And who was that, pray? *That* wasn't a porcelain frog, was it?"

"No, a friend."

"Wait!" Grijpstra shouted and looked at his watch. "It's nine-fifteen here. It must be around three o'clock at your end. Three in the morning. You are in bed!"

"In a way."

"In a way," Grijpstra repeated. "So that's what you are doing. Do you know how busy we've been? I've spent a whole week working on an atomic warfare professor. A Polish gentleman. Came here for a congress and suddenly, whoof, gone. A tremendous stink. Kidnapped, of course. Everybody blaming everybody. Even our very own Secret Service woke up and began to sniff around."

"Did you find him?"

"Eventually. We traced him to a nightclub. He got drunk there and left. Then we traced him to some illegal afterhours porno joint. He got drunker there and left."

"Usual thing?"

"Sure, but try and tell that to a Secret Service vice admiral or to an East Block ambassador. We dragged the canals and found him. The professor tried to piss into a canal and reeled right in. Drowned, sunk, and got himself attached to at least three dumped bicycles. He would have popped up again, but bowel gas takes a few days to form. We had every detective in the force on the job plus all sorts of extra help. If you'd been here you could have been of use. But you weren't here. Now tell, me, Rinus, what have you been doing?"

"I killed a man."

The telephone was quiet.

"You there, Grijpstra?"

"Yes. You wouldn't joke about killing a man. What happened? Are you in the clear?"

"Yes. Self-defense and the man was crazy. A deranged gardener with combat experience in the Vietnam jungle. I think he took me for a woodchuck."

"What's a woodchuck?"

"I haven't found out yet. Small, a rodent, eats shoots and buds. Got big teeth, slightly protruding."

"So you *did* work," Grijpstra said. "I am sorry. I might have known. You were with the local police, weren't you?"

"Yes. How are Tabriz and the flat?"

"All right. Cardozo moved into your apartment. I didn't have time to go there every day to feed Tabriz, and Cardozo gets tired of living with his parents sometimes."

"Didn't mess the place up, did he?"

"No, I checked. He did very well. All right, Cardozo, don't pull faces at me. I won't tell the sergeant about the tea on the wallpaper and the kitchen fire and the holes in the carpet."

"Give Cardozo my regards. See you tomorrow."

"Dutch is a terrible language," Madelin said and patted his chest. "You sounded like you were throwing up. The only word I caught was 'woodchuck.' "

"There is no Dutch for woodchuck, I think. We don't have them in our woods."

"Kiss me, Rinus."

"All right."

She sat up and shook him by the shoulders. "Cut it out, sergeant. I turn you on, I know I do. Stop pretending you are a self-sufficient ice floe, being happily arctic. I'll be seeing you off on the airstrip and I'll cry and I'll come and see you in Amsterdam."

"That'll be nice."

"I won't stay long."

"Stay a week. I can take a holiday and rent a car. If we get up at daybreak and make sure we're back for breakfast we may have some empty space to move around in. I can show you a polder, and birds, and a castle. We might even find a few windmills."

"Anything else?"

"That'll be enough for a week. The birds are best. The herons come right into the city, big birds but exquisite in form, with long necks and tufted head feathers. There are so many herons in Amsterdam that some streets have signs telling you to beware their shit. If it hits you your clothes are spoiled. You'll have to bring an umbrella."

"No."

"True."

"Never."

"It is true. I'll show you a jacket. I still have it. Maybe I can get it repaired. There are holes on both shoulders. And you should have seen what it did to my hair. I nearly had it shaved off."

"I'll believe you when you kiss me without being cold."

"Okay," he said slowly. "Okay. But don't get any ideas. I am like Jeremy, and the older I become the more I will be like him. I'll finish up on an island, far away from here, far away from Amsterdam too. And I'll be alone."

"Yes, sergeant," she whispered. "I believe you. About the herons too. Now come here."